MW00900609

Among the Crepe Myrtles

Letters to Layton
Book One

Kim Williams

Among the Crepe Myrtles
Copyright © 2017 Kim Williams

ALL RIGHTS RESERVED

Front cover by Kim Williams
Interior layout by Jeff M. Miller | FiveJsDesign.com

ISBN-13: 978-1545596937
ISBN-10: 154559693X

For my husband, Lynn. I love you.

In memory of my Nanny Jones.

Among the Crepe Myrtles

Prologue

Two days ago he was a husband.

Today he was a widower, and Ben Williams found himself standing over the fresh grave of his wife.

He felt as though he were on the verge of falling in a deep, dark pit—preventing his son from falling in with him was all that kept Ben from the taunting plunge.

Midday sun beat down on his neck, and underneath his jacket, a white cotton shirt stuck to his back. His brown shoes, scuffed and covered in black Texas dirt, encased his leaden feet. Every member of his body was laden with the burden of Death.

Somehow those lead feet carried him from the graveyard to the desolate boarding house where his son waited for him in the care of a friend—an angel to Ben. He knocked, then waited numbly while Mr. Cramer unlocked the door and let him inside.

Though the windows were open, no breeze blew in and ruffled the curtains or caressed the stale air in the sitting area of the rooms the Cramers called home. Like Ben, as family to the boarding house owner, the Cramers paid no rent and occupied one of the two double-room dwellings in the boarding house. Their families worked around the house for their keep. Of course, that arrangement would change for Ben since his wife had been the blood relation, serving up wonderful meals to the boarders.

Ben gingerly reached down to the blanket on the floor and picked up his boy. At two years old, Sammy was too young to understand that his life had changed forever.

"Thank you for keeping him during the funeral, Mrs. Cramer. My shift on the railroad doesn't start for another four days, so I'll bring him back then. I appreciate you agreeing to care for him when I'm out working."

"Four days. In the meantime, I'm next door if you or Sammy need my help. I'll see you at mealtime." The kind woman who had no children of her own reached up and hugged Ben.

1

At twenty-six, Ben was strong and healthy, but the sensation of his son's little fingers around his neck was enough to make him feel weak and helpless. How could he raise a child on his own? When Sammy would start looking around for his Momma, how could Ben explain to him that she was gone? His son had no concept of death.

He carried Sammy into their rooms at the boarding house and set him down. The little freckled-face, crippled boy looked up at his father and smiled, then began to play on the floor with his train. Ben collapsed on the bed and gave in to the grief that overtook him.

He had no wife. Sammy had no mother. They'd been robbed by the Almighty, a thief no one could catch. And although he was certain his wailing bled through the boarding house walls, Ben realized that Sammy continued to play in a silent world, his deaf ears blocking the sound of a father's broken heart.

Part One

Chapter 1

1918 | LAYTON, TEXAS

Fire!

Smoke filled the sweltering kitchen. Eighteen-year-old Katherine pumped water into the empty tea pitcher as quickly as her slender arms could manage. While coughing into her upper arm, she slung the water into the frying pan. Katherine felt tears roll from her green eyes. The sizzle and steam of water tossed upon fire caused another coughing spell as she pushed open the creaky back door and began waving the smoke outside with her dishrag. "Blast it! I've ruined the bacon. I hate cooking." She hurried through the small four room house and opened the windows.

Her aged house was situated on a plot of flat, black, Texas dirt and was graced by wild flowers, pecan trees, crepe myrtles, and natural overgrown shrubbery. Had it not been for the carpentry skills her brother possessed, the structure would be dilapidated. She knew the home had started as a two-room abode for her great grandparents. Those rooms now served as a front room where the family sat and as a shared bedroom. Eventually, an additional bedroom, stretching the length of the house, had been built on to the back. Years later, a kitchen had been adjoined against that bedroom with a back porch attached to the right of it. Katherine thought the house looked like a square with a bump protruding from it.

The abode was crudely crafted and had little frills. The ivory wallpaper with large green leaf patterns her mother had added in the front room was now faded to a dingy yellow; water marks stained one corner of the room. Katherine remembered watching the water run down the wall; for an eight-year-old girl, the sight had been a distraction from the heavy rain, wind, and thunder raging outside—a howling Texas storm. She also recalled watching her Mama stand in a chair trying to patch the culprit hole in the ceiling. She'd been mesmerized by her mother's arms as she stretched to do the work, revealing their full length.

There were no hallways in the interior, so the family meandered from room to room through open doorways covered with curtains. Katherine had brightened the dim house last year by sewing new curtains in bright floral patterns. The expense had required six months of mending money. Sound carried throughout the entire residence, and although she had known no other living arrangement, Katherine longed for privacy.

Her thoughts were interrupted by the sound of the train whistle announcing its arrival on this hot Friday. Her Texas town of Layton was a flag stop on the Cottonline Railroad system, so the train only stopped when people or supplies were requested to be picked up or dropped off. This evening's stop signaled the delivery of her brother who'd walk the mile from the small depot to their home. Joe worked on the railroad and was gone for days at a time and then home for days.

Katherine tugged nervously on her ears as she headed back into the kitchen. She smirked at herself when she realized she was tugging. What an odd habit she'd inherited from her mother. Katherine supposed she'd never rid herself of it. She stood in the kitchen and surveyed the results of her cooking efforts. Her shoulders sagged with disappointment; all she had to offer for her afternoon in the kitchen were burnt bacon strips and burnt biscuits that were cold by now because she never timed her cooking in the right order. She threw the ruined bacon into the slop bucket on the back porch and set about scraping the pan, hoping the eggs she would fry next wouldn't absorb the taste of burnt bacon.

"Land's sake! Who set the house a fire?" Katherine jolted, dropped her spatula, then turned at the sound of her brother's voice as he paraded through the middle bedroom into the kitchen.

"Hush, Joe! You'll wake the dead shouting like that. The house is not on fire. I just had a little mishap, that's all. Wash up and…" Katherine froze as a stranger stepped into the kitchen behind her brother.

A visceral flutter swept through her being. Mesmerized, Katherine shook her head to break her stare from the tall man, then somehow remembered to sweep a hand across her forehead to clear the flour. She was certain that she had never seen such broad shoulders. His brown eyes crinkled as he smiled—his smile reached the width of his entire face. The wear and tear on his features made her guess he was older than both she and Joe. Katherine thought that at twenty-two, Joe still had some hint of youth in his pale, but weathered skin, despite the wrinkles around his blue, beady eyes that were frequently blood shot. Joe was small framed and had a habit of running his fingers through his dark black hair. Her brother appeared pathetically weak standing next to the stranger.

"Katherine, this here's Ben. He'll be staying with us this weekend. Stop your gawking." Katherine felt her cheeks flush. Her brother glanced at Ben and explained, "This is my oldest sister, Katherine McGinn. She usually don't have flour on her forehead and smell of smoke. I reckon she's the one that cooked." The stranger smiled and pulled his hat from his head, revealing light brown, wavy hair. "Nice to meet you, Miss McGinn. Pardon me for barging in on you. Seems you didn't know I was coming." She saw him glare at Joe.

"You're welcome here, mister."

"I'm Ben Williams, but I'd be obliged if you called me Ben." In response, Katherine shrugged her shoulders and gave what felt like to her a childish, awkward smile.

"Where's Lena?" Joe bent over the wash bowl, rinsed his hands and seated himself on one of the benches at the table. "Ben, Lena's my other sister, the real cook in the family."

"Lena's run a fever all day, so I sent her to bed. I don't want her getting too active and messing up her breathing. You know how her asthma acts up when she's under the weather."

"Course, the smoke in the kitchen won't help her none either if it seeps to her bedroom."

"I know that, Joe. Before I sent her to bed, I gave her coffee to open up her lungs."

Katherine cleared her throat and then turned to address the stranger. "Mr. Williams—Ben—pardon such private talk. Why don't you take a seat across from Joe?"

The trio sat down with Katherine seated across from the two men. Joe passed the platter of cold biscuits and eggs around the table. Katherine bowed her head and said a silent prayer. She knew better than to pray aloud and risk embarrassing Joe in front of the stranger.

Lena and Katherine went to church every time the community's traveling preacher was in town. Educated through the fifth grade, Katherine had learned to read and write and tried to figure out the strange sentences in the family Bible she kept. She surely hoped the good Lord didn't mind her talking to Him sort of like He was sitting in a rocker next to her because that's what she did.

Katherine knew that Joe, on the other hand, didn't give any thought to so called religion; he'd reminded her of that many times. She wondered where Ben stood on the subject and just as quickly wondered why it mattered to her. Eyeing him as she looked up from praying, she saw him already chewing a mouthful and noticed his fork, heaping with eggs, was heading toward his lips. Must not be the praying type.

"My apology for no bacon this evening, Joe. But, Lena did bake a blackberry pie yesterday. I can serve you both some of that if you like. She spent yesterday afternoon pickin' the berries."

"A man needs his meat, but I reckon pie will do tonight. Ben, it'll be mighty good coming from my youngest sister."

"I appreciate everything set before me at the table." Katherine blushed, touched by the apparent kindness of the stranger who extended a nod toward her as he spoke.

"Joe, might I ask how you two men came to know each other?"

"Ben works for the Cottonline too." Katherine knew what Joe did as a railroad brakeman. He threw the switches to guide the train to the proper tracks. She wondered if Ben did the same thing, and with just a hint of embarrassment, she cleared her throat and asked him.

"Are you a brakeman, Ben?" He smiled at her and she liked how his eyes sparkled when his lips spread. "No. I'm a road fireman." Katherine smiled shyly in return. "What do road firemen do?" Both men began to answer at the same time, but Joe halted, and his friend explained. "I shovel coal into the furnace to give the train its power." Katherine felt her brows wrinkle. "That sounds dangerous." Ben chuckled. "It can be. It's also hot and messy." The guest indicated the black smudges on his clothing. Katherine hadn't noticed the dirt until then.

"He lives in Commerce, 'bout forty miles from here." Joe entered the conversation.

"So, your family lives back there, Ben?"

"Katherine, Ben's a widower with no family. He lives in a boarding house." Katherine felt Joe's eyes staring at her. He had a way of making her feel childish and chastised, yet he was the one who uttered the awkward explanation. Ben could have given his own preferred answer had Joe not spoken for him. She returned his stare and controlled her irritation before eyeing their guest.

"I am very sorry about that, Mr. Williams. Forgive me. I feel quite ashamed of my question now."

"It's no bother ma'am. You didn't know, and it's a natural question."

Katherine felt vindicated and smiled at the stranger. She found herself too shy and too embarrassed to speak any further in the presence of the two men. With no one else to talk to, she listened politely as Joe and his friend talked back and forth about the railway—a world Katherine knew little about. "I've never ridden on a train, but tonight, I'm so flustered, I'd ride one as far away as the tracks would take me." Katherine hoped she'd expressed those thoughts in her mind and not out loud, but a look at the stranger's raised eyebrows and smirk made her think she hadn't. At that same moment, Katherine realized the men had finished eating and seized the opportunity to take attention away from her muttered comment.

"Well, how about I get you both a piece of pie to enjoy while I clean up. Coffee? Milk?"

"Best go with milk, Ben. I am." Joe chuckled. Katherine tugged on her ear, wondering why Joe seemingly took pleasure in her inadequacies as a cook.

"Suit yourself, Joe. Maybe I ignorantly let the milk sour just enough to curdle in your belly. Mr. Williams—Ben?"

"As much as I'd love a cup of your coffee, Miss Katherine, don't go to the trouble. Milk's good."

As she handed each one his plate and his glass, the men excused themselves to sit on the front porch steps. Katherine pumped water into the sink and began to scrub the dishes and pans, finding her mind traveling to her deepest thoughts—wanting a family of her own to love and nurture, but wondering if a man would ever want a woman like her.

When she examined herself, Katherine felt she was lacking. An awful cook. Rather plain looking. She huffed a breath and considered the good she would bring to a marriage if given the chance. She would do her share and more of work needed to run a home. She'd be devoted and do all she could to please her husband. She'd try to learn how to love him in the way only a wife should. She'd honor him. She'd pray for him.

Joe had a way of making her doubt that her strengths would be enough to lure a man. But—Joe wasn't the Almighty. She hoped the good Lord had made an honest, nice man who could put up with the likes of her.

Before heading outside to enjoy the last bit of daylight, Katherine grabbed her mending, then stepped into the bedroom she shared with her twelve-year-old sister. Lena appeared to be sleeping. Katherine felt Lena's head and was satisfied the fever was gone.

She moved to the doorway of the front porch and stood with the screen wide open. With her eyes closed and face titled up, she let the breeze cool her down before she sat in the rocker. She spotted the empty plates and glasses on the porch step. Stitching a tear in one of Joe's shirts, she hummed and, despite herself, felt slightly comforted by the voices of the men nearing her as they came from the garden at the side of the house. She bit her lip when she overheard Ben say that they had a mighty fine garden. Did Joe mention that I was the gardener?

"Thank you for the pie, ma'am. It was mighty good." The man who was capturing her thoughts patted his stomach.

"I'll be sure to let my sister know you enjoyed it, Ben, or perhaps you can tell herself if she is better tomorrow." Katherine smiled at Ben and he reacted with a big grin. She felt her cheeks warm. The handsome guest filled the moment with words. "Let's hope so. I'd like to meet her."

The two men seated themselves on the porch. Katherine tried not to stare at Ben, but she did. His eyes were roaming around scenery. "I've never been to your town Joe, other than passing through on the rail line. How long you all lived here?"

"Three generations of McGinns born and brought up on this very soil. My Irish great Grandpappy moved here from Illinois and became a sad legend in his own right. Supposedly, he had money and wanted to be a mighty cotton farmer, but wasted most his money gambling once he got here. Lost our fortune and made us all into common, working folks. Ain't that right, Katherine?"

"Our great Grandpappy left behind a two-room house and four surviving children." She chuckled. "Of course it's not two rooms anymore. Since then, this home was made bigger over time and housed our grandparents, and then our Papa and Mama, and now us. I reckon Joe's right. We're just common, hardworking folks, not owning much more than what was handed down our way or a new piece of furniture Joe crafts from time to time. Maybe an occasional luxury like the water pump." Did I just ramble? She cast her eyes toward Ben and caught him looking at her. He smiled.

"If Grandpappy hadn't gambled and lost his money, this town and others in the community might not be part of the 'Forder Empire,' but the 'McGinn Empire' instead," Joe grumbled. Katherine reflected that their father had also risked the income he made for his family. It appeared Joe didn't even try to hide his disgust with the social status passed down to them. Considering Joe had the same habit of letting money slip through his fingertips when he gambled, Katherine viewed his apparent disgust of their Grandpappy's habits as mockery.

She looked up from her mending just as Ben once again removed his hat and ran his hands through his hair. "Why, the Forder Empire, as you call it, expands as far out as Commerce where I live. Hired laborers fill up the black dirt fields as far as any eye can see across the flat land." He smiled at Katherine. "Communities just like yours here… with homes spread miles apart across the fields, a store, a church, a school. Hard, simple life. I live it too."

Katherine was amused. She'd learned more about her surrounding community from a few sentences with a stranger than Joe had ever taken time to share with her. She hadn't really known what the term "Forder Empire" meant until this minute. Her travels had taken her no further than five miles away to the town of Evan for the annual brush arbor revival meetings where the surrounding communities all gathered outside under a makeshift structure with log seats to hear the guest traveling preacher shout and sweat through his sermon.

She forgot her shyness and spoke directly to the stranger, eager to share her own knowledge about the area. "Mr. Forder and his family make their home here in Layton. Did you know that, Mister, uh, Ben?"

"I'd heard it, but never firsthand. I also hear they have quite a big house."

"More than plenty for their small family," Joe huffed.

Katherine swatted her hand at her brother. "It's a beauty. Been there one time when all the women folk at church had a picnic. No matter rich, poor, or poorest, Mrs. Forder invited us all. We see them at church every time we meet. They're nice folks. Treat us all kindly. Well, except for their orphaned niece who came to live with them. She snubs just about everyone. 'Course, I'm gossiping now."

Her cheeks heated, Ben chuckled, and Joe looked as though he were going to speak, but he didn't, so she continued. "I hear tell our town of Layton boasts the largest store across his so-called empire, due to his living right here and all. He's got the nicest folks running it too—Mr. Justice and his wife. Our store even has a small diner in it. And, a main road to Dallas runs through our town. Well, I've never gone to Dallas, but I hear it gets folks there eventually. I reckon that's important for Mr. Forder so he can take care of business matters in the city."

"You seem content, Miss Katherine."

"I suppose there's comfort in the familiar, Ben. But I don't know that familiarity and contentment always go hand in hand." Katherine turned her eyes back to her mending. By his very presence, this stranger made her long for more than she had day to day, but she felt powerless over her future. Resignation settled in.

"Good insight, Miss Katherine." She politely returned his smile.

"Well, Ben, I tell you. Layton's a fine town, but if you wanna have fun, you gotta travel up the road about four miles to the dance hall in Nelson." Joe elbowed his friend in the side. "Course, Katherine don't know about that kinda fun. You and I will head that way tomorrow evening if you're in for a good time."

"I got a lot I want to stop thinking on for a bit, and a good time is just what I need."

"Count on it then," Joe boasted. "And," he spoke in an exaggerated whisper, "while we're there you might just get to meet that orphan niece who Katherine just accused of snubbing folks. She's all grown up and she's a beaut!" Joe let out a whistle and wiggled his eyebrows. Katherine thought he looked like a salivating dog.

"Well, I don't know if a good time and a beautiful woman always go hand in hand," Ben retorted in the same exaggerated whisper. Katherine reacted with a chuckle to his words—an obvious mimicry of her own statement. A warmth spread through her body. Had Ben understood her thoughts? Did he agree with them? The unmarried eighteen-year-old glanced at the new acquaintance. He was smiling at her; then he sent a gentle nod her way.

She returned the nod and felt more flushed than she had when there was smoke in the kitchen.

Chapter 2

Coffee. That's what he needed, and from the pleasing aroma, he knew some was brewing. Rising from the spare bed in the plain, stark bedroom Joe called home, Ben stretched and let his eyes acclimate to the unfamiliar surroundings so he could make his escape from the annoying cadence of Joe's snoring.

The sound had kept him awake. Of course, he knew that the snoring was not the only culprit that had prevented his rest. It had been two years since he'd become a widower, so it had been two years since he'd had a full night's sleep. But, he wouldn't think about that right now because in the next room, a woman had made some coffee. *Yep, just what I need—coffee, that is.* A twinge of guilt for thinking of that woman on the other side of the kitchen doorway knotted his stomach, but the subtle tug at his heart intrigued him. He felt as though an unconscious part of his being had tried to awaken.

Ben walked into the warm kitchen, but saw no one there. The hint of disappointment he felt amused him. He picked up a rag crumpled near the stove and used it to grab the hot coffee pot then took a white chipped cup from the small shelf above the stove and began pouring the aromatic beverage. "Good morning, and by the way, you're welcome!" An unfamiliar, feminine voice caused Ben to jump and coffee to spill on his hand. "Ouch!" Ben set the mug on the edge of the stove and shook hot coffee from his hand.

"Oh my. Here, Ben, wipe your hand with this cloth and then put it in the bowl of water on the counter. The cool water will help." He recognized Katherine's familiar feminine voice and turned to face her as he took the cloth. "Thank you. Pardon the mess."

He turned toward the figure standing at the back porch doorway. She was shorter than Katherine, but had the same lanky build, almost to the point of appearing sickly and gawky. Her facial features still had a hint of childhood to them. An image of Sammy came to mind and he pushed it away. He wasn't ready to risk sharing that part of himself with this family. Her hair was black, like Joe's. The young girl lacked the natural beauty that Katherine possessed, but she had the same beautiful green eyes. He was amused by the sparkle in them that hinted of mischievousness. "You're welcome? For what?"

"The blackberry pie." Ben saw a large smile cross the girl's face and her bright green eyes widen.

"Ben, meet our younger sister, Lena. Lena, this is Mr. Williams, who you owe an apology."

"Didn't mean to startle you. We were on the back porch when you walked in. Nice to meet you, Mr. Williams."

"Nice to meet you too." Ben pulled his hand from the cool water, dried it off, and reached for the mug he'd set down. "I guess your sister here told you how much I enjoyed my piece of pie."

"No, I overheard you talking about it."

Ben coughed on his sip of coffee and frantically replayed last night's conversations in his mind as he heard Katherine sigh. Whew! The worst Lena had heard was her own brother setting him up for the dance hall.

"Guess Katherine didn't notice yesterday that I'd opened both porch windows from our bedroom. I could hear just about everything. And, I wasn't sound asleep."

Ben laughed good and hearty. "Well, thanks again, face to face. And I guess you're feeling better. "

"Yes, she is," Katherine said as she scooted her sister toward the stove. "How about some bacon for our guest, Lena."

Lena slid a pan of biscuits she'd prepared into the oven as she spoke, "Extra crispy bacon this time, Mr. Williams?" Ben watched Katherine tweak her sister's cheek. "Mind your manners!"

"I'll take it however you fix it." He lifted his cup of coffee toward the ladies in a gesture of appreciation. "Good coffee too. Thank you. "

"Katherine made it," Lena pointed out.

"Would you like curdled milk with that?" Katherine didn't crack a smile as she rolled her eyes and spoke. Ben let out another hearty laugh. "No, black is fine." A good cup of coffee made by the woman of the house. Ben liked that thought and let it settle in his mind for just a second, then pushed it away.

He enjoyed every bite of his breakfast. Indeed, Lena was a good cook. He also thought she was feisty and must test the patience of her older siblings. Lena had tried give her opinion of the Forder family, but when she mentioned the niece named Faye, Katherine swatted her with a dishrag she was holding and scolded, "If you can't say something kind, then don't speak." Lena had responded with an eye roll. Ben hadn't been able to prevent his chuckle at that interaction. He'd listened to her and Katherine spar back and forth like that all morning. Ben formed the opinion that theirs was a unique relationship—sister to sister and mother to daughter—at different times.

It puzzled him that he'd been captivated by Katherine's presence the first moment he laid eyes on her. Tightness had spread through his chest as he sensed a connection with her. He'd startled at the feeling that his life was being altered at that very moment. Ben thought she'd been flustered by his unexpected arrival, and he'd admired how she seemed to recover. She'd appeared to hold her own throughout the evening, even with the attempts her brother obviously made to belittle her.

Joe's cutting comments to her had rubbed Ben the wrong way. He felt sorry for her, admired her backbone, and felt the need to protect her all at once. He had been especially startled by the emotion to protect. He'd never had a sister and thought maybe some untapped brotherly instincts had surfaced. That tug at his heart snickered at such reasoning.

Joe had said his oldest sister was plain and reserved. He'd found her to be wholesome looking, chatty, and even insightful. Her russet hair, twisted into a loose bun at her back collar, was complimented by green eyes that set perfectly in her narrow face. He thought her tall, slender build afforded her a graceful look. She'd captured his eye.

After breakfast the group separated as the women went about their chores, and Ben accompanied Joe with his tasks. "Katherine reminded me that the shed door is loose and rotting. I'm gonna head out and work on it. You handy with a hammer or saw?" Ben answered him as they walked down the back porch steps and headed to the shed. "Hammer? Yes. Saw? No."

The July morning was hot and sweat had already begun to roll down the back of Ben's neck. He pulled out his handkerchief and ran it across his face and neck. To his right, he noticed the ladies already in the garden with sun hats on their heads and baskets on their arms, gathering vegetables.

His mind went back to eight years ago. A lady wearing a sun hat had been the scene when he'd first laid eyes on his wife. She was working the garden of the boarding house he had moved into. The widower let his mind relive the memory for just a moment.

"Good afternoon, ma'am." The young woman jumped and dropped the tomato she was holding. Yellow tendrils of hair peeked out from her sun hat and light brown freckles graced her nose. "I didn't mean to startle you." He reached down to pick up the tomato and handed it to her.

"It's no problem. I was lost in thought," she spoke quietly. "I've not seen you. Are you the new boarder?"

"Just moved in this morning. I'm Ben Williams. How about you?"

"I'm Addie. I've lived here quite a while. My cousin, who passed away, his wife is the owner, and I'm the cook. I'll be keeping you fed I suppose. "

"Well, I'm looking forward to eating whatever you cook up. I'll see you around, then."

He walked away and couldn't resist looking back for another glance at the delicate being and was quite pleased to see her watching him. At his backward glance, she lifted a hand and gave a wave.

Ben shook his head and came back to the present. He had married the delicate creature three months later. She'd died six years after that. In between, she'd given him a son, so a part of her was still alive in the boy's eyes. He knew he wasn't a religious man and supposed he couldn't expect an answer from the Almighty as to why, but he felt angry even now that the good Lord would take such a fine woman so early in her life. He'd robbed a little boy of his mother and left him a father who depended on a kind neighbor to care for him.

He resented that the Lord had given and then taken, forcing one of his worst fears upon him—loss and the longing for what might have been.

He smiled to himself realizing that in this present time, his senses were keenly aware of the russet-haired young woman in the garden. *Would that same Almighty allow me another chance for a wife and a family? Do I even need to worry about the Almighty? I'm a level-headed man who can decide on his own.* And right now, he found himself longing for someone to love, care for, and come home to. This longing had been sickly and weak but now growled with hunger, demanding to be fed.

Ahead of him was a large shed that housed a horse and a two-wheeled cart. "Here you go, Ben, take this tool. You pull this old shed door off and I'll start cutting the wood for the new one." Ben did as Joe instructed and tugged at the hinges and began to pull them loose. "I heard Katherine mention you make furniture from time to time." Joe didn't look up from his work. "Sure do. Kitchen table and benches. The rockers on the porch. That bed frame you slept on, it was my first creation. Katherine says we can't part with it." Ben smiled, thinking that "slept" was an exaggeration. Joe carried on. "Can't ride the rails forever. Maybe one day, I'll go into business for myself."

Ben considered his friend. They'd worked the same shift for the past nine months. He knew him as a hard worker who did his job well. On the nights they slept in temporary boarder housing or waited long hours at the stations between routes, Ben, Joe, and the other crew members passed the time playing cards, talking idly about their families and how they spent their time when home. Most of the men also drank—Joe especially.

His friend hadn't shared much about himself other than he lived with his two sisters. Like Ben, maybe Joe had a secret to hide. When the invitation came to spend this free time in Layton, Ben had been surprised but happy to accept, especially since the route was by-passing his hometown this leg and he wouldn't get to spend time with Sammy. Though he was surrounded by others in the boarding house where he and his son still lived, Ben led a lonely life. Meeting new people had sounded like an adventure. Katherine had certainly proven to be just that.

The morning rolled by pleasantly as the two men built the new door. "What's that you're humming?" Joe's question startled Ben from his thoughts. "Well, I didn't realize I was humming, so I don't rightly know. Most likely something I made up."

Ben chuckled and smiled at Joe. He could not say for certain, but he felt this was the first time he'd hummed in a couple of years. The significance of that hit him square in his chest. As far back as he could recall, singing, humming, whistling, or tunes played on his harmonica had always come from him when he felt happy and content.

"Well, don't mind me. Keep on humming. Kinda soothing."

"Yep. I agree." With that, Ben had just started in on a new tune when a feminine voice got his attention. "You and Lena could have a humming contest. She's always singing or humming or tapping out tunes on the counter." Katherine lifted a ladle filled with water from a pitcher. "Water?"

Ben and Joe each took a sip, then Joe retorted, "Lena's singing is enough to get on a man's nerves though—all high pitched and always hymns or a love song she's heard her friends sing."

"Joe, you just hush. You benefit from Lena's humming more than you know. When she's cooking at her best, you can know it, because she's humming away. Kinda helps her think, I suppose. Besides, it's nice to hear. Speaking of food, lunch will be in a half hour." Katherine turned back toward the house.

"Thank you, Miss Katherine," Ben offered. When she smiled at him, he locked eyes with her and held them, gave her a slight nod, and returned a smile that he felt from cheek to cheek. He resumed humming, a little more heartily than he had earlier.

As the evening came about, Joe and Ben wrapped up their chores. Ben was amused as Joe took extra effort to clean up for a night at the dance hall, even taking a bath and offering the same to him. He'd refused kindly and just washed himself down, shaved, and changed into his other shirt he'd brought along.

Joe had headed out to the shed to obtain the horse and wagon for the ride into Nelson. Ben emerged from Joe's bedroom and into the front room where the ladies were rocking and stitching. "Well, ladies," Ben cleared his throat, "reckon I'll be seeing you when we get back. Have a good…"

"Not likely. Might not see ya anymore," Lena uttered.

"Pardon me?" Lena's comment flustered Ben. He was already struggling between his desire to socialize at the dance hall or socialize with the young woman sitting nearby that had captured his attention. Ben rubbed his forehead.

"What Lena means, Ben, is that Joe won't have ya back here until the wee morning hours. And then, we two will be headed to church before you ever wake up. We only get church here about once a month on Pastor Carlson's circuit, and tomorrow's Layton's turn. You're likely to be back on the train before we get home."

"We'll be eatin' dinner at the church before we come home," Lena added. "I'm making vegetable soup to take." Ben acknowledged Lena with a nod when he saw her look up at him. He wished Katherine would look up as she spoke to him. Instead, he saw her pinch her lips and raise her eyebrows.

Katherine's apparent disapproval of the dance hall agitated him. He chided himself, knowing that her opinions shouldn't be his concern. However, Ben felt his stomach clench. A night at the dance hall had lost some of its appeal. He couldn't very well stay here with just the two women—could he? He offered a weak smile. "I see. What time do you ladies depart for church?"

"Like I said, earlier than you'll be stirring. Night Ben."

"Well, uh, night Katherine. And Lena. Thank you for everything." With that, Ben walked to the front porch and away from the tension he felt. The two women didn't know him well, so he figured they naturally assumed him to be like Joe, who apparently returned from these evenings in a condition of which his sisters didn't approve.

He'd been happy this weekend and didn't want to leave with them thinking less of him. Walking down the porch steps, he paused. *Why does it matter to me what Katherine thinks?* He shook his head and started toward the wagon. Somehow, though, her opinion mattered very much to him.

Chapter 3

As the wagon came into Nelson, Ben observed that the town was like Layton. Cotton fields spread as far as the eye could see with houses dotted in front of them along dusty, bumpy dirt roads. About a mile into the town, Joe turned onto a dirt road that led to apparently nothing. Thick trees and underbrush pressed in and the road narrowed. About a half mile into the thick trees, a whitewashed two-story structure sat back in a wide clearing. The name High Cotton was painted across the front. Wagons, horses, and even a couple of autos were parked in front of it. Light and sound seemed to bulge from its interior.

Ben perked up at the sound of the piano and of the deep female singing voice he heard coming from inside. He saw Joe look around the lot and then smile and point to the side of the house. "See that there auto? Fancy. That means Faye Forder is here." Ben shrugged his shoulders, curious what type of female got Joe's heart racing. Judging by the auto, apparently a rich one. What rich girl would give working men like themselves the time of day?

He and Joe found a table in the back of the smoke-filled room. As soon as he was seated, Ben's fingers began tapping on the table to the best of the music. "I'm stepping up to the counter to order. Ain't gonna wait on anyone to come to me. What'll you have?" Ben had never been a drinker. His Pa had abused the stuff and done awful things to his Mama and to him until the day Ben grew big enough to fight back. "I'll take a cola. Here ya go." Joe laughed out loud. "I'm serious," Ben stated. "I don't touch the stuff." Ben handed a bill to his friend, watched him walk away with a look of shock and apparent disgust, then reached for the deck of cards left on the table and began to shuffle. He'd try to enjoy himself and stop wondering what Katherine was doing back at the house.

When Joe returned, Ben had dealt for a game of poker and had rounded up two more players. Between games, Joe would head to the counter and return with more to drink. Midway through the third game the singer thanked the crowd and left the stage, then the piano player changed to an upbeat tune. The tables began to clear as couples took to the floor.

Joe stood and spoke to Ben. "To your right. There she is." Ben looked, and indeed, a beautiful woman stood near the stage. She was dressed in a silky, shiny short dress, a pair of heels, a headband, and a long necklace. She pulled a cigarette from her bright red lips that sat upon her painted face and blew out smoke. "That's the Forder's wayward niece." Ben heard Joe cackle and then blow out a flirty sounding whistle that blended in with several others. Faye moved to the stage with a slow, seductive walk that left Ben with a sinking feeling in his stomach. For the next hour her sultry voice filled the dance hall and flirted with his ears.

Although Ben enjoyed every note she sang and recognized what a beauty she was, he didn't think himself to be a fool. He figured a woman like her could take what she wanted from a situation and then move on to the next opportunity.

As the seductive singer finally left the stage and moved through the crowd, Ben thought Joe looked like a pathetic child waiting to be noticed. Much to Joe's obvious delight, Faye stopped at their table. Her scent filled the air around the men. "Joe McGinn, fancy seeing you here. It's been a while. Good to see you enjoying yourself." She touched his shoulder. "Still risking your life on those rails, I suppose?" Ben felt a knot come in his stomach because just as Joe was about to reply, Faye switched her attention to him, walking away from Joe and leaning over the back of Ben's chair. Her cheek brushed against his and her hand slid up and down his arm.

"Well, I don't believe I've ever met you. I'm Faye."

"I'm Ben. Mighty fine singing, ma'am." He didn't turn his head to look her in the eye when he answered.

"Oh, I'm no ma'am. Quite the opposite really." She laughed and changed her position to face him directly. "I prefer a fun time far too much to be considered a polite ma'am. Are you new in our lovely, exciting community?"

"Just visiting." Her perfume was inviting and wickedly alluring, but the alcohol and cigarettes on her breath nauseated him.

She turned back to Joe, "Bring him to town more often," and then walked away.

Joe looked at Ben, stood, and headed toward the bar and Ben heard him mutter, "Don't think I will!"

Joe returned with what looked like whiskey. Ben had lost count a while ago as to how many drinks his friend had consumed, and yet Joe kept his senses enough to play a couple more rounds of cards and win, even though he'd lost most everything that evening. Ben had pulled out after three games when the stakes were more than he was willing to pay. He was surprised by the amount of money Joe had gambled. "Got your great Grandpappy's blood in you, I see Joe," he blurted out on the last round of cards. He saw anger cross Joe's face at the comment and determined his friend's spending habits were none of his business.

As the midnight hour came upon them, Ben suggested they leave; Joe didn't hesitate to let his friend drive the wagon. Ben lit a lantern and started out. It was too dark in his opinion to safely drive this distance on such rural roads, but they had no choice.

"So, Faye's got an eye out for ya. Don't think I won't fight ya over her." Ben laughed loudly. "Joe, there won't be any fighting over that woman. I'm not interested in any kind of woman like that."

"Ya got eyes, don't ya?" Joe practically shouted.

"I do. Yep, I do. She's pretty, alright."

"You're strange!"

"That woman will give men like us nothing more than a good time—and only if she wants to."

"So?"

"I'm just saying I want a woman I can settle down with and have a family."

Joe jeered at him. "I don't want responsibility. I just want what I want from a woman and be done with it."

"What's Faye doing hanging out at a poor man's dance hall when she could probably be a Dallas socialite?"

"She owns the place. Claims she bought it with part of her inheritance from her daddy who passed when she's about twelve. Soon as she was old enough to control her money, she did as she pleased. Set it as close to the Forder Empire as she can, I reckon, to rankle her mighty uncle." Joe exaggerated his last two words.

"You're pathetic, Joe." Ben looked his friend in the eye and shook his head.

"Make that happily pathetic, Ben. You some kind of preacher or something, talking all goody two shoes?"

"I'm far from being a preacher. Now, get some shut eye; I remember how to get us back."

The lantern on the cart was lit, but the darkness of the night felt heavy to Ben once they were a distance from the dance hall. Crickets chirped and the wheels creaked, but the only other sound Ben heard were his thoughts. After the noise of the dance hall, the quiet was a welcome change. The area between Nelson and Layton was desolate except for cotton fields stretched for miles. Ben had noticed them on the ride in, but in the dark of night, the area appeared devoid of scenery. The cart dipped to one side when it hit a pot hole and Ben felt his bottom rise from the seat and come down with a thud.

Despite being worn out, Ben lay wide awake in his bed; it had been a short, restless night. He wondered if Joe ever came home more drunk than he was tonight and the thought concerned him, for Joe's safety, but also the safety of his sisters. Daylight was about an hour away and thinking of the sisters, he was struck with an idea.

Rising from the bed and throwing on his clothes, he pushed aside the curtain in the doorway and headed into the kitchen. Just as he'd hoped they'd be, vegetables were set out on the counter. As Ben began to chop carrots, celery, and onions, he hummed contentedly. Not long after it became bright daylight, he had a hearty vegetable soup simmering. Next, he put coffee on the stove. Pleasant aromas began to fill the air. Tossing the vegetable skins into the slop bucket, he then set out for a brisk walk to enjoy the cool morning air. He felt rather pleased with himself and spoke aloud. "Miss Katherine, as you can see, I'm sober and wide awake."

The truth is, Ben needed fresh air to clear his mind. His anticipation of getting to see Katherine was making him jittery. He reflected on the time spent in Katherine's presence this weekend and his heart beat faster in his chest. Had she felt any sensations in his presence? Did she wish for him to visit again? He hoped she approved of his making soup for them. Ben curled up one side of his lip as he imagined her tasting his creation.

When he returned through the back porch, he was rewarded with a sight that gave him pleasure. Katherine and Lena stood at the stove staring at one another. At the sound of the screen door, they jumped.

"Ben! You scared us to death," Lena giggled.

"Guess you had it coming to you after yesterday morning. Mind if I have some coffee?"

"Ben, did you do all this? The coffee? The soup?" Katherine gestured toward the stove. Her face was flush.

"Yes ma'am."

"A man in the kitchen! I can't believe it," Lena interjected.

It amused Ben to see Katherine bring her hand to her throat as she whispered, "You're up already. How'd you learn this?" Ben reached for a coffee cup, poured, and extended it toward Katherine. "Here, I think you could use some coffee. And, yes, I'm awake. And as to the cooking, someone close to me taught me. Lena, do you drink coffee?"

"Of course. I'm not a little girl."

He heard Katherine slurp and then let out a small gasp.

"Well pour yourself some, Lena, but be careful. The coffee is hot." He smiled and winked at Katherine. "Just ask your sister." The russet-haired beauty bit her lip and shook her head in agreement.

"You ladies don't mind me for breakfast. I had some bread and jelly already. Maybe you can gossip a bit before you head out to church. I think I'll sit out on the porch and enjoy the morning." He nodded them a goodbye and headed toward the outside.

"Ben!" He turned at the sound of Katherine's voice.

"Good coffee. Thank you."

He memorized her smile so he could have it with him when he left on the train that morning. If he had anything to do with it, this would not be his last visit to Layton.

Chapter 4

"And they lived happily ever after." Katherine laughed as Lena draped the clean damp sheet around her like a royal robe before pinning it to the clothes line. They'd spent the morning washing and ringing clothes with Lena telling tales of love and romance.

"Lena, all your stories end that way. Every one of your lady characters gets rescued from laundry, and chores, and cooking to go live in a big house with some handsome husband and fine clothes."

"Of course, they do. What good is a husband if he isn't rich and handsome?" Lena splashed sudsy water onto Katherine.

"Well, a husband might be good for loving, and talking to, and depending on."

"And piling up more laundry! Katherine, will you marry some day?"

"I reckon I will; that is, I hope I will."

"Will you be in love when you marry?"

"Well, I hope so. I want to marry someone that I love and who loves me." She fanned herself with her hand as though she were faint. "I guess I long for happily ever after."

"There's not one handsome man in Layton, so you best give up on that part of your happily ever after."

"What makes a man handsome to you may not be the same thing that makes one handsome to me."

"Ben is handsome." A tingle ran through Katherine. "Ben lives forty miles away, Lena." A lump formed in Katherine's throat. "But he's handsome. Don't you think, so sister?" A smile formed on Katherine's lips. "Yes."

"Maybe you could marry Ben." Katherine tugged at her ear. "And maybe I could live in a big house, wear fine clothes, and drive a fancy automobile while you wait on me hand and foot."

It had been almost two weeks since Joe had come home with the stranger named Ben, and it had been almost two weeks since Katherine had gone a day without thinking of him. For the entire weekend visit he'd seemed talkative and easy to be around. She was certain he'd intentionally tried to soften the harshness of Joe's words toward her. She suspected he didn't have

26

any liquor at High Cotton the night before. She pondered what losing a wife does to a man's heart. Of course, Katherine felt silly thinking he had singled her out during his visit; he'd been just as thoughtful and engaging with Lena. Ben seemed to be a nice, good-hearted man who happened to be handsome.

No need to dwell on him; I'll most likely never see him again.

"Katherine, did you hear me?"

"What? No, I was lost in thought."

"About Ben?"

"Never mind. What'd you say to me?"

"The flour will only last another two days."

"Oh. I'll ride to the store this afternoon and get some from Mr. Justice." She shrugged her shoulders and sighed. *Meanwhile, my mundane life goes on.*

The bell jingled as Katherine walked through the doorway of the store. To her immediate right sat the cola cooler. A counter boasting a large cash register sat on the left wall. Newspapers, jars of candy, medicines, and smokes were neatly arranged on shelves behind it. Four aisles were to her right. Perishables sat stocked together on one aisle. Basic toiletries and various personal luxuries were nestled together on shelves. Fishing gear, hard wares, sewing notions, and fabric sat next to each other for some reason. One aisle containing books, pencils, stationery, and even jewelry tempted the playful side of Katherine. She breathed in the smells of fresh fruits and vegetables displayed in baskets. A small post office lined the back wall. The aroma of cinnamon cake and coffee wafted from the small diner in the far-right corner of the building. Katherine's stomach growled. One day, when she could stash some mending money, she was going to bring Lena here to be waited on and taste someone else's good cooking.

"Afternoon, Katherine. Always nice to see ya."

"Hello, Mr. Justice. I need a ten-pound bag of flour."

"You wait right here; I'll bring it to your cart. You got your cart here, right?"

"Yes, it's tied up out front." Katherine meandered around the store, thinking of anything else she might need to buy. "Oh my. Look at this pretty tin of lotion and the wrapped soap." She reached toward the display and brought a bar of soap to her nose. The paper that surrounded it was white with drawings of lavender flowers. Katherine inhaled the scent and looked at the price to see how much mending money she'd need to purchase such delightful treats. Goodness—a month's worth!

"It's all loaded up, Katherine. Need anything else?"

"No, thank you. Can you put the purchase on our account?" Katherine watched his smile fade and felt a knot in her stomach.

"Katherine, the account is past due. I can't add anything to it."

"You saying that Joe didn't pay in full when he was in town a couple weeks ago?" She reached up to tug at her ear. Anger at Joe knotted her stomach. Worry caused perspiration to break out on her forehead.

"Joe didn't pay a cent. I've already extended grace to you and Lena with the few items you purchased last week. I didn't want to tell you then. I'm sorry, I just can't do that again."

"Oh, of course not. Mr. Justice, you've been more than kind. Would you please remove the flour from my cart? I'll be back in a couple of days with money to make my purchase."

Katherine let the tears fall down her cheeks as she drove the cart back to her home. She was humiliated. Three times now Joe had left their debts unpaid and she'd born the embarrassment. How dare he go into Nelson for a night at the dance hall to drink and gamble then leave his sisters to handle the mess he created.

Katherine supposed Joe was like their Papa. She hadn't understood until she was older that gambling had impacted her life growing up. Her Momma took in extra work while her Papa would pander his handmade furniture. "A sale is good money," she'd heard her Momma say to her Papa many times, "but you're losing too much of it." As a child, she had figured her father was literally losing money from his pockets. When she became older, she began to realize he was losing it at the card table.

Katherine knew the debt had to be paid, but she didn't have mending money stashed away and didn't have more mending waiting for her to get done. Her mind wondered to the field wagon that passed her house each morning, carrying laborers to the cotton field. Tomorrow she'd catch the wagon with the workers and ask the foreman to hire her on for a bit. It wouldn't be the first time she'd had to ask.

Among the Crepe Myrtles

It was dark outside when Katherine got out of bed the next morning. Throwing on her work dress and pinning her hair in a tight bun on top of her head, she walked through Joe's empty room and headed toward the kitchen. "Blast you, Joe McGinn." She reckoned Lena would be upset that she didn't wake her before catching the wagon, but she knew the girl would have enough to do the next few days, carrying the workload of the house and garden by herself. She grabbed the lunch pail Lena had prepared last night, then went out through the back porch where her sun hat, yard apron, and cotton sack hung on a nail and grabbed those as well.

Dressed for a day in the hot Texas cotton fields, she made her way to the front of their yard. Dread for what she had to do and contempt for her brother accompanied her. In the still of the morning hours, she heard the wagon heading toward her.

"Whoa," the driver, wrinkled by sun and hard labor, commanded the horse. "You heading toward the fields, ma'am?"

"Yes, I am."

"Hop on in."

Katherine hoisted herself into the back of the wagon, pulling her weight and tall frame inside the best she could. Tomorrow wouldn't be so easy doing this, with the cuts and blisters she was sure to have on her hands. She pushed the unspoken thought aside as she seated herself near the front and smiled at the other occupants. Most were men, some were women, and a few were children who clung shyly to arms of the women sitting next to them. She was the only fair-skinned rider.

All the riders were quiet, so Katherine followed their example. A warm morning breeze soothed her face, and she relaxed in the simple pleasure of it. A large hole in the road caused the wagon to jerk, and her back slammed against the wagon's side. "Blast you, Joe McGinn." Her lips had no sooner muttered the words when she felt a tug at her heart. *Dear God, I need strength for my body today. Lena needs some too. And God, I got some anger toward Joe, so the best thing I know to do is pray for his heart. He's not doing right by Lena and me and Mr. Justice and you neither. I pray he'll turn from his ways and turn his heart to You. Oh, and please let the foreman hire me. Amen.*

The sun rose over the horizon just as the wagon stopped at the field. Katherine stood to leave the wagon, when a young boy's voice broke the silence, "Hep ya out, ma'am?" Katherine took the small dark hand he extended. "Yes, thank you."

Feeling anxious over how much she needed this work, she headed to the far side of the field where she saw a tent set up. Inside, a thin, middle-aged man sat at a table, tobacco juice oozing from his bottom lip. Katherine recognized him as the foreman from the other times she had come to work the fields. "Excuse me." The man wiped the juice with the back of his hand, spit, and then looked her in the eye. "I was hoping to get hired on for a bit." She wondered if she looked as out of place as she felt, for the man wrinkled his eyebrows and tilted his head before speaking.

"Have you ever done field work?"

"I have. You've hired me before."

"Name?"

"McGinn, Katherine."

The foreman shuffled some papers and then addressed her. "A'right. I see your name here. You work the rows in the far left back. I got one worker out injured for a few days. Water will be brought by every couple of hours, and we stop one hour for lunch. We work until the cotton wagon bed is filled and can be driven to the gin. I reckon that's around 4:00 pm. You take care of your personal business before you start, at lunch, and at afternoon water break. Pay is $2.00 a day. Pay you at the end of the week."

"I understand. Thank you." Katherine cleared her throat, then roused up her courage. "Might I ask if I could receive my pay for today and for tomorrow at the end of each day?"

"Pay is at the end of week."

"But, I need flour and…" She fought back tears.

"Them's the conditions. Take it or leave it. And if you are so inclined to leave, you got a long walk ahead of you. Wagon don't pull out 'til the day is ended."

Katherine walked the edge of the field and made her way to rows the foreman had indicated. She found herself working near a family of four—a papa, a momma, and two young boys that looked to be around eight years old. She tugged on a boll with four fluffy heads to it and began her work.

By the time morning water was wheeled up in a wooden wagon, Katherine was in pain. Swiping her hand across her forehead, the sting of salty sweat mixed with the cuts on her fingers caused her to yelp and release the tears that had filled her eyes all morning. Her back throbbed so much that her hand shook as she took the ladle and sipped the warm water from it. When lunch hour came, her eyes searched the area for a spot of shade. "Ma'am, we's rest under that tree. You's welcome to come." She recognized the face of one of the young boys she'd been working near. "Thank you."

She tried to eat her biscuit but couldn't because blood dripped from her raw fingers. Of course, she'd forgotten to bring rags to wrap around her hands that were not used to the prick and cut of the crop. "I'm Celeste." The kind woman sitting next to her spoke as she tore a jagged piece of cloth from her own rag and wrapped it around one of Katherine's hands. "Ouch!" Katherine winced. "Best hold still," the lady smiled. Katherine didn't figure Celeste to be more than ten years older than herself, but it felt so good to be mothered by her. "Thank you. I'll be better prepared tomorrow."

The lunch hour passed with Katherine and Celeste chatting as women do about the things common to most all of them. By the time the workers were loading back into the wagon that hauled them home, Katherine could barely stand up straight. She was at the mercy of two kind men to help her in and later out of the wagon. The ride home was silent other than the hum of a man seated near the back of the wagon and the clop of the horse hooves on the dusty, black ground. Children slept or made quiet gestures and facial expressions to one another.

Katherine smiled at the sight of her sister waiting on the front steps. Lena must have heard the wagon approach. As two kind men helped Katherine down, she saw Lena run toward her then heard a gasp. "Your hands! Give me your things and sit down in the kitchen."

Katherine trudged through the house and collapsed onto the kitchen bench, resting her arms and head on the table. She held back no emotion and wept for the pain and fatigue her body felt. Lena bustled about and Katherine heard the pump and water flowing from it.

31

Soon Lena came to her with a warm, wet cloth and gently wiped down her hands. Next, she poured heated water into a bowl. "Let me unbutton your dress for you, and then I'll leave so you can wash yourself down."

"I don't think I can." Katherine's voice was a whisper as she felt the humility of what she was saying. Katherine watched as Lena walked away and returned with a cotton gown in hand. Katherine felt her sister carefully pull the filthy dress over her head and wash down her neck, arms, back, and face. Katherine felt the gown slip over her head, and she pushed her arms into the armholes.

"Here, let me rub some salve on your fingers." Lena's gentle, massaging touch was soothing. Her sister wrapped small cloth strips around each of Katherine's fingers. Then she sat a bowl of soup and a plate of cornbread before her.

"I don't get paid until the end of the week. You'll run out of flour by then."

"I can work wonders with corn meal. Thank you, Katherine, for what you're doing."

By the end of the week, Katherine's fingers toughened up, and she'd made friends with the family she worked alongside. The thoughts that passed her time had focused less on bodily pain and frustration with Joe and more on the man who'd visited them three weeks ago now. When would a widower be ready for another wife? Could a widower love another woman like he loved his first wife? Would Ben ever show love for God? Was there really a happily ever after possible for a girl who worked a cotton field?

Saturday morning, as Lena led the reins, Katherine rode the cart to the store and once again went in to purchase flour. "Good morning, Mr. Justice. I'm here for some flour." The kind middle aged man smiled and then loaded a bag onto her cart while Katherine waited at the counter.

"That'll be half a dollar," His breath caught. Katherine looked to see him gawking at her hands. "Katherine, my dear, you've been working in the fields to earn money?" She saw tears well up in his eyes. She thought him such a kind man. "Why, what's a scratch or two, Mr. Justice? Here's your money for the flour and partial on our bill. I'll be back next week to pay the rest. Thank you."

She turned and walked out, but not before she heard him say under his breath, "Joe is a scoundrel." No feeling of blood loyalty rose in her at his statement. "In fact, I feel the words are justified." She ignored Lena's question of what words she was talking about as she joined her back in the cart.

One week rolled into two, and soon another Saturday morning was upon her. "Lena, time to head to the store for our groceries." Lena wagged a finger at her sarcastically as she came from the bedroom, "And bill paying."

Although Katherine saw gathering groceries as a chore, she knew Lena loved picking up the vegetables to smell and to touch, selecting spices, and determining how much bacon, salt, coffee, and other what nots were needed. As Mr. Justice totaled the sale, Katherine counted out the dollars and change. She was left with two dollars to pay off the bill when its balance was four dollars. "Lena, we need to put some things back and save them for next time." She was grateful the feisty young thing didn't choose this moment to be dramatic. She knew Lena understood the situation and smiled at her. "Quit tugging on your ear, Katherine. Stop worrying."

As they were considering the items on the counter, the train whistle blew. Katherine jumped and then looked at Lena. "Blast it. You think that's Joe coming in? I wasn't expecting him until next week."

Since the depot was next to the store, the ladies hadn't finished their shopping when the bell over the door jingled and in walked Joe. Anger at him caused Katherine's body to stiffen when he approached.

"Joe! I wasn't expecting you until next week."

"Well, hello to you too, Katherine. Our route's needing repair. Shift got cut short a couple of days. What's Lena doing, taking things back to the shelf?"

"We can't afford all we need because you left the bill unpaid." She lowered her voice somewhat as she raised her hands for him to see. "This is how we've managed in your absence. "

"What's that supposed to mean?"

"You know good and well what it means, Joe McGinn. I've worked the cotton field to earn money for what we need and to try and pay off our debt to Mr. Justice. A debt you didn't pay a cent on the last time you were in town!" She turned toward Lena. "Bring those items back up here. Joe is here to cover all the expenses." With that, she grabbed the two dollars lying on the counter and stuffed them into her pocket. "While he and Mr. Justice settle up, let's you and me get us a cola at the diner." She smiled at the kind shop keeper who lowered his chin and smiled back. Then she turned toward the diner and ran smack into broad shoulders and a big smile.

"Ben!"

Chapter 5

His breath quickened. He'd spotted the McGinn cart as he and Joe came to the front of the store because among the others, one cart and horse was vaguely familiar to him. His heart beat faster with the thought that he wouldn't have to wait the mile ride to the house to be near her. After all, she was the reason he was in Layton again. His thoughts had been filled with her for the last four weeks and he needed to lay eyes on her again.

Entering the store, those very eyes fell on her immediately. She had her back to the door and was standing at the counter with goods in front of her. He watched her turn and was disappointed to see what looked like anger cross her face. She had noticed Joe, but not him and as the siblings began to exchange words, he hoped he'd blend into the scenery as he stepped down an aisle so as not to overhear. He overheard plenty though, and anger at Joe rose inside him. He watched her grab money from the counter and then turn and head toward the diner on the very aisle where he stood. There was no time to move, so he'd just enjoy the moment. He let a smile overtake his face in anticipation of her impact. She exclaimed his name.

"Miss Katherine." He quivered as her upper arm grazed his chest and his hand clasped her elbow to steady her in their brief collision. Her high-pitched gasp and the flush of pink on her cheeks both amused and excited him. He already knew he found her attractive, but now realized he thought her adorable too.

He saw her bring her hand toward his shoulder in what he figured was an attempt push away from his body. He grabbed the wrist of that hand and murmured, "Careful of your fingers," then gently released his hands from her elbow and wrist, giving her freedom to step back, which she did. He felt the gap between them and had to wrestle his mind to tell his feet to stay put and not close it.

"It's good to run into you ma'am. Hello." He tipped the edge of his hat and gave her a nod and a wink. Her cheeks reddened. Adorable!

"Hello. I'm surprised to see you, Ben. I, uh, wasn't expecting Joe so soon."

"Nor me, at all, I suspect. I hope our arrival is a good surprise." He winked at her.

"Joe? No. You? Yes." He chuckled as her hand flew to her mouth, and her eyes bugged out. "Don't worry," he said as he leaned into her ear, "your secret is safe with me." A little squeak came from her throat, and her hand moved to her ear and tugged.

"So, a cola. Turns out I'm thirsty for one myself. Mind if I join you and Lena? My treat. Lena! Over here."

Apparently twelve-year-old Lena had already spotted him, for when she came to them, her surprise was so pathetically feigned that he laughed out loud. "Ladies, after you." He raised his eyebrows at Katherine, and she finally began to move toward the corner diner. Ben seated them at one of the small tables, headed to the counter to order colas, and then joined them. "Sincerely, pardon me for showing up again unannounced. When we got the unexpected leave, I asked Joe if I could come. I'm being assigned to a new crew and won't be working with your brother. So, I couldn't pass up the chance to see, uh, Layton again."

Ben chuckled to himself. *I actually stammered. Who is pathetically feigning now?* He felt like a shy school boy. *If it is obvious to the ladies that I am obviously trying not to be obvious about coming to see Katherine, I can only blame myself.*

Lena filled his awkward moment with words. "We're glad you came. Aren't we Katherine?"

"Yes, of course. You're always welcome here."

Joe sauntered to the table. "I got the cart loaded. Y'all ready to go?"

Ben cleared his throat. "Still working on our colas. I'd be happy to walk your sisters to the house if they don't object. Or, wanna join us?"

"You all keep each other company walking back. I'll enjoy the ride by myself."

"Bye, Joe." Lena waved, took a sip of cola, and smiled at Ben. "How long will you two be in town?"

"Today."

Katherine choked, then hiccupped. Ben grinned and concurred. "I couldn't agree more, Miss Katherine. The visit is far too short."

Lena giggled.

When they finished their colas, Ben purchased the shave cream, headache powder, and chewing gum he'd come into the store for in the first place, then led the trio out. He kept them chatting about the town, what they enjoyed when they had time to relax, his crew change—just about anything but the cuts and tears on Katherine's hands and fingers.

As much as he wanted to ask Katherine about her time in the cotton fields, he restrained himself, not wanting to risk embarrassing her. As soon as he could get Joe cornered, Ben planned to confront the man. There was no excuse in Ben's mind to justify a man not providing for those under his care. He had dismissed his earlier notion of Joe's finances being none of his business.

How he'd love to rub salve into Katherine's hands to show concern for her welfare and irritation that she was put in such a predicament, not to mention how much he'd enjoy the touch of her fingers on his. He was jolted by his desire to touch her and wondered if there was shame in a widower feeling this way toward another woman. He shook off the question.

"So, Lena, when you make up those stories you just told me about and act them out, I figure Katherine must play the lead woman in love." He donned a roguish grin.

"Oh! Not just the lead—" hiccup "but sometimes I have to play more than one part because—" hiccup "she's quite demanding—" hiccup "when's she's in charge." Hiccup.

"I think I'd enjoy seeing an original play by Lena McGinn starring the one and only Katherine McGinn." He rubbed his palms together to show his anticipation, just as another hiccup sounded in his ear.

"Yes! Let's do that!" Lena jumped up and down.

"No—" hiccup "let's not!"

Adorable!

Mid-morning, Ben and Joe packed a lunch and jug of water and set off for some late morning and afternoon fishing in the Layton Pond, a quarter mile walk from the McGinn house. The men pulled in blue catfish and a few white bass. Ben's mouth watered thinking of fried fish for supper, so when Joe shared that he had other plans for the two of them that evening, Ben felt annoyed.

"Every time I've hooked a fish, I've practically tasted it fried up and hot. I don't want my supper at the dance hall. Besides, what are you gonna do with these fish?" He motioned toward the hook containing their catch.

"Ben, I've set my money aside for a night of cards, drinking, and a good bowl of dumplings. Not to mention a glance or two at Faye Forder. We'll ice the fish, and the girls can cook 'em for themselves on Sunday. Take it or leave it."

"I'll leave it. If you and the women don't mind, I'll clean the fish and fry 'em up myself and just hang around the house tonight." Awareness of the awkwardness in the suggestion set in. "And… I'll wait on the porch for you to return."

Ben watched as Joe wrinkled his brow before he spoke. "I reckon your intentions is good toward my sisters, and since you don't partake in drinking, well, suit yourself, my goody two shoes friend." Joe's comment about good intentions irritated Ben. The time to confront the scoundrel was now.

"So suddenly you have concern over the welfare of your sisters? Hypocritical if you ask me."

"I didn't ask, and what are you talking about anyway?"

"Joe, I overheard Katherine in the store this morning and obviously have seen the wrappings on her hands. How could you leave your sisters with a debt they had to pay off before they could even buy supplies?"

"None of your business."

"You saw Katherine's hands. The cotton fields? Joe, aren't you the least bit ashamed for putting her there?"

"I didn't put her there."

"Your decision put her there."

"My money affairs are none of your business."

"I reckon you're right about that, but I also reckon when a friend sees his buddy gambling and drinking away his money but leaving his debts unpaid, he ought to speak up."

"You're right about one thing. You're a friend. And I don't like being judged by a friend. But since I owe you a judgement, here's one. So suddenly you have concern over the welfare of my sisters? I think you deceived me and asked to come back to Layton for reasons that have nothing to do with our friendship. Hypocritical if you ask me."

Ben literally bit down on his tongue. Joe was on to him. And since Ben had said his piece to Joe, he let the conversation end with a smirk and nod of his head. If Joe recognized the response for the acknowledgement it was, so be it. He'd handle whatever Joe dished out about his interest in Katherine; however, if Joe didn't catch his meaning, Ben wouldn't clarify it.

Back at the house, Ben gutted and cleaned the fish while Joe apparently bathed in aftershave. The smell was so strong when he came to bid Ben goodbye, he covered his mouth to cough. Lena fried up the fish, and Katherine mashed some potatoes with milk and butter. The three of them enjoyed the fresh catch and lumpy potatoes then headed to the front porch as darkness set in.

Ben took in the natural surroundings. Crepe myrtles lined the far edge of the yard. Crickets chirped. The stars were out in numbers tonight. As though she had read his thoughts, Lena challenged him and Katherine to find a shape in the stars.

"I spot a bluebonnet. See it's there to the left, over the chimney." Katherine pointed. He noticed at that moment that she was finally free of her hiccups.

"You think that's a bluebonnet? Well, I see it as a sword. Miss Lena what do you think?" Ben chuckled.

"I think I'm smart enough to find my own constellation and not answer that question." Ben felt at ease and happy as they all three laughed.

"Speaking of a sword, there was this old man that lived in my boarding house. Kind as he could be, but his mind wasn't right. Most of the time he felt certain he was a pirate and called himself Hanging Johnny, after a song, and all us boarders had to call him that too when he wasn't thinking right. Always talking about treasures he had locked away in trunks in his ship, you know, his room. He had the landlord put an extra bolt inside his door to protect his loot from us robbers. He'd always sing 'Blow the Man Down.'"

"I like that tune." Lena began humming.

"Did he have a sword and a patch?"

"Alas, Miss Katherine, sadly he did not."

Ben pulled a harmonica from his pocket and began to play along with Lena's humming. The ladies smiled at one another. And although he was not a church going man, when Katherine asked if he could play her favorite hymn, he knew the tune. A feeling moved through him that he recognized as contentment. He hadn't felt it for a couple of years.

"I can't imagine what it would be like to own one of those phonographs," Katherine sighed. Ben stopped playing. "We have one at the boarding house where I live. Our landlord owns three records and plays one after supper each night. It's nice."

"Did you go off to the war, Ben?" The abrupt change in subject jolted him. Ben looked at Lena and nodded his head no. "Oh. Joe didn't go either because of us—being our provider." Ben laid the harmonica on his leg and cleared his throat. "It was the same for me. I was responsible for my family…" His stomach lurched at his error. "…uh my wife, as provider and care taker. She'd gotten pneumonia our fifth winter together and it weakened her, so when it struck again, she was bedridden." Neither lady seemed to notice his blunder.

"Is that what took her?" The question was spoken by Katherine in a voice as thin as the air around him. He looked her way to try and gauge her emotions. He thought he saw apprehension; she had her chin down and eyes looking up at him. Did she wonder if the question would upset him? What he didn't see on her face was pity. He had grown weary of pity. The fact that someone had stepped through the door he'd opened and asked about his wife—especially this someone—touched him.

"Yes." He opened his mouth to say more, to tell her his wife hadn't left him completely alone, that he was a Papa, but the words became paralyzed in his throat and he almost choked on them.

"I shouldn't have asked, Ben." He collected his thoughts. "I'm glad you did. Most everyone shuns the question as though not asking will change the past."

"Ben," Lena smiled, "did she hum and sing too?"

He literally laughed out loud at the memories of his wife singing and doing so evoked a longing for her. Lena didn't know he couldn't dig deeper down in his being right now without risking being pulled in two by the desire to share his soul with Katherine and the desire to remain loyal to his deceased wife and mother of his son?

"Goodness, yes, but she couldn't carry a tune in a bucket and she knew it," his fingers thumped the harmonica on his leg, "but it didn't matter to me." He pulled the harmonica back up to his lips. "How about another request, ladies?"

It became time for Katherine and Lena to go to bed. Ben felt loneliness seep in at the thought of ending the evening. "Thank you for lunch and supper ladies. It was good to see you again." He'd felt dead inside since his wife died, and he wanted to say how he'd begun to feel alive again when he was around Katherine. He wanted to say that he'd miss her. Instead he said no thank you when she asked if he wanted to join them at church the next morning. "You ladies go on inside the house and hit the hay. I'll be waiting out here for Joe." The girls spoke their good-nights and headed in.

Alone on the porch Ben let himself feel the emotions inside. His mind slipped back to the day his wife had died. He knew a part of him had ceased to breathe along with Addie. Was that part of him waking up, gasping for air? It felt like Katherine was air coming back into his lungs, but there was pain in breathing it in. The very thing he needed to be alive again was coming at him faster than he could inhale it.

The creak of the screen door shook him from his thoughts, and he turned to see Katherine standing there. She held a quilt. His heart skipped at the sight of her; he felt divided between two women.

"Here, Ben. Take this. You'll get chilly out here."

"Thank you, Katherine." He reached to take the quilt, keeping his eyes locked with hers. His action was slow and deliberate as he slid it gently from her grasp and brushed her hand in the process.

"Ben, might I ask you something? Something very personal?" Her voice was just above a whisper.

"Yes."

"Do you believe in God?"

He paused before answering, letting the reality of the answer sink into him. She'd risked embarrassment and his possible anger by asking him. He wanted this woman to hear the truth, even if his answer put their friendship at risk—a fragile friendship because it was so newly formed and yet, for him, had so much at stake. And the fact that he felt that way surprised him.

"I believe in God. I just don't understand Him." She remained silent, but tilted her head to the side. He read that as curiosity she was too polite voice. "God took a young woman in her prime. Not only that, He took her from me and from… Well, I reckon I'm holding a grudge. Not just for taking her, but also for the scoundrel my Pa was. He was in church every Sunday, but would hurt his family all through the week. I determined a long time ago that God didn't play fair and confirmed that when my wife died." He took in a large breath, never letting his eyes unlock from hers. She seemed to consider his words and the jagged vulnerability he'd just shown her. Far too soon?

She gazed at him. "I'm sorry all that happened Ben. Seems like a heavy burden for a man to bear." She brought her hand to her heart, turned toward the door, and then paused. Her eyes met his again. "Might I be praying for you?"

Ben felt relief. He didn't sense judgment or withdrawal from her. He sensed concern. And it felt good to his soul. She didn't have to ask for his permission; she certainly could have prayed without his ever knowing of it, so he felt her question as a connection between them, and he imagined himself grabbing it and holding on. And deep inside where his soul rested against eternity, he knew he needed someone praying for him.

"I'd appreciate that. Thank you, Katherine." He forced his hand to stay at his side rather than reaching out to touch her cheek. He felt drawn to her.

"Then count on it. Night Ben."

"Night Katherine."

Ben wrapped himself in the quilt and settled into a rocker for an uncomfortable doze, hoping Joe came home much sooner than midnight. Overhearing whispered conversation, he realized the rocker he sat in was in front of the ladies' open bedroom windows and a little too close for his mind not to wander where it shouldn't go. He moved himself to a rocker on the other end of the porch.

His eyes were heavy, but his thoughts were wide awake. He settled in on the thought that Katherine would be praying for him, and the idea soothed him. He knew he wasn't a religious man, nor did he see himself as a particularly moral man. He knew that anything others may see as good and moral in him was, in his mind, just a practical decision that worked for him. He was driven more by reason than morality or spirituality or emotion. *Miss Katherine, reckon I'll feel the effects of your prayers?* He smiled to himself and gave in to sleep.

A clatter awakened him, and Ben jumped. He shook off the fog in his head and realized where he was as his eyes focused on Joe coming on to the property in the cart with the lantern lit. He unwrapped himself and headed toward him. "Here, let me help you settle the horse for the night." Joe didn't reply. He slid from the cart and raised a fist. The impact was intense and knocked Ben off balance. Catching his footing, he grabbed Joe's wrist and blocked the next punch. Searing pain came from his eye and the jaw below it. "Joe! What was that for! It's me, Ben"

"I know it's you! That was for stealing my girl."

"You're drunk."

"Faye asked me to dance tonight, but all she wanted to talk about was where was my friend I brought in a few weeks ago and oh, how much she would like to see him at her place again." Ben released Joe's wrist but stepped close enough to smell his liquored breath. "I don't care for the likes of Faye. Back off." Just as Joe raised his fist again, Ben heard the screen door slam shut. "What's going on?" The voice belonged to Katherine and he sensed fear in it.

Joe began storming toward the front porch and screaming at her to mind her own business. Ben felt fury engulf him instantly. He yanked Joe by the back collar. "Don't you lay a hand on her; I'll beat you to a pulp, you drunk." He wrapped both his arms around Joe's chest from behind and held him firmly.

"Ben!" He looked up when Katherine called his name. She moved to the edge of the steps. "Ben, he won't hurt us." Her voice was calm, though slight. "He never has. He just needs to get in bed."

Ben was breathing heavily with his lips pursed tightly. He took in Katherine's words and slowly released his grip on Joe. With her robe tied around her and her hair braid draped across her shoulder, Katherine turned and opened the screen door. "Come on in, Joe. Lena, back to bed." Ben hadn't noticed the younger girl until that moment when he saw her slip her shoulders back through the open window. He willed himself to calm down and escorted Joe up the stairs.

Chagrined over his reaction in front of Katherine, he wished he could explain himself to her, but now was not the time to discuss his childhood and drunken father. Maybe she'd recall what'd he'd shared about him and understand his heightened emotions. When the two men entered the house, he heard Katherine gasp.

"Ben. Your eye! What happened out there?"

Joe interjected, "Just two men talking," and moved on to his bedroom.

Ben gave Katherine a half smile. "Just a misunderstanding. He's likely not to remember it in the morning."

"I'll get you a wet cloth as cold as I can get it."

"Thank you, Katherine, then you head on back to bed. I'll care for the horse and cart."

Following Katherine into the kitchen, Ben was relieved as he crossed through the bedroom and noticed Joe had simply stretched himself across the bed and become silent. Katherine looked Ben in the eye. "Ben, he's never been violent toward us. He just comes in and falls onto his bed when he comes home drunk. Tonight was different somehow."

"I reckon I startled him by being outside and one thing led to another. I'm sorry."

"No harm. Well, except to your eye." She handed him the cloth. "Goodnight, Ben." She smiled. "Thank you."

Just like he had four weeks ago when he visited, Ben awoke to the smell of coffee. Making himself presentable, he walked into the kitchen. A covered plate of biscuits and some bacon sat in the middle of the table and coffee cups set upside down to dry were next to the sink. "They've eaten." The realization pushed him out the backdoor, and he trotted to the front of the house. There was Katherine sitting in the cart holding her Bible in her hand. He saw no sign of Lena.

He had something he wanted to ask Katherine, and he best do it now.

"Katherine?" At that moment, he heard the screen door creak open. Lena was approaching.

"Ben. Your eye's all swollen shut!" He realized that he must look horrific, but he couldn't worry about that now.

Resting his forearms on the edge of the cart where she sat, he leaned toward her, looked up, and locked his open eye with hers as she looked down into his face. "Katherine, might I write to you? A man gets lonely on the rails and weary of talking with crude and brute males, and well, I'm on a new crew and don't know anyone, and…"

"Yes." His heart thudded as he watched her smile fill her face and touch her cheeks that had just turned pink.

44

He returned the smile, and without a thought, he touched her arm with the hand he'd be using to write her. "Should I beg your post number from your brother?" She tugged her ear. "Eighteen." Then she whispered. "Same as my age."

He was ten years older than her. More than half her life span. And in the near balance of that span, he'd loved a life, created a life, buried a life, and lived a death.

Ben removed his hand just as Lena stepped up to get in the cart and noticed his face. "Ben, your eye looks awful. What'd you say to Katherine to deserve that?" She smirked and moved her eyebrows up and down. He took her mood and tossed it right back at her. "None of your business, Lena, but it was worth it."

He painfully winked at the feisty young girl then turned and whistled all the way back to the house. He overheard Lena ask her sister in a high-pitched voice if he'd kissed her. He chuckled when Katherine replied, "None of your business." Adorable!

Could he revive a life?

Chapter 6

It had been a long time since she had seen him, but Katherine was grateful Gabriel Hawkins had been at church last week. He was on his way to her house, but she was not looking forward to his coming.

He was due at noon and she was waiting for him in the shed. Lena had looked surprised when Katherine asked her to walk to the post office and get their mail. They both knew that mail delivery day was a highlight for Katherine, but today she had something awful on her mind to tend to, and she would rather Lena not know until it was done.

She turned at the sound of footsteps. "Well, Buster, he's here." She ran her hand down the mane of the weak horse. She'd miss him. Buster had been vital to the family as he pulled their cart or used his strength to help till the garden.

Her mind flashed back to the day her father had left with their cart loaded with handmade chairs and the mule tied and ready to pull the weight. She'd overheard her mother and father speaking before he left on the delivery. "Josiah," she'd chided, "return with all the money. We need it for some groceries, and our oldest boy and girl has outgrown their shoes. Do you understand what I'm saying? There's no hand me downs to give those two."

That night her father had returned with no money, but instead with a tall brown horse pulling the cart. Katherine had been so excited over the horse that it never occurred to her to ask what happened to their ugly mule. What poor, rural, immature, girl wouldn't be proud of the prestige that came from owning a horse?

However, at the same time, a realization had nagged at her pride and happiness—she'd be going through the winter with boots that rubbed blisters on her heels and toes from being too small. Years later Katherine had become wise to the fact that her father regularly gambled away most of the money he made selling his handmade furniture, leaving his family to live on meager income.

It was then she reckoned that Buster had been part of a bet with some other man who bid away too much of his money and offered up his horse as a chance to keep playing the game. Her Papa had been lucky enough to play the final best hand. When the cares of the household had fallen on her shoulders after the passing of her parents, she also wised up to the financial strain the upkeep of a horse could be to a meager income.

"Afternoon, Gabriel. Thank you for coming." Gabriel smiled. The few teeth he had were grown in crooked and set below a clef palate. A purple birthmark covered the entire left side of his face. He was a lonely soul, Katherine thought, placed upon the earth with seemingly no kindred human being formed for him. Katherine had known Gabe so long that she was used to his appearance. What she never got used to was his taking a liking to her.

"I'm happy to help ya, Miss Katherine. Sorry though about Buster." They entered the shed. Gabe rested his head against the animal. "Sure is struggling to breathe, ain't he?" Katherine nodded her agreement. Gabriel didn't have much of a way with people, but he had it in him to work with animals like no one she had ever met. "I got your mule tied up to my wagon. I'll just trade him and Buster and be on my way."

"Will Buster make it to your place without...without dying?"

"Yes'um, he's got enough life in him for the short trip, and then I'll take him out to the woods, end his misery, and bury him. Don't you fret none for his care. I'll respect every bit of what I's about to do."

"I know you will Gabe. Thank you. Bring the mule around and tell me all about him. I'd like to be done with this sad business. I got your partial payment ready. Thank you for letting me pay the rest later."

"Miss Katherine, you know I'd do whatever I can for ya. You just owe me for the mule; my services are free to you. You're the best lady in the county." Oh my, she didn't want to be beholding to this man, but no need to argue.

"Well, go on about our business now, ya hear me Gabe?"

The exchange took place and Katherine noticed and smelled the sweat rolling down his face and neck and soaking his arms. She didn't have it in her heart not to offer him some sweet tea before he set out, which of course he accepted. She sat on the front porch enduring talk of cows, longhorns, coyotes, and other sorts of animals. Apparently, he'd taken in an injured armadillo as a pet. "Your Momma good with that thing in her house?" He replied that his mother was as much taken with the thing as he was, which, she supposed, is what any mother with a comely, lonely, and odd son would feel. Eventually he left when she reminded him that Buster was very ill and needed the good mercy that Gabriel would be bestowing on him.

Katherine breathed a sigh of relief that Joe would be back in town in time to pay the rest of the money owed for the mule and that she wouldn't have to interact with Gabriel. She was determined that she wouldn't go work the fields before her brother's return to make money for the rest of the payment. That would be Joe's matter to clear up. She sighed. Getting around was going to take longer from now on depending on a mule.

Gabe had just started down the dirt road as Lena made it back from the post office, and Katherine knew she'd seen him with Buster in tow.

"Katherine, what's Gabriel doing with Buster?" Ugh. Her day had just gotten worse. She spent the next half hour or so explaining the matter to Lena and comforting her for their loss. It seemed Lena felt the loss of a beloved pet more than of a working contributor to the family. Her sister had retreated to her room to mourn or so she stated.

Katherine needed to get her mind on something other than Buster, so she began to press their clean clothes that were stiff and wrinkled from drying on the line outside. About an hour later, Lena popped into the front room. Evidently her mourning was behind her for she'd emerged with a broad grin.

"Don't you want to know what was in the post office box?" Katherine had forgotten all about the mail.

"Yes."

"Well, maybe I should wait for a while. After all, we are in mourning."

"Hand me the mail. Crying. Smiling. I can't figure you Lena! You certainly made a quick recovery from our loss and seem a might too interested in this week's mail."

Lena stood with her hands behind her back and told Katherine to pick an arm. Katherine rolled her eyes but played along. She picked the left. Lena brought forward a *Farmer's Almanac*. "That's certainly not what's got you grinning! Show me the rest."

Lena acted as though she were deciding about what to do when she finally brought forward her other arm. Katherine saw an envelope. Lena smiled, "It's addressed to someone named Katherine McGinn and it's postmarked Commerce. Now, who would we know from Commerce that would be writing my own Katherine McGinn?"

Katherine dropped the hot iron on top of the shirt she was pressing and let out a high- pitched squeal at the same time. She grabbed for the envelope. Lena was laughing heartily. "Here, take it. Go read, I'll rescue this shirt and finish up the rest. Oh, my goodness, Katherine, this is better than a fairy tale. I must be told every word he writes!" Katherine took the envelope and pressed it to her chest. "Only if you poison me, make me sleep for a hundred years, and find the letter where I hide it, Lena McGinn."

The screen door slammed as she rushed through the doorway and sat in her favorite rocker. She ran her finger over the entire envelope, savoring the experience, taking in the small, heavy handed curves and lines of his penmanship, thinking that his hand and mind had worked together to form her name, evidence she was in his thoughts. And maybe his heart.

She pulled the envelope to her nose to inhale any of his scent that might be lingering on the outside. Pulling open the flap, she slid the thick pages from inside, graced her lap with the envelope, and then unfolded the letter in ritualistic, reverent motions despite her heart racing.

She read the letter once silently. Then she brought it to her lips and kissed it before reading it again outloud.

August 15th, 1918
Commerce, Texas

Dear Katherine,

I hope this letter finds you and your sister well. As I write, I am seated in my room at the boarding house and the sound of the phonograph is coming through the walls. I smile, thinking how much you and your sister would enjoy hearing the music.

I hope that your hands are healed. Have you had to work the fields again? I hope not. My eye has healed. I am sorry that Joe and me argued, but we did make things right later that morning. Maybe he has told you that.

I have not seen Joe since we left Layton. I am getting used to my new route and the crew. They are good, hardworking men. All but one is married and he is younger than the rest of us and stays homesick for his sweetheart. Most the crew give him a hard time for it, but I don't 'cause I know how unwelcome loneliness is for a man.

I have seen some new cities on my route. I travel as far as Pine Bluff, Arkansas most the time. That's a far piece from Layton where you work your garden and make your coffee.

I will end my letter now. It is time to sleep. I will write you again in a few days. I am counting on those prayers you mentioned. Give my hello to Lena and to your brother when you see him. Find a new picture in the stars.

Your friend,
Ben Williams

Katherine read the letter two more times before she gently placed it back in the envelope. Her thoughts swirled in her head, going first one direction and then another. It was certainly the letter of a friend; he'd even signed it that way. But her heart fluttered when she read the lines that spoke of the time he'd shared with her. The music that evening on the porch. The star gazing. True, Lena had been there too, but he didn't close by saying he wanted her and Lena to find another a picture in the stars. He wrote the words to her.

He was counting on her prayer. She imagined his smile as he wrote those words. Awareness hit her. It could be the face of a man who had suffered great loss that she would see. If so, did the eyes of that face hint at any interest and hope as he wrote to her?

Katherine had been true to her word and hid the letter without Lena's getting to read it. A short summary and passing along his regards had not satisfied her sister, and for the past two days, she'd dramatically not spoken to Katherine unless the words were necessary. Katherine found her over-exaggerated huffs, silence, loud banging, and similar actions as humorous, which only irritated Lena more. Katherine didn't let Lena annoy her. On the contrary, each time she read the letter, which was every morning and every night, her happiness grew.

Lena's devastation was quickly laid aside when the following week an invitation came in the mail for the sisters. In two weeks Mrs. Forder would be hosting another gathering for all the women folk in the community. It was to take place on the lawn of the Forder home, weather permitting. The Forder Gin wagon would come through the community and pick up those who needed a ride and waited outside for it to come by. It would also make a stop at the Justice store. Others were welcome to walk or use their own wagons, carts, or autos. Katherine laughed at the thought of poor, rural women having access to an auto. She figured that the only folks with an auto were those hosting the party. She would need to decide if she and Lena should ride the wagon or take their cart with its new slower pace as Gitter, the mule, led it.

The sisters had worked hard to get ahead of their chores so there would be no excuse to miss the gathering scheduled for the day after next. In the meantime, Joe had been home for a couple of days and settled with Gabriel. He never mentioned anything about the day he and Ben had parted from here, and Katherine didn't ask about it. Before his arrival, she had told Lena to not mention Ben's letter. In time, if Ben kept writing, Katherine would tell Joe about their own separate friendship. Thankfully, Lena reminded her that she loved a good secret and would happily be a part of one.

"Lena, I'm heading out to the store for supplies and to check the post box. Need to add anything else to the list?"

"Fancy soap so we can smell good at the social."

"Have you ever tasted soap? 'Cause if I spend our money on that fancy stuff at the store, that's what you'll be eating. Can't afford to smell flowery and eat too."

Lena came and stood at the back porch screen with hands on hips, "I could learn to cook with soap, Katherine McGinn, and make it so tasty you'd beg for seconds."

Katherine gathered her items, and while Mr. Justice added them to their account, she walked to the post office boxes. As she did, the allure of the flowery soaps and lotions drew her to the display where they taunted and smirked at her. She sniffed the fragrances so much that she sneezed. "Lena couldn't handle the smell, with her poor breathing and all. Just another reason to stop eyeing such fancies."

Katherine noticed a sign at the post office counter. Expansion was coming to the general store. She read the dates on the sign. By Thanksgiving three rooms and a common bath would be built onto the backside of the store. By the new year the diner would be enlarged with more tables and menu choices, and a gasoline pump would be added at the front of the store. The Forders were making Layton into a place to dine and sleep on the route to Dallas. Katherine found she liked the idea of the town expanding.

Mrs. Justice appeared behind the counter. "Big news about our little store, don't you think, Katherine? The Forders are gonna have to hire us some help, that's for sure." She smiled and extended her hand with something inside it to Katherine. "Yes, Mrs. Justice, it's exciting news if you ask me." Instinctively Katherine reached for the item from Mrs. Justice. It was a chipped bar of soap that smelled like honeysuckle.

"I can't sell damaged goods, so I was wondering if you could take this off my hands. Don't really want to throw it away." Mrs. Justice smiled, and Katherine thought that if her own Mama were still alive, it would be that same kind, loving, motherly smile she'd see on her face.

"Thank you. That's very kind of you, Mrs. Justice." Katherine smiled, hoping it was a smile like a daughter would share with a mother. She'd been out of practice being a daughter and to feel like one at the moment was comforting.

"Don't think me nosey, but I did fill the postal boxes this morning and put a thick letter in there addressed to a Katherine McGinn." The short, round woman grinned and walked away.

Katherine felt heat rise to her cheeks just as her heart sped up its beats. Sure enough, her fingers pulled out a letter postmarked Pine Bluff, Arkansas. She pulled the letter to her heart, sniffed the soap, and hurried back to the counter. "You're all loaded up, Miss Katherine, and your account is in good order."

"Thank you, Mr. Justice."

"You have a good day now, Katherine, and thank you." Mr. Justice waved.

"I will!" With that, Katherine swung open the screen door of the store, jumped onto the seat of the cart, placed the soap in her lap, and then sniffed the letter she held—a scent of honeysuckle on her hand. My scent and his, mingled. She laughed at her silliness and opened the envelope. Good thing nothing in the cart had to get home immediately.

August 20th
Pine Bluff, Arkansas

Dear Katherine,

I trust this letter finds you well. I've seated myself in the parlor of the boarding house the railroad uses in Pine Bluff. I don't know anyone except the crew, since this is our first stay here since I came on board. There is no music playing in this parlor like at home. My crew and the other folks are all in bed and I reckon I am feeling a might lonely. I'm thankful I have you to write to. I hope you don't think ill of my writing you again.

Do you remember the young man on our crew I told you about who was missing his sweetheart? Turns out he's engaged to marry her and once he gets back to his hometown, he's quittin' the rails. Says her papa has a job for him on his turkey farm. What about that! I rather liked having him around in a brotherly sort of way.

Katherine, I have something bothering me and want to explain. When I came after Joe that day in your yard, I was reacting to his hollering and coming at you 'cause it roused something in me. My Pa was a drunkard. All my growing up years he'd beat on my momma and me until the day I was old enough to beat him back. He claimed he was a Christian. Had us in church on Sunday, but beat on us Monday through Saturday. So, you see, when I saw Joe behaving like he was, I got angry. Forgive me for scaring you.

Since I said this much to you, I reckon I'll keep telling. My Mama died of a weak heart when I was thirteen. I think she maybe died of a broken heart though, if a body can do that. I cried like a baby.

My Pa's liver was a mess and finally made him bedridden. A spinster cousin of our neighbor would care for him so I could work the gin in his place. He died when I was almost twenty. I didn't shed one tear. When he passed, I wanted out of that house that was nothing but walled in hurt to me, so I gave it to the spinster. I suppose that was crazy. After giving away the house, I moved into the boarding house and met my wife.

I just wanted you to know, Katherine, that I'm not a man that angers real easy. I'm not cruel or violent. I'd never beat my family. I'm not a drinking man. I'm not like my Pa. I think I'm a better man without religion than he was with it. God is supposed to be my Father, but my mind can't reason why He didn't take care of Momma and me and stop my Pa from beating us? What good father would not take care of his family?

I hope I'm not wrong to write you this about me.

Have you seen a picture in the stars? Katherine, I would be so glad if you would write me at PO Box 22, Commerce, Texas. Please write and tell me something about Katherine McGinn.

Say hello to Lena. I am happy in Layton and would very much like to visit there again.

Your sincere friend,
Ben

P.S. My mind also reasoned there was no harm in you praying. My heart knows I want it.

Katherine wiped the tears from her cheeks then tugged at her ear. Even though he'd signed the letter as a friend, his words were very intimate. She felt surprised by the risk he took to share such personal thoughts when he didn't know if she would be repulsed by them. She wasn't repulsed. She was humbled and delighted by his trust in her. He'd opened his soul and gave her another piece of himself to understand. His wife. His father. The man carried these burdens alone, without family and without God. What other burdens might he be bearing that she knew nothing of!

54

She wished he were sitting next to her so she could tell him to his face that she was certain she'd never tire of his sharing his thoughts and his story with her. She imagined if he were here, she would be so bold as to reach over and touch his arm or take his hand and squeeze it or touch his cheek to give him comfort.

The longing to release her care toward him caused literal pain in her chest. She had to give life and breath to the longing. Snapping the reins, she turned Gitter toward home. She must write Ben a letter—an invitation. The desire to connect with him was so visceral she felt the health of her continued existence depended upon her writing that letter.

And once the task was completed in the still night of that day, she allowed herself to rest and to dream—of him.

Chapter 7

The day of the social arrived boasting breezy warm dry weather. The letter to Ben having been posted a day earlier, Katherine found herself feeling as pleasant inside as the day was outside. She and Lena would take their own cart to the party. Smelling of honeysuckle soap and dressed in their Sunday attire, the sisters rode to the Forder home, looking forward to chatting and giggling with friends, some whom they saw only at monthly church services or the annual brush arbor meeting.

As they rounded the bend in the road, the Forder property came into view. The large gate that boasted an iron F encircled with iron flowers was opened for guests to freely enter. As Katherine guided Gitter through the gate, the left side of the large home stood five hundred yards in front of them. The road to the house was lined on both sides with sycamore trees. It eventually split into two directions. The left road led to the carriage house, the garage, and the barn. The right road circled toward the front of the home. A Forder employee met them at the split and assisted them to their feet, then directed Katherine and Lena to the front lawn as he hopped into the cart to park it somewhere.

"This place is more beautiful than I remember."

"Yes, it is, Lena. I don't know that I'll ever see anything more luxurious," Katherine sighed. "The scene is breathtaking." She stood with her hand covering her lips in an attempt to hold back the gasp that was fighting to be released. Katherine wanted to display the most dignified version of her common self that she could muster.

The great front lawn was green and plush with grass. Tables adorned in blue linens and fresh flowers and filled with delicious sweets, meats, and beverages, lined the edge of the lawn. A stringed quartet was placed under the large pecan tree at the front of the grounds. Their music mingled with the soft voices and gentle laughter of the chatting females who were scattered across the lawn.

The white two story home was adorned with a front porch that ran its length and proudly displayed four large white pillars. A balcony extended over the porch and provided a place for residents in the upper rooms to step out through the large shuttered windows and enjoy the view.

"What force do the Forders have that brings field workers and farm wives to the same level as landowners for a day without embarrassment or hesitation or judgement?" Katherine asked the question, not intending an answer from her sister.

"It's the invitation. We're equal today because we all received the same invitation and chose to accept it."

"Like Cinderella."

"Alas, without the handsome prince to set one of us apart."

"Oh! Lena, come with me. I see Celeste, my friend from the cotton field. I want you to meet her."

Katherine took her sister's hand and guided her across the lawn toward her friend. Seeing Celeste helped her relax and not worry so much about being all dignified. She reckoned she would just be herself. The day passed in much that same way, flitting from person to person, talking, nibbling on food made by the Forder's cook, and enjoying music. Mid-afternoon, Katherine spotted Lena sitting alone in the shade under a tree. Katherine interrupted her conversation with Mrs. Justice. "It's not like my sister to sit alone; she's at her best among people. Asthma!" As the thought struck Katherine, she walked briskly, approached Lena, and heard the wheezing.

"Lena, we should head home and get you indoors. You need coffee to open up your lungs."

"Goodness child, are you not well?" Katherine turned to face Mrs. Forder.

"Lena's asthma is acting up. I need to get her indoors, so we better head out."

"I...had...a...good...time," Lena wheezed and smiled.

"Yes, we did, Mrs. Forder. Thank you from both of us." As she spoke, Katherine pulled her sister to her feet.

"She can't leave with her breathing like this. You said she needs the indoors. I insist you go inside. Does she need anything else?"

"Ma'am, that's very kind, but we can't impose."

"You're not imposing on me, but if you don't come inside, you'll be insulting me." Mrs. Forder took Lena by the arm and walked into the house.

Katherine followed, relieved and a little nervous. She'd never been inside such a large home. "Coffee helps her, Mrs. Forder." Mrs. Forder turned toward her and smiled.

Katherine was sure her breathing was as loud as Lena's as the entryway came into view. A winding staircase, a large chandelier, a rug, and plants greeted them. Katherine was amused when she realized even Lena seemed speechless at the sight. Mrs. Forder led them into a sitting room, seated them on a green velvet couch, pulled on a string connected to a bell, then instructed the woman who appeared to bring the guests some coffee and a cool cloth.

"Stay as long as you need, but please tell me goodbye before you leave. I want to make sure my patient is well enough to travel home." She smiled and headed back to the entry.

"We will. Thank you. Mrs. Forder."

Katherine tugged on her ear and noticed Lena biting her nails, both eyeing the room. "It's breathtaking, isn't it, little sister." Katherine giggled and elbowed Lena, trying to lighten the moment. She was greeted with a roll of the eyes and a coughing fit. The coffee arrived and the ladies sat quietly so Lena's lungs could settle down.

Katherine had felt a part of things out on the lawn, but inside the house she felt awkward and anxious to be in her own surroundings. As though she couldn't feel more out of place, she saw Faye Forder come into the room from the hallway and notice them immediately.

"Oh, I didn't realize guests were indoors and not just on the lawn. Katherine and Lena, you surprised me." Faye's brow was wrinkled and her left hand rested on her hip. Her right hand held a cigarette. "Your aunt sent us in so that Lena's breathing could get under control. We'll be heading out; she's just finished her coffee." Faye's eyes widened in what appeared to be realization of Lena's condition and she put out the cigarette.

"I need a second cup," Lena smiled at Faye then leaned toward the coffee tray and poured herself another cup. Katherine recognized the smile as conniving. If Lena was attempting to make Faye feel uncomfortable with them being in her home, the attempt apparently failed. Katherine, on the other hand, wanted to disappear.

"By all means, drink all that you need." Katherine was surprised when rather than leaving them, Faye sat down in the plush chair across the room. "I wonder if I might ask you ladies about someone." Faye's bright red lips spread into a smile. As Katherine answered her with a verbal "of course," her mind couldn't imagine whom Faye could possibly want to ask them about.

"It was such a pleasure meeting your brother's friend a few weeks ago. Ben, I believe, was his name. I wonder if you know when he might be visiting again."

Katherine felt her hands go clammy and her stomach recoil. She hoped the contents of her day would stay put rather than rise to her throat. Katherine heard Lena choke and spit coffee back into her cup. Perhaps the widening of Faye's eyes had been more about seizing an opportunity than being concerned for Lena's asthma. Ben? *He's my Ben.* Katherine recognized her own jealously and possessiveness at the mention of him.

"I don't really know. The rail men have such odd schedules, and well, Mr. Williams does not live nearby. I—I didn't realize you knew my brother's friend." Katherine's insides were in knots. Her hands were clasped together tightly. She hoped her voice sounded calm and would not betray her.

"Oh, I met him when he was in town and came to High Cotton with Joe. And I am certain I would love to lay eyes on him again—such an attractive man." Faye's hand adjusted a curl that was already drooped perfectly on her temple.

Lena stood. "Katherine, I am done with my coffee now, and we should really head out to be home by dusk. Lovely seeing you again, Miss Faye."

Katherine felt appalled, but touched, at her sister's apparent attempt to rescue her.

"Lena, why don't you let Mrs. Forder know we are leaving? She'll be glad to know that you are well enough to travel. Then you can ask for the cart to be brought around." Her sister pursed her lips together and turned to leave.

Faye seemed undisturbed by the interruption and relentless in her questioning. "I can't imagine what it must have been like to have such a fine-looking man visiting your home. Tell me, Katherine, is he as charming as he looks?"

"Mr. Williams was a thoughtful and friendly guest and quite easy to be around." Katherine felt heat rise in her cheeks. She looked away from Faye and took a sip of coffee that had gone cold.

"Well, if you know that he is coming to town again, you must certainly try to get word to me. I'd like to offer him an invitation to dinner, here, of course, with my aunt and uncle. Do you think he'd have dinner attire with him?"

Katherine banged the coffee cup against the saucer and turned to look Faye in the eyes. "I can't say when Ben, uh, Mr. Williams, will return or what time he would spend away from our brother if he were to come, and I certainly don't know what attire he has. But I'll remember your offer." *Boy, will I!* "Thank you for your hospitality. I should excuse myself and get Lena home. Bye, Faye."

Faye stood, looked Katherine up and down, and then spoke without expression. "Yes, well, I'd be grateful if you would remember it. Goodbye, Katherine." The siren departed while the guest sat motionless.

A thought pierced Katherine in the heart. The letter! She'd mailed Ben an invitation to return for a visit. Had she not done so before today, she knew she would never have mailed one after the conversation with Faye. Katherine reasoned Ben must have no idea that the wealthy, attractive Faye had interest in him or he'd never asked to write her instead. If beguilement entices, does purity repulse? Katherine assumed the answer was yes.

As she suspected it would be, the ride home felt endless. Katherine could hardly wrap her mind around her own thoughts on the conversation because Lena filled the minutes with huffs, questions, and exclamations.

"I can't believe that snooty lady wants to lay claim to our Ben!"

"Our Ben? Lena, we have no claim on Ben."

"We most certainly do. Well, you do at least."

"You're making up another story."

"Did I make up the letter I brought back from the post or imagine Ben flirting with you the Sunday we pulled out in the wagon? No. I didn't. There's a spark there. I know it. You just want to be proper and boring about it."

"Cautious. I just want to be cautious about Ben. Besides, let's see what Joe knows. He should be home tonight for a stop over." *Cautious? No, I want to fling myself into his arms.*

"At least you didn't deny there is a spark. Listen to your heart more than you listen to your head."

Oh, little sister, I fear I already have.

Katherine was relieved to find Joe already home when they arrived. Insisting Lena tend to the mule, she wasted no time confronting her brother even though he was shaving.

"Joe, does Faye Forder know Ben?" Joe literally dropped the razor he was holding, cursed, and wiped at the blood coming from his chin.

"Katherine, you scared me to death! Look what you made me do!" He reached for the cloth lying on the table. "What are you talking about anyway? Ben?"

"Yes, Ben. Does he know Faye Forder?" Her words were pointed and deliberate.

"I can't say he knows her. He's met her."

"At High Cotton?"

"No, at church," he smirked. "Of course, at High Cotton. Why?"

"At the social today, Faye asked about him and told me to let her know when he was back in town. She wants to invite him to dinner."

Joe laughed loudly. "Well, that won't happen. Ben's likely not to be here again anyway."

"Why couldn't it happen?"

"Faye flirted with Ben when he went with me to High Cotton that night. Made me angry, if you want to know the truth. It's like I vanished from the table when she spotted him."

"Flirted?" She felt her heart race.

"Ben didn't take the bait though. For reasons beyond me, he didn't seem the least bit interested in her. Said she's not the kind of woman he'd be after. Darn fool if you ask me. But, maybe that makes my chances with her better." Joe slid the razor down his neck. "Remember the fight in the yard last time he came? I was angry at Ben because Faye asked about him. He told me again he wasn't interested. Then you came out, and you know the rest."

Katherine mellowed, thinking that perhaps purity did entice Ben Williams. She let a flicker of hope light her heart, recalling that he'd spent his second trip here with her and Lena at night rather than returning to

High Cotton. She thought of his letter telling her he had wanted to protect her from Joe. Could he feel that way toward her and at the same time have interest in the beguiling Faye? She determined that no he couldn't.

"Faye Forder, cast aside." She chuckled.

Joe looked her in the eye, something he rarely did, and she saw in them the questions he wouldn't speak.

"Joe, you're wrong about one thing. Ben could possibly come back."

"I ain't been in touch with him."

"I have. And I invited him to come visit again. To come visit me."

With his face still covered in shaving cream, Joe yanked hold of her hand and led her to the front porch. "Start talking, Katherine."

She did.

Chapter 8

Ben reached down and pulled his son up to his chest. How good it felt to hug his tiny frame. He'd missed him. The days away from him on the route were becoming more difficult to endure. Once he'd allowed Katherine to open his heart, his emotions seemed to stretch themselves from the cramped quarters he'd forced them into and fill him to overflowing. Loving Katherine—yes, he loved her—had intensified his love for his son.

He shifted the small boy to rest in his arms. Sammy smiled at him, and in it Ben saw the words his four-year-old son couldn't speak. He knew Sammy had missed him too.

Looking at Sammy's smile surrounded by light brown freckles, Ben sighed and ran his hand along the side of his son's face, reacting to the sadness of knowing this little boy would never hear life. Scarlet fever had spared Sammy's life but robbed him of hearing. Ben considered his deafness more than an injustice. He viewed it as pure, mocking cruelty from God, who had destined the innocent child to be born crippled and then ruthlessly silenced his world all before taking his mother from him.

"How was my little fella these past days, Mrs. Cramer?"

"Why, Mr. Williams, he was good as an angel. I didn't have any trouble with him at all. He and Mr. Cramer even whittled a small train together. I'm sure my husband couldn't have made it without his help."

The middle-aged woman rubbed Sammy's head and chuckled, then pulled a small wooden train from her apron pocket and handed it to him. Sammy laughed with a loud, screeching sound, and Ben knew he was proud of his creation. Ben took the train into his hands and examined it. Giving Sammy another hug, he smiled and handed the train back to him.

"We'll add it to his collection of train cars, Mrs. Cramer. Thank you."

"It warms my heart to see him happy. Childless like we are, we got lots of love to give him."

"I know he loves you both too. I just hope he misses me while I'm away." Ben laughed.

"Oh, Mr. Williams don't be silly. I think he misses you more and more the older he gets. I reckon he's come to understand time now, and I suspect the days you're away seem longer to him. We mark them off on a piece of paper and every morning it's the first thing he wants to do when he wakes up. Today, he knew you were coming back, and he smiled and looked to the door all day long."

"Thank you, Mrs. Cramer. It's good to be missed. He'll be back on Friday. See you at supper."

Ben and the gentle woman who boarded next to him said their good-byes. Then he wheeled Sammy across the hallway to their own rooms. He felt a kinship of sorts with the couple since Mr. Cramer was the grounds and maintenance keeper for the house and had known Sammy's mother long before Ben came into her life.

Tossing his traveling bag on the bed, Ben sat down on the floor and removed his son's shoes to massage his feet. To his astonishment, he noticed that the boy was growing quickly. He needed new shoes from the Sears catalog. Ben would ask to borrow Mrs. Cramer's catalog tomorrow.

They played trains together until supper time. The meals were some of Sammy's favorite times; Ben was certain. The boarders all made a fuss over him with smiles and treats and pats on the shoulder. His humble son seemed to enjoy being the center of attention, which did Ben's heart good. The frail human being deserved recognition.

When the residents gathered in the parlor for after dinner conversation and music, Ben and Sammy headed back down the hallway to their room. "Sammy, I got a letter to read. It's burning a hole in my back pocket. Let's get you ready for bed, and then I'll see what Miss Katherine McGinn has to say." Sammy smiled. Ben was aware his son didn't hear his words, but he understood the routine of bedtime after supper.

With Sammy sleeping soundly next to him, Ben opened the envelope from the woman in Layton. "She's got good handwriting," he noted aloud as he unfolded the letter. Warmth spread through his body as it reacted to the words she'd written him.

"A butterfly. Sammy, she saw a butterfly in the stars." Silence met his words, as he knew it would. He read aloud.

"You asked to know something about Katherine. I'm fragile inside. People don't know it, but they can break me deep inside where my feelings live. I keep this hidden behind hard work and a sense of humor. I guess I have my earthly father to thank for all that. He didn't care for his family as he should and I felt betrayed by him. I knew I couldn't trust him to meet our needs. My Momma made up for the difference. I still don't know how she stretched our meager income to meet our needs. But, Ben, as much as I couldn't depend on my earthly father, I know I can trust on my Heavenly Father."

Ben laid the letter on his lap, feeling unnerved by what he'd just read aloud. Could a woman who loved God as much as Katherine seemed to give her heart to a man who doesn't love that same God? A man who held a grudge against that same God. Yet, a man who now found his heart open to being prayed for.

He looked at Sammy. He couldn't imagine not doing his best to protect and provide for his own flesh and blood. Katherine's father hadn't done right by the McGinn family and although the actions were different, Ben's own father had not done right by his family. He exhaled. Ben still couldn't reconcile a Heavenly Father not doing all he could to protect his children on Earth.

Ben read on, and it was as though Katherine had anticipated his reaction. Her words responded to the deep emotions he'd shared with her when he last wrote—emotions he was feeling again at this very moment.

"I understand why you can't reason God's choices for your life. I think that some things just come with life and being human. We can usually accept those. Other bad things seem pushed upon us by God and those are hard to accept. The Good Book says that His ways are not our ways. Ben, what human can understand the mind of God? It also tells us that God is just and loving and merciful. I reckon when we can't understand His mind, we should choose to follow his heart and character.

I always trust that God is at work, even when the sorrows and difficulties are confusing. It seems a might unfair that humans seem to accept good things from Him and then judge His love when bad things happen. Stop asking your questions and just be quiet before God. I hope you don't think me too bold in saying that."

Ben released the letter and let it drop to the bed as his hand fell to his thigh. "Katherine," he uttered, "you've written truth. I have a mountain of resentment in my soul, and I must choose to climb it if I want to see the other side. You're a bold woman." He closed his eyes to hold back the tears he felt come. "A bold woman that I love." He continued to read aloud through misty eyes.

"Well, I've had a busy time since I last saw you. Our horse died and now we got a mule named Gitter. Mrs. Forder had another social for the women folk. Lena and I enjoyed it, but had to leave early when Lena's asthma came upon her."

He held the letter closer to the light, trying to figure out a line she had written and crossed out, quite aggressively it appeared. Someone had asked about him…maybe? He couldn't make out the words. "I bet she tugged on her ear after she wrote that line then set to blotting it out."

Reading the last line of the letter, Ben jumped from the bed in excitement and read it again out loud. "Joe will be home for a few days three weeks from this Saturday. Perhaps you could visit us. Visit me."

His mind was now too active to sleep, so Ben made his way to the small table in his room and began to pen a letter. He wrote slowly and deliberately, then read the lines aloud to feel their sound on his own ears.

Dear Katherine,

I desire nothing more than to visit you again. But I will not.
That is, unless you embrace a truth I have held close, but now offer you.
I am a father. I have a young son. He's not well and whole.
I cannot come to you without him.
Forgive me.
Sweet Katherine, a word from you will bring us or keep us away.
Lovingly,

Ben

P.S. Joe does not know.

The next morning before Sammy awoke, Ben placed the letter with the mail for the local carrier to pick up. All night he had tossed and turned, wondering how Katherine would respond when she learned what he'd kept from her. He hoped she wouldn't feel betrayed or tricked. "Now I wait," he whispered.

He knew he hadn't much to offer her—a broken heart, a little money, a struggling son, a grudge against God, and love. *Will my love be enough to outweigh my weaknesses? Will she realize I love her? Now that I've opened my heart, the thought of not having her is agonizing.*

Breakfast came and went. Ben had no appetite, but he ate anyway, enjoying the leisurely time with Sammy. Most of the borders had eaten earlier and headed out for their work day. When his second cup of coffee had gone cold, Ben reckoned he and Sammy should clear out and return to their rooms. They stopped at the Cramer's rooms and borrowed the Sears catalog

"Sammy, let's find you some shoes in the catalog." Sammy clapped his hands when Ben held the book out for him to see. "You love looking at the pictures, don't ya?" Pulling Sammy next to him on the floor, he thumbed through the pages. When they came to the shoes, he pointed to Sammy's feet, tickled them, and was rewarded with a smile. He chose a size and color. With that task complete, he turned a few more pages and found what he was looking for in the women's section and added a hair clip to his order. "It has a butterfly painted on it. Do you think she'll like it, Sammy?"

A man can be hopeful and that is exactly what Ben determined to be as awaited Katherine's reply. After another trip out on the rails and another return home a week later, Ben was greeted by a postcard with a picture of bluebonnets sketched on it. He stared at the words.

"Come. I am waiting for you both. Katherine."

"She wants to meet my son!" Ben wept. Embarrassingly.

Two days later Ben stood behind his son's wheelchair in the parlor of the boarding house as Mrs. Cramer gave Sammy a hug and a kiss on the cheek. Ben wanted to reach out and wipe away the tears that streamed down her face, but he restrained himself.

"Mr. Williams, I'm afraid he'll be so confused when the train pulls out of town. I'm concerned for him—such a small boy and so many challenges." Her eyes were locked with Ben's.

"Mrs. Cramer, I did what you taught me to do. I drew him pictures." He pulled a piece of paper from his shirt pocket, unfolded it, and placed it in her sweaty, plump hand. "See, I drew a train on a track with a man and a boy figure beside it and a suitcase. I pointed to it and to us and I think Sammy understood the picture was about us. I drew a woman at the other end." He smiled. "I think he understands."

Ben took the paper back from Mrs. Cramer who nodded her head yes and touched his arm. He put his hand on her shoulder. "Thank you, Mrs. Cramer. We'll be back soon."

"Mr. Williams, may I ask a personal question? I care for Sammy so much, and well…"

"I know you care and, yes, you can ask me anything."

"Have you met a lady friend?" Ben felt heat rush to his cheeks and his mouth drop open. He laughed heartily.

"Why Mrs. Cramer, I guess it's true that women have a sixth sense. I do have a young woman in Layton that I am interested in, and it's time for her and Sammy to meet." He shrugged his shoulders then became amused when Mrs. Cramer lowered her head and tried to wipe tears from her eyes.

"Mrs. Cramer, this won't be the last time you see Sammy. No matter what happens between the lady and me, my boy and I will be back here—to live or say good-bye. I assure you. "

"Then, Mr. Williams, I wish you the best. Sammy deserves a family, and well, Ben, you do too. A man shouldn't be without a woman."

With Sammy holding their small bag in his lap, Ben pushed his wheelchair, and the two of them waved at Mrs. Cramer in the doorway then headed down the street to the train station. The warm morning breeze lifted Sammy's hair as he turned to his father with a smile, and Ben tousled the flowing head full.

"Let's get to the train. The lovely Katherine McGinn wants to meet my son."

Ben hummed loudly. Embarrassingly.

Chapter 9

"Any moment now I'll fall to the floor." Katherine stared in the mirror and fanned herself. "My goodness. That bath has made me hot all over. Lena, can you find my silver hair clip? Oh, and I need some help with these buttons on the back of my dress."

She heard Lena giggle and clasp her shoulders from behind. "Katherine, you're not going to faint. You're just excited. Now, take a breath, my nervous princess, and let it out slowly while I button this for you."

Katherine inhaled, and as she began to exhale, Lena broke out in another giggle. "What's so funny, Lena?"

"Well, beside the fact that we're running around the room on tip toes and whispering so we won't wake up Joe, the drunk dance hall king, I found your clip…in your hair."

At that Katherine faced her sister and covered her own mouth, her shoulders shaking with laughter.

"You make me smile. I love you, Lena."

"Well, that's all sweet and stuff, but save those smiles for your handsome prince."

As Lena spoke those words, a wave of nausea came over Katherine. "I need to tell you something, Lena. No, what I mean is that I want to tell you something. But it must stay a secret from Joe until I'm back from the depot."

"I'm all ears!" Lena clapped her hands, then rubbed them together quickly. "This is fun!"

"This is serious."

"Are you secretly getting married?" Katherine felt the full force of Lena's arms embracing her neck. She pulled away from her sister and held her by the shoulders.

"No! But this is about Ben." She released one shoulder then tugged on her ear. "He has a son…"

She was interrupted by Lena's gasp, that could surely awaken the sleeping brother. "Katherine, don't tease me. Your joke is not funny!"

Katherine noticed the tears that welled up in Lena's eyes, so she reached over and drew the young sibling to her chest. "I'm not playing a joke on you.

Ben wrote and told me he has a son. He says he's not well and whole. I don't know what that means exactly, but, I will soon." She saw the question in Lena's furrowed brow. "I don't know why Ben kept his son a secret. Even Joe doesn't know. He seemed to understand I'd be shocked, so he left it up to me whether to come visit again. I told them both to come. Ben's bringing him!"

Katherine heard silence. Deafening silence. "For once in my life, I think I've made you speechless Lena McGinn." She rubbed her sister's back and kissed the top of her head. She felt Lena's body relax and pull away to face her.

"I'm excited to meet him, Katherine."

Katherine pressed her palm to her heart. "I know. Me too. I need to leave. I can't be late."

Katherine scurried to the front door, down the steps, and toward the cart that Lena had already hooked up and brought around from the shed. As she seated herself, commotion at the front door caught her attention. Joe.

"Blast it! All this noise! What's going on round here? Where you going, Katherine?"

Katherine thought how unkempt and foolish Joe looked standing there in his drawers. She pulled the reigns so Gitter would start moving then shouted back to her brother. "I'm headed to the depot to get someone."

"To get what?"

"You mean who."

"Who? What do you mean who?"

"Ben! I'm going to get Ben." Katherine heard her brother curse and run a hand over his face and through his hair. "Talk to Lena; she knows. Ben's coming to see me." As she pulled away, she threw him a mocking kiss that turned into a wave.

Katherine arrived at the depot just as the train whistle blew. Scooting down from the seat and shaking off the dirt, then straightening her skirt, she headed to the small depot porch to wait. "There's the train!" Katherine was embarrassed when she realized how loudly she'd proclaimed those words. Her hand went to her ear and began to tug. Goodness! She hoped her hair wasn't blown too much out of place!

"Good morning, Miss McGinn. Didn't I see your brother come home yesterday?" She turned to face the kind depot attendant. "Yes, Percy. Joe

70

came home yesterday." She smiled and felt her cheeks heat up. "I'm here for someone else. Well, two people. We have guests coming to town." As she spoke the whistle blew again, hiding Percy's reply. The train began to slow to a stop. Katherine turned toward what she hoped was her future, clasped her hands under her chin, and bounced up and down on her toes. She felt her smile reach from cheek to cheek as she waited for him.

If time had ever stood still for Katherine, it was at this moment when Ben stepped from the train. Her heart fluttered and her breath caught. She was captivated. His presence. His smile. His shoulders. His arms…and in that very same instant of pure pleasure, awareness set in. Without being told, she knew why the boy wasn't whole. He appeared old enough to walk, but his father carried him sideways. His legs hung loosely over Ben's arm.

She felt her knees buckle and caught herself on the depot window seal. She managed to keep her eyes focused on Ben and saw that his face went crestfallen. He instinctively stepped forward to steady her, though carrying his own flesh and blood would have prevented any rescue. Had her response disappointed him? Feeling her eyes swell with tears that she couldn't hold back, Katherine recovered her footing and brought her hand to his forearm. Touching him gently, she longed to redeem herself.

"Ben." She took in the smile he now offered as though it were lifesaving. "I'm so glad you're both here." Katherine turned her eyes to the small, freckled face boy. "And, such a fine, handsome young man. I'm Katherine. What is your name?" For an answer, she noticed the boy turn to his father, just as Ben's whispered words floated into her ears.

"He can't hear you. He's deaf."

She felt her throat tighten causing a raspy, whispered voice. "Oh, Ben, I'm so sorry. And I'm so sorry for my reaction. Please let me begin again. It was the shock of it—that's all." To keep the sobs from coming, Katherine took a deep breath and then released it. "What's his name?"

"Sammy." Ben nodded his head toward his son, and Katherine felt some measure of grace. Giving her best smile, she looked at the child and waved. "Hello Sammy." The beautiful, innocent face offered a slight smile in response then leaned into his father. The eyes of man and boy caught, and Katherine surmised some silent communication must have passed between them, for Ben nodded a yes and the boy seemed to relax.

For the fourth time in a day, Katherine felt she would faint as Ben moved the boy to his hip and gently pressed his freed hand to her cheek. "It's so good to see you Katherine. I'm happy to be here." As he leaned his forehead against hers, Katherine had no words. She simply touched his shoulder with one hand and rested the other on the back of Sammy.

Katherine knew she was in love—with a man and his son.

She felt Ben readjust his son in his arms as he spoke. "Well, shall we load up?"

Katherine smiled and pointed to where Gitter stood in place. "The cart is right over there." Ben moved in that direction as she followed alongside him, thinking that he must carry the child everywhere they go. Just as the thought struck her, he hoisted the young boy onto the middle of the cart seat. "Will he be okay sitting by himself?"

His smile warmed her, but she thought he must be amused at her question. "He'll be fine. It's just that his legs are too crooked and frail to hold him up. Let me help you up, then I'll get our bag and his wheelchair loaded."

Some form of relief swept through Katherine when she heard the word wheelchair. *Of course. A wheelchair.* She smiled at Ben and then felt his hand grasp hers, and before he assisted her to the seat, he drew her to himself and pressed her against his chest. "Katherine, thank you. I know this must be a shock. Are you okay?" Katherine turned her face up to his and slipped her arms around his waist. Never had she been so bold in a display of emotion. "Yes, Ben. I'm very, very happy."

She longed for him to kiss her, but instead he touched her. She felt his hand on her neck and then her cheek and then her mouth where his finger traced her lips. She watched a suggestive smile take over his face as he tapped her nose then moved to get her seated.

While Ben retrieved his things and loaded them into the cart, Katherine sat on the seat next to the small boy. He looked at her and then pulled a piece of paper from his pocket. Handing it to her, he smiled and transformed himself into a tiny image of his father. A warmth spread through Katherine; she thought it must be her heart melting. She opened the paper and the drawing made her breath catch.

Looking at Sammy, she grinned, then pointed to the drawing of the woman at the end of the railroad tracks and then to herself. Sammy seemed to understand her question and answered with a back and forth nod of his head. Yes, the drawing was her, and Sammy must realize why he was here—to meet this woman sitting next to him. Katherine wondered if he knew the significance of meeting the young lady in the drawing. She brought the paper to her heart to show her joy, then handed it back to him.

So, this was how Ben communicated to his son...in pictures. She ruffled the boy's hair just as Ben placed the wheelchair into the cart and spoke. "Alright! We're loaded up. Who feels like a cola before we head to the house?"

"We do!" With that simple declaration, Katherine realized she felt connected with the small son of the man she loved.

As the trio headed toward the store, Katherine's earlier boldness waned, and she found herself feeling shy to be around other folks with Ben and Sammy before she'd faced her siblings. As though he sensed her uneasiness, Ben slowed to a stop at the side of the store and turned to her. "I think I'll go in and buy our colas. We can drink them on the way to your house. Do you mind?"

Katherine wondered if a woman could fall more deeply in love in a wee moment of time. "I think that's a good idea. You fellas must be tired after traveling."

Ben's laughter delighted her as he reached his hand over Sammy to touch her shoulder. "I'm so tired, sweet lady, that I don't have it in me to sit at a table in a diner and drink a cola while folks stare at me. I might snap a head off." Katherine felt her face get warm as she retorted. "By all means, we must not let that happen!" She watched Ben point to the store and then to himself as Sammy eyed him, and moments later they were all three sipping colas while Gitter led the cart toward home.

"I saw the work getting done on the store. Motor lodge rooms, Mr. Justice told me. He and his wife both said hello to me. They remembered me for some reason. Can you imagine why?" Ben teased. Katherine rolled her eyes and chuckled.

"Sammy's such a handsome little boy, Ben."

"I have to agree. He takes after his Momma."

"Then I know she was a lovely woman. But his smile… it comes straight from his Papa." Ben turned and smiled at her. She looked at Sammy who was eyeing the sights around him with big eyes. He was tucked into his own silent world. Katherine felt a sense of hopelessness surge through her. This little boy, so close, yet so far. How could she ever get inside his heart and mind? As quickly as the hopeless feeling overtook her, she shunned it with the hopefulness of a new life that seemingly was in her future.

She hadn't seen any of this coming—an instant family with a man who took her breath away and a little boy who needed to embrace the love and care a mother could render.

"I brought you a gift." Ben's husky voice grabbed her attention.

"A gift? I love gifts!" She clapped her hands in delight, and the motion caused Sammy to startle and look at his father. Ben winked at his son.

"Yes, a gift, my lovely eager Butterfly who smells of honeysuckle. And I'll give it to you when I feel like it." This time, his wink was directed to her. As delighted as Katherine was that he'd thought enough to bring her a gift, the sound of his calling her his own butterfly was sheer pleasure. She breathed in the joy and let it fill her being.

"Katherine, I know you must have questions about Sammy. And well, I don't want you to think I hid him from you the times I came before. That first visit, I never expected, I mean…I never thought. I'm trying to say that I never expected you."

"Me?"

"You and…this between us. You and me."

"I know, Ben. Neither did I."

"And when it came, well, I didn't know how to handle it. So, I decided to try and discover if you maybe you felt the same way."

"And what did you discover, Mr. Williams?"

"I discovered that you did." He looked at her, and his vulnerability almost undid her every ladylike manner. She resisted the urge to reach over and kiss him deeply on the lips.

"I do." The phrase sent instant heat into her cheeks. She saw Ben's mouth twitch.

"And only then was I ready to let you see me as the father I am."

"I wrote you that my heart was ready for you both. It still is. And one day, Ben, when you're ready, you'll tell me the story of Sammy. For now, I'm thankful you trust me enough to bring him here."

Sammy chose that moment to expel a lengthy, loud burp, and the man and woman fell into laughter. Sammy joined them, and his loud laughter made Katherine's body jump. She guffawed and snorted. "Lena's gonna love him." Katherine looked at Sammy who seemed to be trying to expel another burp. "I have to agree Katherine. He might be the match your feisty little sister never expected!"

With that happy moment settling into her soul, the cart rounded the curve, the house came into view, and the eighteen- year -old woman fought off the nervous little girl tucked inside who was afraid to face her big brother. Would he disapprove of his friend loving his little sister? She smirked at that little girl inside her—after all, it had been the big brother who introduced them.

Ben had just slowed the cart and hopped from the seat when Katherine noticed Lena push open the screen door, jump off the porch, and take off toward them. "Ben!" She heard Lena exclaim as she watched her hug him at full impact. Katherine laughed as Ben struggled to keep his footing and speak to Lena.

"Excuse me, Miss, do I know you?"

"No. I call all strangers 'Ben' as I hug them."

Katherine laughed along with the two people she loved. As she did, she felt Sammy move closer to her side. An instinct that must be motherly surged through her, and she looked to the young boy. Was that fear and shyness mingled in his eyes?

The two people she loved pulled away from one another and Katherine saw Ben place his hand on Lena's back to direct her toward the cart. "It's good to see you, Lena. I want you to meet someone."

"Your son?"

As Ben turned to her, Katherine gave a smile to acknowledge that she had indeed shared the news with her sister, and then she nodded toward Sammy. Ben seemed to immediately realize what Katherine had seen in the boy's eyes. She watched as he stepped back into the cart and pulled Sammy onto his lap. Then he turned them to face Lena.

"Yes, Lena, meet my son. This is Sammy."

Katherine covered her mouth with her hand and gave a deep, gratifying sigh when Lena spread a beautiful smile across her face. Her sister looked Ben and then Sammy in the eyes. "He's deaf," Ben told her.

To Katherine's astonishment, Lena reached into her pocket and pulled out a small wooden train car. She'd forgotten all about that toy—it had been Joe's, and when Lena had come along, as prissy as she was, she'd taken a liking to it and had made it her "princess train." She realized it must be one of the secret treasures Lena kept in her trunk. Her sister made her feel proud.

As Lena held the train toward Sammy, Katherine watched him smile. She kept her ears on the conversation.

"Ben, would he like to sit on the porch and play with me?"

"Yes. He loves trains. We brought some from home."

Katherine and Ben looked at one another before he cleared his throat and spoke.

"He's crippled, Lena."

"I thought so," the young girl whispered as she glanced at the wheelchair.

"Thank you, Lena." Ben patted Sammy on the head as he spoke.

"Sweet Sister," Katherine interjected," why don't you get the extra quilt in our room and lay it out for you two to sit on." As Lena looked at her, Katherine threw a kiss her sister's way and mouthed a silent thank you.

"Oh! Where's Joe?" Katherine heard the panic in her own voice.

"He's round back, cleaning out the shed. He didn't go back to sleep after you left. Only reason I got out of helping was because he needed his breakfast."

Katherine exhaled. Joe wasn't watching for their return.

As Ben placed Sammy back on the seat to sit, Katherine caught his eye and noticed that hers weren't the only eyes filled with tears. With Lena out of earshot, Katherine spoke.

"She has a tender heart, that sister of mine."

"Yes."

"She hides it a lot behind her sass, but that is who she is." They chuckled. "I told Joe about us writing letters, and he knows I was going to pick you up, but I didn't mention Sammy. I thought maybe he should hear about him from you. I hope you don't mind."

"You're right, Miss McGinn. The news needs to come from me."

Ben unloaded the cart and placed his bag and the wheelchair on the front porch while Katherine sat with Sammy. Ben came back to the cart and reached to help her get on the ground. Standing next to Ben, Katherine's heart stirred as she watched him tenderly lift his boy from the seat and carry him in his arms. She wondered if Sammy's earlier uncertainty subsided when his Papa held him. The two of them seemed to communicate in silence.

She helped Lena spread the quilt before Ben settled his boy onto it and pulled his trains from their bag. The crippled, deaf boy and the feisty, talkative young lady began to play. Katherine stood to watch for a moment. Words were not necessary. Ben's breath warmed her neck as he leaned in to whisper.

"I think I'll go find Joe."

She turned to him and tilted her head to the side.

"Alone?"

"Alone."

Ben Williams crouched down next to his son, patted his hand, and then pointed to the side of the house. Sammy seemed to understand or at least to be unconcerned, for Katherine watched him nod to his father then hold up a train for Lena to see. Katherine's eyes met Ben; he acknowledged her then headed out back.

"Katherine, do you love Ben?'

"Lena!"

"I'm not talking about a fairy tale right now Katherine. I'm talking about if you love the man, can you also love his son?"

"What a deep question. My little sister has grown up this instant before my very eyes."

"Well, do you? "

"Yes, I love Ben. And though I've only known him moments of time, Sammy has filled my heart."

"With pity?"

Katherine considered the confrontation.

"No." She bit her lip and glanced at Lena. "I'm certain it's love too."

Katherine felt Lena squeeze her arm as she offered up a smile, "Well, I think he's precious!"

Katherine sat down on the quilt to join in the play. Her anxiety over what Joe and Ben would say to each other made time crawl. Finally, she heard them coming from around the side of the house. The eighteen- year-old woman looked at her brother and felt heat in her cheeks. She tugged on her ear as the siblings stared at each other briefly.

"Katherine. Full of surprises, are we?" Her stomach tightened until her brother smiled then turned his attention to Ben who tapped his son on the shoulder.

"Joe, this here's Sammy." Katherine felt instant pity for her awkward brother who began to speak then hesitated. He put out his hand as though he were meeting a grown man, then drew it away. Had Joe suddenly recognized Sammy's condition, or had Ben told him and Joe had just been struck by the reality of it? The boy looked up at him expressionless.

Katherine stood to be eye level with Joe. "How about a wave and a smile," she said while Ben, who was standing next to Joe, gave him a friendly pat on the back—a signal to Sammy, no doubt, that this man was a friend. The boy smiled and offered a wooden train car to Joe who took it, admired it, and returned it with smile.

"He's a fine-looking boy." Joe's words edged their way through a croaky voice.

"Thank you, Joe." Bolstered by her sibling's complimentary words, Katherine smiled and looked at Ben as he spoke to her brother. "And I was wondering if you'd like to fish before lunch time." Her delight transformed into disappointment.

Katherine knew that Ben only had today and until midafternoon tomorrow to spend with them. Why would he choose time fishing with Joe over time with her? She crinkled her brow. Was Ben looking for a caretaker for Sammy and not a wife to share his life with?

Joe agreed to fish, and Katherine gave Ben a stare that she hoped made him feel shameful to the bone. She yanked open the screen door and stepped inside the house. She felt like a foolish little girl.

Anger and humiliation pulsed through her, and all Katherine could do was pace in the kitchen and tug her ear. Her thoughts, spinning like a tornado, rushed her mind.

She was in love with Ben, and because of that she couldn't bear to be with just to care for Sammy, no matter how precious the little boy was. To do so would be torture.

And why had Ben set his sights on her? He had told her Sammy had a caregiver back where they lived in Commerce, so what would make Ben turn Sammy's world upside down to find another caregiver? Katherine stopped in her tracks at the only explanation she could decipher. The kitchen walls seemed to close in on her as panic and anger set in. Ben's caretaker was a middle-aged married woman. In contrast, Katherine was young and single. Ben was looking for a caregiver for Sammy and an eligible woman to satisfy his own needs whenever he pleased.

"He's lied to me!" Speaking the words aloud moved her anger into sadness. She shoved the covered plate of biscuits to the other side of the kitchen table then plopped herself down on the bench. With her head cradled in her arms, she let tears flow. Her shoulders shook in rhythm with her muffled sobs.

A moment later, she felt a warm hand clasp her shoulder and turned to see Ben standing beside her. Before she could speak a word, he pulled her gently from the table and into his arms despite her resistance. Her moist cheek nestled on his chest against the cotton fabric of his brown shirt. Her tears mingled with the sweat of his body heat. Despite her despair, she felt comfort in his closeness. *Fickle emotions!*

"Whatever's upset you, whatever you're thinking, Butterfly, make sure you understand something." He drew her head away from his chest, and his hands enveloped her face. Their eyes locked—resistance and reassurance stared at one another. "I love you, Katherine McGinn. You hear me? I love you and that's the reason I'm here."

Katherine closed her eyes and shook her head side to side as he held it. "I think you love the idea of someone taking care of Sammy and also meeting your needs."

"You're wrong. I love the idea of sharing my life and my heart with you. No other woman. No other reason. "

"But you just got here, and you're going off with Joe."

"Katherine, I want to be here—to stay for the rest of my life. If you must know, I just wanted time to speak with him about us. I think I should show him respect man to man, you see, since you don't have a father to grant us his blessing. I could do that right here in this room if that makes you feel better. Don't let your thoughts tell you otherwise as I suspect they already have." She felt him pull her against him again. A whisper escaped her mouth.

"You love me?"

"I do." At that, he pulled her face up to meet his, and she watched as he lowered his lips to hers.

Katherine McGinn was being kissed for the first time, and she felt the pleasure of it sweep through her being. Her body relaxed, and her soul came out of hiding. Body and soul joined forces as Katherine slid her arms around his back and returned his kiss.

When the lovers parted, she felt his breath on her lips as he whispered, "On second thought, I don't want to be more than a few feet from you this entire visit."

His second kiss nearly brought her to her knees.

Chapter 10

A shuffle of feet signaled that Joe had made his way to the kitchen doorway just after she and Ben pulled away from their second kiss. Katherine felt a small measure of guilt when Ben told Joe he'd changed his mind about fishing. He'd said he didn't want to leave Sammy and that putting him in a cart to travel to the fishing pond would be too much after the train ride.

She watched the men return to the shed for tools. Joe needed to repair the steps at the back porch. From the laughter reverberating from the front room, Lena and Sammy seemed captivated with one another, so Katherine remained in the kitchen to cook lunch. She took a deep breath and tugged her ear. Being a happy nervous wreck with Ben and Sammy here might not fare well with her poor cooking skills.

"Bless you, Lena." Katherine stood motionless and savored the sight—a pot of chicken and dumplings sat on the stove. She hadn't noticed before in her frustration—and passion. Her only task would be cornbread. She bit her lip and put her hands on her hips. She'd done cornbread many times and not burnt it; she could do it again. After all, she was feeding the man she loved. "And besides, he loves me already, despite sampling my cooking."

The kitchen was warm so Katherine propped open the back door, hoping some outside air would wander through. It did and brought with it the sound of male voices. Katherine gasped as the words she heard flirted with her heart; she shamelessly did nothing to prevent overhearing the two men talk.

Joe's voice carried through the open window and screen door. "Ben, how long you gonna stay here?"

"If she'll have me, I'm here to stay." His declaration rang with enthusiasm. Katherine clasped her hands under her chin.

"Needin' a momma for that boy?"

"That's not it at all. I fell in love with your sister."

"That simple, huh? Not sure I believe you."

"Truth is, it's not simple at all. Sammy's got a caregiver he loves. I'd be taking him from her and from the only home he knows. But right here with her sister is where Katherine belongs, and I want to make that work for her—for us. So, I'll uproot Sammy and put down roots with Katherine."

81

"Love or not, you're placing a big burden on her caring for a deaf and crippled child with you off riding the rails."

"I've thought about that. I got experience working the gin and plan to visit the Forder gin while I'm here. Joe, the only thing selfish about my intentions toward your sister is the fact that I want to keep on living, and I'm not sure I can do that now without her."

Katherine overheard silence until Joe responded quietly. "You love her. You're making plans to care for her." She heard Joe clear his throat. "I reckon I won't argue that with you. If you're wanting my blessing," a pause lingered in the air, "well, you got it."

A squeal escaped Katherine, and goose bumps hugged her all over. "Mrs. Katherine Williams." Her words tickled her tongue. Dropping her wooden spoon, she braced herself on the counter and remembered how to breathe.

The next sound she heard was Ben whistling a happy tune. A moment later she turned at a rustling on the back porch. Ben stood in the doorway with a look on his face that told Katherine he realized she'd overheard his conversation. Grinning, she pressed her palms to her cheeks. Ben replied with a wink.

The afternoon became evening. Crickets chirped. A light breeze weaved through the open windows. Somewhere in the distance, an owl hooted. As usual, Joe was spending his night in Layton at the High Cotton. Katherine realized that the house was filled with the four people who would transform it into a new home. She played trains with Sammy while Ben and Lena challenged each other in checkers.

When they all tired of those activities, Ben pulled out his harmonica, and the ladies sang. As they did, Katherine couldn't keep her eyes from wandering over to Sammy and a knot formed in her stomach. He played with his toys, completely lost to the sounds in the room.

Her heart ached at the sight, and she felt ashamed. Maybe Lena had been right. Maybe what she felt for the boy was pity and not love. Sammy looked up and smiled at her. One look at the young face whose smile transformed him into Ben was all it took to remove Katherine's doubt. She didn't pity Sammy; she loved him. Maybe the sadness she felt was that of a mother who wanted the best for a child.

An ear-piercing squeal shook Katherine from her thoughts, and she and Lena both stopped singing. At the same moment, the sound of the harmonica stopped suddenly.

She watched with big eyes as Ben stood and picked up his son. "Mother Nature calls. Guess we'll take care of that and then I'll get him ready for bed." Katherine shook her head yes in frustrating silence as he spoke to her. She wanted so badly to not be shaken by what was happening in front of her. As Ben walked through the doorway of Joe's room, she collected herself.

"Can I help?" Her eyes locked with Ben when he looked back over his shoulder. "Could you soap up a cloth for me so I can wash him down before I put him in the bed?" She smiled and began to stand. "Yes." Ben moved through the room and toward the back door in the kitchen.

"I want to help too," Lena stated and rose from the floor.

"You want to help, but I need to help. I have to learn."

"Need?"

Katherine rolled her eyes at Lena and propped her hands on her hips. "Want and need." She despised the uncertainty she heard in her own voice.

Lena had said her good nights to Sammy, and as Ben tucked his son into the small bed the two of them would share tonight, Katherine stood next him. It felt strange not to put him to bed with prayers like she'd always done when Lena was young. The reality that Ben was still struggling with God nagged at her, but when Sammy looked to her and spread a big smile on his face, she allowed the nagging and her earlier uneasiness to give way to tenderness.

She kissed her finger, leaned over, and touched it to his cheek. A small hand came from under the sheet and touched her face in return. Katherine felt Ben's arm come around her back and pull her close to him, then felt his lips touch her lightly on the cheek. Her heart jumped. The man holding her close to him reached down and kissed his son good night. The realization sank in. Ben had displayed his love for her to Sammy and confirmed her place in their lives. The tiny hand on her face told her the young boy already knew the three of them belonged together.

As they left the bedroom, Ben's voice whispered in her ear, "Come with me, Butterfly." With her hand clasped in his, she let him lead her outside to the front porch and away from Lena's open bedroom windows. The sky was filled with stars. They spoke in whispered tones.

"What do you see in the sky tonight, Katherine?"

"More stars than I can count."

"I see a Butterfly. A beautiful Butterfly," Her skin prickled because his eyes were not on the sky, but on her. "It's time for your gift." With that, she watched him pull a small cloth bag from his pocket and felt him take her hand and place the soft cloth in it. "Open it."

Katherine pulled the drawstring bag open and reached inside. She pulled out a beautiful gold hair clip with a butterfly painted on it. Yellow, red, and blue wings adorned the creature. Katherine had never seen a lovelier clip, much less owned one.

"It's so beautiful, Ben. Thank you." She held the clip in her hands and pulled it to her heart.

"Can I put it in your hair?" Without waiting for an answer, he began to turn her. She instinctively handed the clasp to him, so delicate in his masculine hand. The intimacy of his fingers in her hair made her insides quiver. She felt the clip close tightly.

As she turned back to face him, he held her face in his hands and kissed her lips lightly. "Good night, my beautiful Butterfly." He backed away and went inside the house. Katherine stood frozen except for the smile that spread across her face. "Good night." She wasn't certain if her voice or her heart had spoken the words.

As though she flitted through the air like a butterfly, she made her way to the bedroom, washed in the dark, slid on her cotton gown, and rested beneath the covers. The sounds of the night and the ticking of the clock would surely lull her to sleep where pleasant dreams should be waiting, but in the dark depths of the night, Katherine awoke and sat up in bed; sweat was rolling down her face, and her heart was beating rapidly.

Sammy! She watched as the boy leaned over the bank's edge to pick up a rock. He'd reached too far! His fragile body made an explosive splash. She plunged into the waters. Katherine strained against his weight but couldn't lift him. His gasping and choking penetrated the air, frightening a flock of birds who screeched and fled from the horror. Screaming, Ben ran madly toward them from the opposite side of the pond. He frantically shoved Katherine aside, and she became lost in the murky water that suddenly engulfed her. It was then that she remembered she couldn't swim. Katherine could hear Joe on the bank mocking her for being unable to care for herself, much less a crippled boy. Distanced from those she loved, her body and soul gave way to the calm darkness of the water and rested in its beguiling escape.

The nightmare jolted her. The scene wasn't real, but the question was. Could she give her life to the care of his son? Fear settled in and lurked in the recesses of her heart.

Chapter 11

When he'd last squinted to look at the clock, it read three in the morning. He felt like Katherine's presence from one room over had seeped into him and heightened his senses. The sheet felt heavy; Sammy's breathing screamed at him; the breeze was a twister. At last, Ben's eyes became too heavy to stay open, and he felt himself sleep though his body tossed and turned and his mind taunted him.

Ben entered the garden outside the boarding house, and she smiled at him. "I'll love you forever," he told her.

His eyes were locked with hers as she walked down the aisle then stood at his side. "I'll love you forever," he told her.

He ran his hand over the bulge of her middle where his unborn child rested. "I'll love you forever," he told her.

His head lay on her chest as she fought for every breath of dying life. "I'll love you forever," he told her.

Her cold, decaying hand touched his face. "Not forever, Ben" she told him.

A butterfly flew in and lighted on her pillow. He scooped it up and brought it to his lips. A flutter of wings. A gentle kiss. "I'll love you forever," he whispered to it.

Ben jerked awake and covered his mouth to keep the moan from escaping. His sweat soaked the sheets. His guilt made the air heavy. If it were not for Sammy lying next to him in the bed, he'd flee to the outside to clear his mind of the haunting images sleep had brought.

Once his breathing returned to normal, Ben embraced Sammy—the fruit of his crippled first love. A first love—but not his only love. Tears welled in his eyes. He realized that a first love would never cease to play a starring role in his life, but it would exit the stage and gracefully make room for a second star. Ben felt Guilt slip out the open window. Hope sat down on the edge of his bed and smiled. He slept until the sound of morning birds awoke him.

Ben's mind went to the plans he had for the day. His proposal day. He dismissed the dream and savored the excitement of asking Katherine to be his wife. Eventually both Sammy and Joe stirred, and they all three began to prepare themselves for the day.

"Mind if I borrow the cart today, Joe? I'd like to make my way to the gin after breakfast and then take the ladies and Sammy on a picnic. I'll be back before three when I have to catch the train to Commerce."

"Help yourself. I reckon my part in your matrimony plans is done." Ben shook his hand. "I'm honored to have your sister, Joe, but your part isn't done. We got to talk about living space."

"You and your boy moving in?"

"If you'll have us. Like I said, I don't want to take Katherine away from her sister. Sammy can room with me and Katherine at first, but I got an idea to propose about adding a room or two off the kitchen."

"You want to add on to the house?" He chuckled as Joe ran a hand through his hair causing it to stick out in odd places.

"Yep. Thought I'd leave the plans I scribbled for you to look over. I want to surprise Katherine. I got some money from my cousin in Galveston. Our great uncle had no family and passed his house to us. My cousin lived there, but now he's marrying and sold the place, so he wired me my part of the money. It should cover supplies and still leave me a good amount of money to put away. I'd do as much of the work as I could on my own, but I'd need your permission and your skill. In the meantime, I worry about Lena's space."

"She's already made her plans. That girl don't want nothing keeping you from marrying her sister. She wants to run a curtain in the front room and move her bed and trunk in there. I reckon the small dresser too."

Ben smiled. Katherine was his soft Butterfly. Lena was his cool breeze.

Ben dressed Sammy and the three fellas set out to the kitchen where they found Lena preparing pancakes for breakfast.

"Sammy!" the cook exclaimed. Ben watched as his son reached out his arms to Lena. The two embraced in a hug while Ben held the wheelchair steady.

"Good morning." Ben pulled her into a side hug.

"Lena, where's your sister?"

"She's getting dressed. She overslept. Said she tossed and turned last night. I suppose she has something on her mind." Ben felt Lena's hand pat him on the back.

"Could you pack a picnic lunch without your sister knowing? I'd like to take you ladies and Sammy on a picnic after my trip to the gin." Ben winked at her and watched her answer with a hearty head shake.

A sound outside drew his attention, and Ben noticed Katherine making her way to the back porch. She'd been outdoors without coming through the kitchen? He met her in the backyard.

"There you are, Butterfly. Good morning." His hand caressed her cheek. She felt warm. *Must have been a brisk walk.*

"Morning." Her voice was faint and sounded hesitant to his ears. Her eyes had not met his.

"Are you alright, Katherine?"

"I had a bad dream. Hard to shake it off."

"Me too." A dread came over him. Had doubt plagued her also in the night? Is that why she tossed and turned? Is that why she needed an early walk?

At last she looked up at him. "Are you alright?"

"I am now, here with you." He kissed her forehead. "Miss McGinn, I'm riding to the gin to seek a job." He felt her startle, so he readjusted his thoughts. "That is, if you want me to."

Time paused. The breeze stilled. Ben stiffened.

Katherine raised on her tiptoes and placed her hand around his neck. "With all my heart."

Time resumed. The breeze blew. Ben relaxed.

"Would you keep the late morning and afternoon free for me? I want to spend all the rest of my time with you before the train whistle summons me away."

"I suppose I could spare the time." He watched a smile pull at her lips and betray her serious tone. He captured the smile with a quick kiss. With his hand on her back, he guided her to the kitchen.

No butterfly clip adorned her hair. Ben felt a hint of disappointment.

With breakfast behind them and Sammy settled with the others, Ben set out to seek a job. After a half hour ride on a dirt road headed north out of Layton, he pulled onto the grounds of the Forder Gin and situated the cart. He noticed a slate blue Studebaker Touring parked in the shade of a large pecan tree. Ben paused to admire it.

Among the Crepe Myrtles

The gin was a large single structure made of wood. A high, slanted, metal roof that peaked in the middle covered the building. Two smoke stakes jutted from its top. Bales of cotton were stacked five or six deep in rows of twenty or more. The sea of bound cotton extended the length of the property on three sides. The fourth side left room for the cotton wagons to line up for inspection where weight and price would be determined. Large barn-like doors were slid open to reveal the entry into the gin. Ben stepped inside and noted two small offices set off by walls, doors, and glass windows. Taking a deep breath, he turned toward the gin office and was met by a man dressed in a suit. Ben connected this sight to the auto parked under the tree and smiled to himself. *Of course.* He cleared his throat just as the man extended a hand toward him.

"How can I help you?"

"I'm here to inquire about a job. Name's Ben Williams."

"Are you new to Layton? Don't know that I've heard the name before."

"Yes. I'm looking to settle here. I come from Commerce."

"Commerce? What brings a man from such a thriving community to settle in our striving town?"

"Hope."

The businessman chuckled. "Hope. We'll I guess we're each entitled to it. I'm Mason Forder. Just so happens I own this gin. Got any experience?"

"I do."

An hour later, Ben walked back to the cart carrying a tune on his lips. A week from today he'd be a shift foreman in the engine room at the gin, and off season he would be a saw filer at the small Forder Mill that primarily provided lumber for the extended community.

As he passed the rows of cotton lining the flat, black Texas fields, his mind wandered to the praying Katherine had been doing on his behalf. He'd come to realize he had gratitude to give and no recipient, and the emotion made him ponder whether God was at work in his life or just simple circumstance? A twinge of remorse pulled at his heart. He was guilty of wanting the good from God and blaming Him for the bad, just as Katherine had written about in her letter. He had to admit he had a lot to learn about an actual relationship with God. He also had to admit that for the first time in his life, he willingly cracked open the door to knowing God personally.

Pulling into the yard, he spotted Katherine shelling peas on the front porch. He jumped from the cart and met her at the front steps. "Katherine McGinn, you are looking at the morning foreman of the engine room." He lifted her at the waist and spun her in a circle.

"Ben, you were hired?"

"Yes ma'am. Hired by Mason Forder himself. And when the gin season is done, I'll be working the mill." He set her on the ground and pulled her into a hug.

"Ain't nothing to keep us apart now, my darling Butterfly." His lips grazed the top of her head. "Are you happy?"

He felt her look up to him. "Yes."

"Could you thank God for me?" He tweaked her ear. "My heart is full of gratefulness, and I suppose it only right to thank Him."

"I'll thank Him on my own account, but I reckon he'd prefer to hear from you directly." Her tweak on his ear felt gentle. The tug he saw her give to own ear didn't appear to be gentle at all. He'd come to recognize that tug as a sign of nerves. Was she an excited bride-to-be or a reluctant one? He'd need to put her mind at ease and propose sooner than later during their outing.

Within the hour, Ben secured Sammy next to the quilt and picnic basket in the back of the cart. The wheelchair lay sideways between his son and Lena, who sat with her legs dangling over the open end. Katherine stood near Gitter as he'd instructed her. Taking the russet haired lady by the hand, he pulled her near the seat and helped her up. Before releasing her, he gently kissed her hand then touched the butterfly clip that now adorned her hair. He was rewarded with a blush.

"I thought we'd picnic at the pond today. Lena can help Sammy fish."

"Are you sure he'd be safe?"

"I'm certain of it. I wouldn't risk Sammy's safety." He felt his brow wrinkle. Perhaps motherly instinct was causing her question.

"I know you wouldn't. My bad dream was about the pond and well, here we are going to it."

"Then we won't go. I'll pick another spot to picnic. Or you can pick. My time with you matters, but the place doesn't."

"No. You're right. Let's go to the pond. Lena will get a kick out of helping Sammy fish." He rested his head on her forehead and she leaned into him and grasped his arm for the remainder of the ride. Her silence was much louder than any he'd experienced with Sammy. And anxiety nagged at him.

Ben felt some relief as Katherine relaxed during the picnic. He pulled out his harmonica and played as the ladies cleaned up, then he helped Sammy and Lena bait their poles. Sammy's loud cry of excitement made the group break out in laughter. Ben put his finger to Sammy's lips as a reminder to keep quiet. How rare the need for him to quieten his son. Satisfied that Sammy and Lena were occupied and safe, he took Katherine by the hand. "Walk with me."

As he'd eaten, he spotted an area surrounded by trees and close enough to hear should Lena express a concern with Sammy, but hidden enough to express his love for Katherine. Hand in hand, he led her there and positioned her to stand against a tree trunk. He kissed her slowly and tenderly while his hands held both of hers. Bees buzzed on nearby wildflowers, and to Ben's delight, butterflies flitted in the air around them. Katherine must have noticed, for he saw her smile.

"Katherine McGinn, I've come to love you, almost from the first time I laid eyes on you. You've awakened something in me, my Butterfly. Death had cocooned my heart and I never thought I could love this way again—the way a man loves a woman. But I do."

He kissed her hand.

"I don't have much to offer you other than my fluttering heart. I give you everything I am and everything I have if you could love a man like me," he went to his knees, "and be my wife."

Tears rolled down her face and dripped onto his hands. He waited, and like earlier that morning, time stopped. The thud of his heart seemed to echo through the trees.

"Katherine?"

"I love you Ben. But, I won't be your wife."

He released her hands and grabbed her waist tightly. His head sunk to his chest.

"You say you love me and then refuse me! How can you do that?"

"It's for the best."

"For who? You?" He looked her in the eyes even as he felt hot tears stream down his face. He had no pride, only heartbroken despair.

"For Sammy."

Ben felt numbness invade him nerve by nerve. Disbelief pushed to become anger, but he refused to let it.

"I don't understand."

"I'm scared to be his mother."

"We've talked about this. I trust you and I'll help you. Katherine, I won't abandon him to you."

She shook her head no.

He rose from his knees and pulled her forcefully toward him, his hands gripping her shoulders then moving to her face.

"Katherine. I love you. I need you. Don't abandon me."

The russet butterfly slipped from his grasp and flew away.

Ben felt his body hit the ground. He wept. Embarrassingly.

With Sammy on the seat next to him and Katherine and Lena in the back of the cart, Ben led the speechless, awkward group from the pond. His stomach churned. The reins felt heavy and cutting in his hands. Every sense seemed heightened despite the numbness that invaded his body. He felt his son's eyes on him, expressing the concern he could not speak. The sniffles, sobs, and whispers from the back of the cart made their way to his ears and tortured him.

When they arrived at the McGinn home, he watched Katherine slip off the cart and run into the house just as Joe came around the corner from the garden. He would never see her again. Ben grabbed the seatback and fought to maintain consciousness when his mind wanted to relieve his heart from the pain.

"Lena, my bag is packed. Could you bring it to me?" He'd miss the puffy-eyed girl who looked at him with sadness etched on her face and shook her head yes.

Ben turned to Joe who now stood with a puzzled look on his face.

"She refused me."

"You certain?" He watched red creep up Joe's face at the ridiculous question.

"Of course, I'm certain!"

"Sammy?"

"You knew?"

"No, but I figured. She don't think highly of her abilities."

The insults he'd witnessed Joe thrust upon her flashed in his mind; his disappointment gave way to anger. "She's listened to your cutting words, Joe!"

With that, Ben turned from the man who had been his friend while "I'm sorry about that" filled the tense air.

"For the refusal or for your influence?" His question was left unanswered.

Lena returned to the cart with his bag in hand. "I'll drive you and Sammy to the depot." He pulled her toward him and gave her a bear hug. "Thank you." Her body trembled against his.

With Sammy seated between them on the cart seat, the irony of the situation was not lost to Ben. He'd left the depot with one McGinn by his side and would return with the other. Silence settled between the riders, but as they came near the store, Ben spoke in a raspy voice.

"We've got a bit of time before the train leaves. Let me get you and Sammy a cola." He helped the riders down and situated Sammy in his wheelchair. Sorrow washed over him as he looked at Sammy. He'd put his son's heart at risk too.

Rather than ordering from the diner, he pulled two colas from the cooler and headed to a table. Getting Sammy and Lena settled, Ben breathed a sigh of relief that he didn't recognize anyone working the store. He was too unnerved to sit, and he wanted to offer Sammy some last moments alone with Lena, so he meandered down the aisles.

As he stood uselessly examining the shave cream, a presence seemed to sizzle next to him. A delicate hand clasped his arm, and a feminine scent filled the space around him. The scent was not that of honeysuckle—sweet and pure like his beloved. It was alluring. Costly no doubt. Demanding a high price.

"Ben, so good to see you." Chills ran down his spine. He turned toward the flirtatious voice.

"I had asked Katherine to let me know when you were coming to town. My intention is to invite you to a private dinner, at my home—the Forder estate."

He kept his features stone cold. He saw a smile and a hint of embarrassment cross the beautiful face.

"You don't recall who I am?"

"Faye." He felt the beauty tighten her grip on his arm.

"Indeed I am. And how fortunate that I was here to view the progress of our expansion and ran into you."

He felt her hand slide down to his own and clasp it. It was soft— untainted by common labor or chores.

"Are you coming or going, Ben?"

He wished he knew.

His mind and emotions twirled. Why had time dropped him in this vulnerable, tempting moment?

He was a rejected man, and she was an inviting woman.

Ben composed himself. "I'm going. My stay here is over."

"Pity. I didn't see you at the High Cotton with Joe." She leaned in closer to him. There was no alcohol on her breath to repel him. "So, what brought you to Layton if not to spend time with him?"

"Katherine."

He watched her brow wrinkle.

"My son and I were here to see Katherine."

He watched her go pale.

"Your son?"

Ben smiled as Lena, eavesdropping no doubt, rolled Sammy into view at that precise moment.

"Miss Forder, meet my son." Ben tousled the head of the young boy who looked at the siren but offered no smile. Faye sucked in a breath and wrinkled her brows.

He heard the seduction hit the ground and shatter.

"Well, Katherine can have you." And with that, Faye released his hand and slithered toward the door.

"Yes, she can. If only she would."

The words were spoken so lightly they fell on deaf ears.

Chapter 12

The screen door slammed shut.

"Have you lost your mind?"

Sobs racked Katherine's body. She lifted her moist face to look at Lena.

"I think so." Her stomach lurched, and she leaned into the bucket Joe had left for her—his one act of compassion before leaving her alone with her misery.

"I was scared, Lena. And now I'm hopeless."

"Go to him. He loves you."

Lena scrambled to their room and returned with a wet cloth. "Wipe your face and eat this." Lena placed a peppermint in her hand.

"She's right, Katherine. Go to him." Joe's deep voice shook her. He cared?

"Can Gitter make it in time?"

"Yes! Go!" Katherine let Lena pull her from the chair.

An instant metamorphosis created a woman insanely driven by passion. Without looking back, she ran to the cart and commanded Gitter with authority. The mule moved at a speed she'd never gotten from him before.

"Please, God, give me Ben. Please, Ben give me grace."

The train whistling in the distance caused Katherine to panic and she yanked Gitter to a stop, jumped from the cart, and ran by foot toward the man she loved. Sweat soaked the back of her dress. Black dirt flew up and covered her hem as her feet pounded against the ground. She reached the store and focused on the small depot just beyond it. The high weeds surrounding the train stop threatened her footing as she ran.

Her breath caught! There he was coming around the corner of the building—a rejected lover; a lonely father pushing his son toward the train and away from the pain.

"Ben! Ben!" He turned toward her commotion just as her body slammed into his. She clung to him tightly.

"I was wrong. Please forgive me." Her sobs returned.

Katherine felt him loosen her grip and her regret caused her legs to give way. His touch was gentle as he steadied her and looked her in the eyes.

"Katherine, what are saying?"

"I'm saying I love you and..."

"You told me that already."

"And I want to marry you." Her eyes searched his. "Do you still want to marry me, Ben?"

His silent stare made her feel like stone.

"I love you, Katherine, but, no, I don't want to marry you—not out some sense of guilt or obligation you feel toward me and my son. I have a caregiver. I want a wife."

"Any wife?"

His look softened. "You know the answer to that question."

"I let fear push you away earlier, but it wasn't fear or guilt that sent me running to you like a crazed woman. It was love." She clung to him and implored him with her body and voice. "Don't leave me. Marry me."

His lips captured hers. With the passion of a woman in love, she returned the kiss until they were both breathless. The world could watch them. She didn't care. She had no pride. Only desperation for him.

"Is that a yes, Mr. Williams?"

"Yes." His gorgeous smile left her captivated. "Will you be my wife?"

"Yes."

Relief swept over her, and she collapsed into his arms and wept. Embarrassingly.

Pulling herself from Ben, she leaned over and embraced Sammy who wrapped his arms around her. She kissed his cheeks then placed her hand on her heart. "I love you." Katherine wondered how much he understood about the scene before him.

The whistle blew again as the train stopped at the depot. "You got fifteen minutes, Mr. Williams, before the train pulls out." Katherine felt her face flush; her earlier boldness was slipping away. "Thank you, Percy."

Ben's fingers laced with hers. "Sit next to me on the step, Butterfly."

She nestled next to him and grabbed his arm with both her hands. She wasn't sure she could ever let go of him and continue to breathe.

"Lena found me sobbing in despair over what I'd done."

His lips brushed her temple. "As soon as she helped me put Faye Forder in her place, she ran out of the store." He chuckled. "As she ran out of the store, she yelled for me to wait and not leave."

"But you were leaving."

"Because it wasn't Lena who needed to ask me to stay."

Despite the moment, the name of Faye Forder made her curious. "Faye was in the store?"

Ben produced a roguish grin. "A curious butterfly."

She squeezed his arm.

"Apparently, you were supposed to tell her when I was in town."

"Apparently, I did not. She has eyes for you."

"Don't worry, Katherine. One mention of Sammy and she disappeared. Besides, I told her I was here because of you."

"You did?"

"I did."

"I love you." Then, "How did Lena help you?"

"Enough talk of Lena and Faye. I plan to be back in a week. We'll talk to the preacher and get married before the next week ends. Can you be ready that soon—rearranging the house like we agreed and whatever else you women folk do to prepare for a wedding?" His warm breath filled her ear when he whispered, "And a wedding night."

"Ben!" Despite her retort, an embarrassing tingle ran through her body, but it clung to a taunting image—Lena, Sammy, and Joe sitting in the front room smiling as the blushing bride and eager groom entered their bedroom. Perhaps a private picnic in the woods would be less embarrassing for the newlyweds? Of course, she had no idea what to expect beyond the moment a newly married couple found themselves alone with no boundaries. She freed one hand from his arm and tugged at her ear until Ben gently pulled her hand away and put it back where it had been.

The fifteen minutes passed quickly for Katherine as the couple made their plans. Reluctantly, she hugged Sammy goodbye then turned her attention completely to Ben.

"Come home to me as soon as you can, Ben Williams."

"It won't be soon enough." His hands covered her face as he bent to kiss her. "I love you, Katherine. You've made me very happy."

The two men folk who would become her very own disappeared from sight as the train rolled down the track. Only then did Katherine think about Gitter, who she'd left untied in the middle of the road. Finding him in the same spot, she gently led him to the store.

She had a thought, an embarrassingly bold thought, and needed to see Mrs. Justice. Although Thanksgiving was a few weeks away, one of the new rooms in the store had been completed, and she thought it could provide privacy for a bride and groom as they became man and wife.

"Katherine, good to see you. Mr. Justice and I have been in the back cleaning all day. So glad I came out to sort the mail." The ladies embraced.

"You got some shopping to do, dear?"

Katherine shook her head no and felt her mouth stretch into a broad smile. "Not exactly. I have news. I'm getting married."

Mrs. Justice grabbed her in a bear hug and kissed her on the cheek. "My dear Katherine, congratulations. Is the lucky man from Commerce?" Her wink caused the bride to be to blush.

"He is. Ben Williams."

"Tell me about him."

Katherine told her mother-like friend about the man and his boy and then posed her idea.

"I was thinking that a wedding night away from the house would be a good present for him." Heat filled her face; her voice could only manage a whisper. "I know things aren't finished around here, but I thought maybe I could rent the one room that is done."

"Well, I hadn't thought about opening a room at a time. Let me see what Mr. Justice thinks. He knows about the permits Mr. Forder got and legal matters like that. You wait right here."

Katherine must have blushed because Mrs. Justice patted her on the shoulder and quietly proclaimed, "Don't be embarrassed about my asking Mr. Justice. He's already given his daughter away, so he can respect the inquiry. Besides, I'll know just how to word it to spare your dignity."

Within moments, she saw her friend return wearing a look of excitement on her face. "We'll do it. And good news, the common bath is completed, so you can use it too."

"Luxury! Thank you." Katherine cleared her throat. "I suppose I should ask the price."

"Consider it our wedding gift."

"But, I should pay you."

"No. You should accept what's offered to you."

Katherine gave in to the delight of the offer. No smiling family members. No private picnic.

"Oh, thank you, Mrs. Justice. If my Mama were still alive, I think she'd be just like you." Katherine paused at her own words. "In fact, I'd be honored if you would be with me and Lena at the house when I get ready on my wedding day."

"I'd be proud to be there."

She kissed Mrs. Justice on the cheek then hurried to the door. "I best get home. I left Lena and Joe in a whirlwind."

Katherine was still guiding the cart into the yard when Lena leapt off the porch and ran to her. She felt tenderness for her younger sister when she noticed tears rolling down her cheeks. Releasing the reins, she jumped down and hugged Lena.

"I'm getting married!" She felt Lena relax against her and heard a soft sob escape her throat. "We've got lots to plan, don't we little sister?" Katherine felt Lena nod her agreement. Momentary silence settled in until Lena released her hold and came eye to eye with her.

"Did he kiss you?" Not even a tint of pink shown on her sister's face. The value of the Justice wedding night gift instantly increased to Katherine, but despite herself, she laughed out loud at Lena's spunk. "Yes. And I kissed him back." They giggled together.

The squeak of the screen door got their attention. "Well, did you fix your mess, Katherine? Ben and you gettin' married?"

"Yes. Week after next." She moved to her older brother and stood before him. "Joe, thank you for giving us your blessing. And, well, thank you for bringing Ben here and for being willing to share the house." Her arms went around his chest, and she pressed into him, her head resting where his heart beat. Proof he had one. His hand felt awkward and hurried as he patted her back, but it comforted her. "I'm happy for you, Katherine." The moment between them flew away and would most likely not return. But it had lit upon her heart.

Two days later changes began to happen inside the house. Katherine admired the makeshift wall that was coming together. Joe had put nails in two opposite walls of the front room and gathered a rope from the shed. When Katherine had placed the last stitch in the two sheets she'd sewn together, she called Lena in from the kitchen. Together the ladies ran the rope through the openings she'd sewn at the top of the sheets, then held the cloth wall steady as Joe climbed onto a chair and hung the looped rope ends onto the nails.

"My own private room!" Katherine giggled at her sister. "It might not be too private, Lena, but you can certainly sit and read all night and not bother a soul with your lamp." Tenderness that came from the place where no words could speak flooded through Katherine. She pulled her sister into her embrace and let the touch speak for her. Lena was feisty, but she was also the most self-sacrificing person Katherine knew. It brought Katherine joy to know that she was giving Lena a brother-in-law and a nephew. Her sister had love to give, and Ben and Sammy were ready to receive it.

As the three siblings were moving Lena's bed into the front room Katherine heard footsteps on the front porch. Katherine looked out the screen door. There stood Mr. and Mrs. Justice. He held a box in his arms.

"What a nice surprise. Come in." A hint of lavender wafted from the box and teased Katherine's nose when the couple entered.

"What's in the box?" Her sister's question popped out before Katherine had time to divert Lena's curiosity.

"It's a surprise for the bride-to-be." Mrs. Justice ran her hand across the lid of the box. Her smile warmed Katherine. "I see we interrupted some moving, but if you have time, I'd like to show you what's inside."

"Plenty of time," said the blushing bride.

"Just us three girls." Mrs. Justice took the box from her husband.

"Let's go to the bedroom." Katherine nodded toward her room, and the trio went inside and pulled the curtain closed behind them.

Katherine had imagined there would be moments in life that encountered her hopes and dreams and lingered with them. When her fingertips touched the white satin dress Mrs. Justice pulled from the box, such a moment existed for her.

"I was married in this dress and so was our daughter."

"I remember how beautiful she looked at her wedding," Katherine answered. Her spoken reply was interlaced with her unspoken question, "Is this for me?"

"We'd like to offer it to you for your wedding day."

"I'd be a real bride." Her left hand went to her heart as her right hand stifled a sob. She heard Lena sigh beside her.

Mrs. Justice chuckled. "Katherine, your heart makes you a real bride. This dress is outside wrapping."

"A way that Ben can see how I feel about him?"

"Yes." Mrs. Justice patted Katherine on the shoulder.

"This is so romantic. My big sister a bride. Try it on, Katherine!"

"Should I, Mrs. Justice? I've not bathed."

"Oh, I'm not concerned about that. Let's try it on and see how it fits."

As Katherine began to unbutton her cotton dress, she watched Mrs. Justice unbutton the satin one.

"It smells good, Mrs. Justice."

"What you smell is something I brought for you to use on your wedding day and wedding night. It's lavender soap, hair rinse, and lotion."

Katherine stopped unbuttoning her dress and took the small square package Mrs. Justice pulled from the dress box. The lid was covered in a layer of white paper with lavender flowers and a gold seal with the name *Sills & Smith* stamped on it. Katherine lifted the lid. Inside the box was a bar of soap wrapped in purple tissue with that same seal; a clear bottle filled with purple liquid lay on one side of the soap, and a round silver tin lay on the opposite side. The seal on the tin read "Sills & Smith Lavender Body Lotion."

"I've never owned lotion and soap quite this fancy. I am going to feel like one of Lena's princesses. Thank you."

Katherine glanced at Lena, then began to address Mrs. Justice.

"Mrs. Justice, I'm afraid I don't," she glanced at Lena again. "Could you excuse us Lena?" Katherine thought her sister caught the gist of her question because she saw red seep up the twelve -year- old's face as she answered, "I'll get some sweet tea ready in the kitchen."

Katherine turned back to Mrs. Justice just as the middle-aged woman sat on Katherine's bed and patted the spot next to her. "Sit by me dear." Katherine sat. She thought for sure Embarrassment huddled in the corner, hiding its face.

"I don't know anything about a wedding night."

"Of course not. Well, your husband does and, I hope you don't mind me saying this, he's already experienced a first-time bride, so he probably suspects how you're feeling. Maybe tenderness and patience will be part of what he shares with you that night."

"Is what happens between a husband and wife a bad thing?"

"No, it's a natural thing between a husband and wife. And your innocence is just as it should be." The nervous bride watched Mrs. Justice blush before whispering to her, "Katherine, time and experience make some things better."

Lena returned with the tea just as Mrs. Justice was helping Katherine into the satin gown. She looked at her young sister for approval. The russet-haired bride-to-be smiled when she saw Lena set down the tea and cover her mouth with both hands while bouncing up and down on her toes.

"Katherine, you look beautiful. Don't you think so?"

Katherine turned and looked at herself in the mirror. "I do."

The three women laughed at her answer then hugged each other.

The next day Lena and Katherine worked to make space in her small dresser for Ben and Sammy's belongings. As she rearranged her personal items into one drawer, she pondered what she'd be placing in Ben's drawer week after week as she did the laundry. She wasn't naive about men's undergarments, but the thought of touching Ben's clothing seemed extremely intimate now. She smirked at herself realizing she may not feel so romantic over his garments when she was bent over a tub scrubbing them.

At Katherine's insistence, Joe had pulled an old family trunk from the shed and cleaned it up before heading back out to the rails. It would be more storage in the room that she would share with her husband and his son—her son. Katherine took a heavy quilt from Lena, who had just walked in with it from the clothesline outside. She sniffed it, breathing in the scent of fresh air. Soon the scent of Ben would linger in its threads. She folded the quilt and placed it in the extra trunk to await the cold weather.

When Lena slipped into the kitchen to prepare supper, Katherine sat on the bed. She was alone in the room, but felt crowded by her emotions that had invited themselves to spend the week with her. Aggravated by her feelings, Katherine gave in to them. She would listen to her emotions and then speak her piece to each one.

Fear was the most wordy. She interrupted it. "I've argued with you once before. The only reason you're even here is because you are holding hands with Unknown. Go away."

Embarrassment had been cowering in the corner, but it came from the shadows and whispered in her ear. Katherine retorted, "Ben will teach me about the things between husband and wife. I reckon you'll be around on the wedding night, but you have to keep quiet!"

Doubt tapped her on the left shoulder. Katherine interrupted it. "Go away. I'll learn to be a mother. "

She sensed a movement, then Doubt tapped her right shoulder. "He doesn't want Faye's beauty. He wants mine… dressed in satin and smelling like lavender, with russet hair and a butterfly clip, tasting like burnt biscuits and good coffee."

The twins Hope and Happiness knelt at her knees and each took a hand. What they had to say didn't require words. "You're both welcome here anytime. I trust you with my heart."

Katherine shook her head to clear her thoughts, then chuckled. "Lena will surely think I've lost my mind if she heard me in here talking to no one."

On the fourth day of Katherine's engagement, rain saturated Layton, so the sisters baked pies in anticipation of Ben and Sammy's arrival. And like two days before, a knock at the door announced the arrival of an unexpected guest. Katherine walked through Joe's room and into the front room. Dread came over her when she saw the visitor.

"Gabriel, my goodness, you're soaking wet. What brings you out this way in the rain?"

"Miss Katherine, I was at the store, standing there waiting for my mail. Mrs. Justice was filling the mail slots and said to herself that she didn't think you'd make it in to check your postbox. I told her I'd be more than happy to drop this by." He handed her a rolled-up bundle covered in cloth. "Can I come in?"

Katherine couldn't dare send the man away, so he entered muddy and wet. To keep him from sitting on the rocker cushion, she escorted him through to the kitchen for a cup of coffee. A trail of black Texas mud followed them.

"Lena, Gabriel was nice enough to bring us our mail from the store. Let's get him a cup of coffee before he heads back down the road."

"Hello, Gabriel. Take a seat." Even as Lena tried to interact with the awkward male, Katherine felt his eyes on her, and they remained fixed as the three of them passed the next half hour with idle talk about how Gitter was doing and about Gabriel's latest heroic act toward an animal.

"Miss Katherine, ain't you gonna look at your mail?" *Just waiting for you to leave.* She held the thought captive in her mind. Katherine untied the cloth Mrs. Justice had placed around the rolled-up mail and discovered an advertisement for a washing machine from the Sears Company. She was about to toss the paper into the garbage when a smaller slip of paper rolled inside the advertisement caught her eye. Katherine recognized that it was a telegram from Commerce. A giggle escaped her; neither Lena nor Gabriel let it go unnoticed.

"It's a telegram from Ben." She read it, but the visitor left no time for her to respond.

"Who's Ben?" Gabriel's question hung in the air before falling on Katherine's shoulders. "Ben is the man I am about to marry."

In all her years of knowing Gabriel, Katherine had never seen him angry, but she watched it flash across his disfigured face and then evolve into sadness that settled in his eyes. He was a mangled boy stretched into a man-sized body, and despite her discomfort with his attraction to her, she didn't want to hurt those childish feelings. "I can't wait for you to meet him and his little boy."

He stood. "Alright, I'll come by sometime and meet 'em. You tell 'em your friend Gabriel is the best person in the county when it comes to animals. Bye now Miss Katherine. Bye Lena." His words and his leaving were simultaneous.

Katherine hollered her agreement and good-bye then immediately read the telegram again—her excitement for Ben much stronger than her pity for Gabriel.

She read aloud. "Arrive Friday 10 AM."

Chapter 13

Time dragged, and later than sooner, Katherine found herself at the train depot two days later. Ben stepped off the train alone and opened his arms to her; Katherine went eagerly into his embrace. After all, she need not worry about Percy seeing them; he had been privy to their boldness the last time the couple met at the depot. Ben smelled of sweat and coal and aftershave.

Her lover's kiss on her lips felt tender and tasted sweet. She ran her fingers through the curly hair at the nape of his neck. "Welcome home." That tingle moved through her again. It was becoming familiar. The wedding night crossed her mind and, enclosed in his arms, she felt more eagerness than timidity.

"Help me with the wheelchair." His raspy voice was warm in her ear. Her eyes never left Ben as he stepped back into the train and handed down the chair. She watched him step inside one more time then reappear with their son resting in the arms that had just embraced her. She and Sammy reached for one another at the same time and fell into their own embrace.

As Ben unloaded his two trunks and a bag from the train, Katherine found herself once again seated next to Sammy in the cart. She pulled a piece of paper from her pocket. Lena was the artist in the family and had drawn a sketch for Katherine to show him. Both Katherine and Sammy smiled as he pointed to the drawing. A mother and father were holding hands with a boy seated in a wheelchair on the front porch of the McGinn house. A young girl was seated nearby playing with a train piece.

Katherine wondered how much Sammy understood about the change in his life. Did he see this as just another visit with new friends? Would he long for Mrs. Cramer? After all, Ben had spoken of the couple with such admiration. Could Sammy open his heart to Katherine as his mother? She took his small cheeks in her hands, smiled at him, and then placed his hand on her heart and her hand on his. Time would answer her questions.

Ben jumped onto the seat. The cart squeaked. "Is Joe in town?"

"Not until tomorrow afternoon. Why?"

"We have a small matter of discretion to discuss, Miss McGinn, between now and the time he gets here."

"Discretion?"

"Well, since Joe's not here, I can't be sleeping in the house tonight. So, here's my plan. Tell me what you think. I thought Sammy could sleep in the bed you have for him. You could sleep in yours—ours—and I could sleep on the porch. With the windows open, Sammy would see me, and I could hear if he needed anything."

Katherine poised her hand on her hip. "Mr. Williams, that's a fine plan, but as the lady of the house, I thought of my own plan. Tell me what you think." They laughed. "I'll sleep with Lena in her bed, Sammy can sleep in his bed, and you can sleep in my...our bed, even after Joe gets home." She touched his arm. "When we're married, I'll join you in the bed." She watched the corners of his mouth curl up.

"But suppose someone misunderstands our arrangements tonight?"

"Who's to know besides us, Percy, and maybe Mr. and Mrs. Justice. If my reputation is that bad, then yours has just suffered a mighty loss."

Ben's hand clasped one of hers, and he rested them on Sammy's leg. The boy's small palm warmed her fingertips as he covered their laced hands.

"Do you think Sammy understands much of this?"

"I can't say for certain, but I reckon he understands most of it and knows a change is coming."

"How?"

"Well, lots of reasons. We packed up all our belongings. He's seen lots of children with both a Momma and a Papa. You all are the only people we've spent time with outside of the boarders and a relative or two. And although I appreciated Mrs. Cramer, I never kissed her or held her hand."

Tingle. Laughter.

"I guess he'll miss her."

"Probably. I know she'll miss him. She never had her own children. She blubbered all during our good-bye."

"I wish I had met her. I bet she's a fine woman."

"She and her husband are good folks. She sent you something. A kind of handmade wedding gift, I suppose, that no one else could give you. "

"I'm curious!"

"She wrote some things in a journal she thought you'd like to know about caring for Sammy. Things like his favorite food, his pastimes, his bath, his habits, and," he winked at her, "nature calling." Katherine smirked at him. "She put some recipes in there too. She also drew pictures and signals she used with him. I think she wanted to share her heart with you."

"She must have a big heart. What a special gift. I know I'll treasure it."

"Katherine, just give Sammy some time. He adores you and I don't think it will take long for him to open up his entire being to you."

Time—it was persistent. It also rolled along, and the week between Ben's arrival—his final arrival now that he was here to stay-- and their wedding had sped by in a flurry of activity.

Her mind buzzing with thoughts, Katherine lay next to Lena who seemed to be sound sleep. Tomorrow was her wedding day. Katherine's mind thought through the past few days that had been filled with preparation—a wedding license, a meeting with Pastor Carlson, washing and ironing clothes for the wedding day, unpacking Ben and Sammy's belongings and making them part of the home, and a surprise shower at the diner with Lena, some ladies from church, including Pastor's fiancé', Mrs. Justice and her daughter, and Mrs. Forder, who gave her the most beautiful gown she'd ever seen. Katherine gloated to herself, "Faye was not invited and not missed."

Her gloating turned to gratefulness as she thought about the generosity of both Mrs. Justice and Mrs. Forder. Because of them she'd be dressed in white satin for her wedding and dressed in white sheer cotton and lace for her wedding night. The scent of lavender would cover her skin.

Her favorite wedding gift sat a few feet away in the front room on a small table in between hers and Lena' rockers. She pulled the covers back and gently got out of bed. Pushing the divider curtain to the side, she stood to admire the present and relive the evening.

Ben had given her a new phonograph and two records. While the rest of the family was occupied playing checkers in the kitchen, he'd whisked her away to the front room then patiently and tenderly danced with her to the tune of Irishman John McCormack's "Foggy Dew." He'd held her close and guided her along the way with gentle touches and whispered instructions.

It was her first dance. And as they swayed, she whispered the secret of her wedding night gift to him. He had responded with an embrace that left little room for air between them.

Replaying the ballad lyrics in her head, Katherine relished the thought that tomorrow night she would be Ben's Irish bride. Her slender body would surely be tucked next to his masculine frame under the covers. Her nerves made her giggle. She heard Lena stir, but not awaken. She hoped his gentle way during the dance was a glimpse of what would be between them on their wedding night, but she had no idea what to expect beyond being tucked at his side. Tugging her ear, she slipped back into the bed and under the covers. Sleep finally came.

The brightness of the sun and the sound of muffled voices woke her. Katherine slid her hand to the spot where Lena had slept next to her. It was empty and had no hint of body warmth. "How late have I slept?" Once again, she pulled back the covers, and for the last time Katherine McGinn, as she had always known herself, rose from the bed. Tomorrow morning another Katherine would awaken and would start her new life.

She followed the smell of coffee and the sound of the voices that led her to kitchen. There stood both Lena and Mrs. Justice pouring steaming water into the metal bath tub.

"Good morning."

"Katherine." Lena placed her empty pitcher on the floor, and Katherine walked into her embrace. "Happy wedding day!"

"Am I really getting married?" Katherine laughed and tightened her hold on Lena.

"Yes, you are." Mrs. Justice had emptied her pitcher and now stood near the bride. Her motherly kiss on the cheek soothed Katherine. "Let me get you some coffee and a piece of cinnamon bread I brought."

Katherine released her sister and walked to the table where the bread sat next to the butter. "It smells delicious." She took the warm coffee cup from Mrs. Justice and took a sip. "I hope my breakfast stays down. My nerves are hard at work."

"Well, your bath will help soothe those nerves." Lena sat down close enough for Katherine to rest her head on her sister's shoulder. She drew a deep breath, inhaling the comfort that was Lena. Katherine's stomach growled. "Guess I should eat." She took a bite of bread and sighed.

"How long have you been here, Mrs. Justice? And, this bread is delicious."

"Thank you. Just as you planned, Mr. Justice dropped me off around eight this morning, and within the hour, he left with all your menfolk."

"Sammy was so cute," Lena added, "looking all proud as he rode off with all the men. I wonder if he even knows what's happening today."

"I can't believe I didn't hear any of the commotion."

"You were snoring—sound asleep."

"Snoring? Lena, I don't snore. Oh, please tell me I don't snore." Her breakfast crawled up her throat.

"Katherine, you snore. Why, I sometimes wonder that the walls don't shake because of it."

"I'll be so embarrassed." Katherine turned toward Mrs. Justice. "Is it awful that a wife snores?" The answer came from Lena.

"I'm sorry, Katherine. I was teasing you. I've never heard you snore. Relax."

Katherine felt Mrs. Justice pat her on the back. "People snore. The secret to not hearing it is to be the first one to fall asleep. Of course, that's also what can get you accused in the first place."

Katherine didn't think she was supposed to see Mrs. Justice narrow her eyes at Lena. By the way Lena lowered her chin, Katherine figured her sister understood Mrs. Justice' message. She leaned over and hugged Lena. "I should've known you were teasing. You couldn't have kept that news to yourself all these years."

She finished her coffee and bread while Lena and Mrs. Justice brought in a cloth, towel, and pitcher of water for the bath. Her box of lavender treats sat beside the tub. When the ladies excused themselves, she undressed and slipped into the tub.

Looking at herself through the veil of the water, Katherine wondered if Ben would find her attractive. She'd seen the only picture Ben had of his first family. Sammy was an infant sitting on his mother's lap. Katherine thought she was beautiful. She thought herself to be plain.

As though they were in the flesh, she sensed Hope and Happiness whispering in her ears that Ben had chosen her. He could have chosen any woman, but he had chosen her—his Butterfly. She closed her eyes and imagined her fluttering wings bringing her to rest in his hand, feeling cherished and safe.

She lathered herself with the lavender soap then slipped her head under the water. The lavender rinse bubbled in her hair as she scrubbed her head. Lathered now from head to toe, she poured the pitcher of warm water over herself. The scent filled the kitchen. She inhaled it and smiled to herself. Why worry? Ben should be very pleased with his lavender Butterfly.

After drying her skin, she spread the thick lotion over her entire body. Her hands had been ripped by cotton bolls, cut by a knife, blackened by the Texas earth, dried out by Lysol, and held by Ben. But never had they felt this soft. She wrapped a robe around her and headed to the bedroom where she would transform into a bride.

Katherine didn't recognize the woman in the mirror. The white satin dress felt soft against her skin, and the neckline that rested on her collar bone revealed her slender neck. "I've never thought about my neckline before. I look elegant." She saw Lena smile in the reflection and hand the butterfly clip to her. Katherine touched the natural curls that fell from her loosely knotted hair. The russet cascade fell against her elegant neck. Mrs. Justice had styled her hair in a way Katherine had never done before and it looked beautiful. She attached the clip in the knot.

Mrs. Justice came from the kitchen with a bouquet of white kidney wood and frost wood wild flowers wrapped in a handkerchief and tied with a ribbon. Katherine whispered through a smile, "Those flowers attract butterflies." And just as she spoke, recognition set in.

"Mama's handkerchief." Katherine felt tears well in her eyes.

"Now she's part of your wedding day," Lena whispered.

"Thank you, Lena. And Mrs. Justice."

Katherine was surprised to find that the men had taken Gitter and the cart earlier that morning, leaving the Justice' larger cart with a cushioned seat for the bride's escort to the church. As the bridal trio entered the dusty, black grounds of the church, Katherine saw their own cart draped in flowers and vines. A quilt lay folded as a pad on the seat.

"Mrs. Justice, look. Who decorated our cart? It's so pretty."

"The men have been busy this morning." The mother figure winked at her.

"It's like Cinderella." Katherine thought Lena sounded like a six-year-old version of herself when she spoke with such admiration. "Today I feel like Cinderella!" She kissed Lena on the cheek.

The bride gasped. "I don't see my suitcase. Did we forget it?" Katherine felt Mrs. Justice's hands clasp her face. Their eyes met. "The men weren't the only ones busy this morning. Everything is taken care of with your belongings. Relax, beautiful bride. It's time for you to get married."

The women entered the small church foyer, barely wide enough for the three of them to stand side by side. A picture of Jesus knocking on a door caught Katherine's eye; she took in the familiarity of it and let that mingle with her sense of the unknown. Mrs. Justice kissed her on the cheek then went and sat next to her husband on a front pew.

Joe must have taken that as a cue, for he opened the door behind the small pulpit area and called to Pastor Carlson, then turned and came to the foyer. Lena patted him on the shoulder and headed to a pew. "You're very pretty Katherine. Congratulations. Mama would be proud." A tear leaked from her eye and she wiped it away. "Thank you." To her astonishment, Joe reached over and kissed her temple before he grasped her hand and slid it into the crook of his arm.

Katherine knew the moment Ben's eyes fell on her. His smile was full of admiration, love, and awe. Katherine clung to Joe's arm as he walked her to stand beside her groom. Lena, Joe, Sammy, Mr. and Mrs. Justice, Pastor Carlson and his fiancé' surrounded her and the man she loved as they said their vows to each other. In a heartbeat, Katherine McGinn became Katherine Williams.

The next hour was a haze for the bride as the wedding ensemble gathered at the diner for strawberry cake, hugs, and celebration.

Warmth spread over Katherine's body when she saw Mr. Justice speak to Ben who nodded his head yes. Within moments, Ben and Katherine said goodbye to Sammy, and as though the building were on fire, the group left the store. Ben walked over and hung the closed sign on the door then locked it. Katherine extended her hand to him as he returned to her. "I love the smell of lavender, Mrs. Williams." His lips met hers and she sensed his anticipation.

Katherine let him lead her to the hallway of overnight rooms. Once again, her husband locked a door. She was swept into his arms and carried into the guest room. For the third time in a matter of moments, a door was closed and locked behind the bride and groom. Katherine blushed. Indeed, Mrs. Justice had made the room beautiful. She noticed her new gown spread across the chair. The bride was keenly aware that she was alone with her groom. Her insides quivered.

Ben stood her on the floor. "You look beautiful." He turned her back to him and she felt his fingers glide over the buttons of the satin gown. Chills ran down her spine. His breath warmed her neck.

The first button loosened, followed by the others. She felt his fingers push the satin off her shoulders. He released the butterfly clip and freed her hair. Softness cascaded her shoulders and back. The groom turned his bride to face him.

Time to dance.

Part Two

Chapter 14

"Reckon this will hold for a couple of years?" Ben spoke through the nails he held in his teeth. He and Joe had replaced the rotted wood platform around the hand pump used to draw water from a well. "Good as new if you ask me." Ben hammered in the last nail then threw the others into the metal bucket Joe toted around when he made repairs. "We're lucky to have a well in the yard. It's a long haul to the community one."

Ben acknowledged Joe's comment with a nod then wiped his forehead with a rag. He blew into his hands to warm them. The day after Christmas was brisk. He and Katherine had been married a little more than a month. They'd shared their first Thanksgiving together as husband and wife. Sammy had easily embraced his new family. Indeed, Ben had never seen the young boy so happy. The leaves had fallen and the bare trees sat waiting for their spring attire. Ben inhaled then let out a contented sigh. "I think I'll wash up and find out what Katherine's up to. She said something about needing to run an errand." The two parted ways, and Ben headed to the back porch to wash down his arms, neck, and face then made his way to the front room.

He saw her before she sensed his presence. The sight of her delighted him, and his being was filled with her essence. Ben stood and stared at his wife, thinking that his first marriage had been like an East Texas summer evening—warm and soothing, yet threatened by life's storms that often rolled in unannounced. Marriage to Katherine felt like the spring—gentle rains, full of color, new life, and promise. But he was not naive. Even spring showers would come with occasional thunder and lightning.

Katherine was reaching to the top of the Christmas tree, apparently trying to remove one of the cloth bows. "Want some help?" He moved to her and pulled her into his embrace. To his delight, she turned to face him and kissed him quickly. "I'd love your company. And yes, I could use your help untying the bows at the top. I'll work the middle and bottom. Just drop them in this basket." "Yes ma'am." He kissed her back and took his time doing so before speaking again.

"I haven't seen Sammy or Lena since breakfast."

"They're in our room playing slap jack with the new deck of cards we

115

gave Sammy for Christmas. I think the Christmas tree is aggravating Lena's asthma, so I shooed them out."

"I should warn her. Sammy turns wicked when it comes to playing slap jack. He's liable to break her finger when they go to slap the card pile."

"I heard that, Ben Williams, and your warning is too late. I don't think I'll be able to cook or clean ever again with this injured hand." Ben laughed out loud as Lena's comment floated from the next room. Sammy's loud laughter trailed behind her words, even though he was clueless to them. His son always seemed happy in the company of Lena.

"Well, since I'm a lousy cook, guess Lena and I will turn the kitchen over to you, Mr. Williams." Ben tweaked Katherine's nose when she smirked at him.

"And the laundry." Ben rolled his eyes. "Get back to your card game, Lena McGinn."

Ben worked alongside Katherine untying the small bows and tossing the strips into a basket. He kept thinking what a good Christmas Day it had been, gathered with his new family. Sammy and Lena had been so excited. And Katherine, well, she—glowed. He turned the thought into words.

"You seemed to glow yesterday, Butterfly."

"It was the best Christmas I've ever had—with you and Sammy and Lena all around me, and Joe too." Ben felt her lean into him. "Sammy was so excited. I think he made us feel a little childhood Christmas magic. It was a good day."

"One of the best days of my life." He had contemplated when to share the house plans with Katherine, and Ben decided now was the time, and he'd baffle his new wife a little in the process. "Even so, I sensed that something was missing." He felt Katherine stiffen next to him.

"Sammy's momma?"

"What!"

"Was she who was missing?"

"No. Life is whole." He bent and kissed the top of her head where the scent of lavender lingered. "Besides, I said something...not someone."

"What?"

"A gift for you." He watched her glance toward the phonograph where the record she'd unwrapped yesterday lay. The player and records were a luxury of sort. He knew she was baffled when he saw her wrinkled brow. "Another gift for you."

She seemed to smile through her lips and eyes then suddenly tug on her ear. Her forehead came to rest on his shoulder. "I don't have another gift for you."

"Is that right? Well, it's a good thing my gift is for both of us."

"Both of us! Ben, what is it?"

"Patience, Butterfly." He thought he probably deserved the pinch she gave him on his arm.

A glance at the doorway, and he saw Lena standing there holding Sammy in her arms; the boy's bottom was sagging almost to her knees. "We want to see the gift." He didn't give her the pleasure of an answer but snickered to himself. *We?*

"All the bows are off, so I'll drag the tree out. Don't we have an errand to run, Katherine?" He pulled her by the hand through the doorway of their room, brushing Lena and Sammy as he went by. He rustled his son's hair. "Bundle up, Butterfly and meet me out front. Lena will sweep up the needles, won't you?" He winked at his young sister-in-law. "And, Lena, Joe's in the shed if you need help with Sammy. I'll tell him we're leaving."

After he pulled the tree to the woods and spoke to Joe, Ben helped his wife into the cart, then jumped up on the other side. He took the quilt she'd brought out and wrapped it around both their legs

"We are heading to the store, right?"

"Yes."

The smell of banana bread caught his attention. "Is that the bread Lena made this morning for breakfast?"

"She made two loaves. This one is for Mr. and Mrs. Justice. I stitched the cloth that the bread is wrapped in. It's a gift for them." He looked at the wrapped loaf when she titled it up. The letter J was stitched across the middle of the cloth. He traced it with his finger. "It's nice, Katherine."

The December wind blew across them as Gitter pulled them along the potted road to the store. Their breath made smoke.

"Are you too cold?"

"No, the fresh air feels good. And I like getting a few minutes to ourselves."

"Me too. Katherine, is there anything you need? Anything you hope for?"

Even in the cold air, the expression on her face melted him when she turned to answer.

"No one's ever asked me that question."

"It should have been asked a hundred times before now."

Her humble smile warmed him despite the cold.

"Needing? I only ask for the necessities of life. Wanting? I never let myself think that way—so I wouldn't be disappointed. Oh! There is one thing I've always wanted." Her gloved hand emerged from under the quilt and gently grasped his. "I always dreamed about a family of my own. And that dream has come true. I know how you feel about God, but I thank Him for you and Sammy. He answered my prayers when he brought you to me."

"I may be more open to God than you realize and far more than I ever expected. Since the time we wrote our first letters to one another, I've continually been more aware of God than I care to admit. I feel so grateful for you have been struck with the thought that no human was worthy of that gratefulness. It belongs to God."

"My prayers are working?" She leaned into his shoulder. Releasing her grip, he put his arm around her and drew her to him.

"Keep praying. Now, about those wants and needs. You sure there's nothing else you want?"

"Some privacy would be nice. And another child. For us. For Sammy."

"Those two usually go hand in hand."

"Ben!"

He pulled the reins and directed the cart off the road and into a small gathering of bare trees near a small stream. In the summer, the large trunks would display beautiful weeping willows, but in the winter, their barren limbs looked more like a veil. He'd spotted the scene on his first ride down this road months ago. He felt Katherine raise her head. "What are you doing? Is something wrong?"

"It's time for our present. Close your eyes." Ben reached into his back pocket and pulled out a folded piece of paper. He unfolded it and placed it in her hand. "Open your eyes."

118

His wife looked at the drawing of squares and rectangles drawn in the layout of their house; each room was labeled. He knew the moment her eyes fell on the new rooms because a smile spread across her face. "You're adding on to the house?" Winter smoke came from her mouth as she spoke.

"Yes ma'am. If you want me to. Says right there 'Ben and Katherine's room.' And right there, that small room says 'Sammy' and that one says 'extra.' And look here. He pointed to two indentions off the larger of the three rooms. Two doorways. One from the outside and one from the kitchen. And those small bedrooms, they'll have doors too."

Katherine wiped a tear from her cheek and pointed to a circle drawn further away from the rest of the squares and rectangles. "What's this?"

Ben laughed. "That's an outhouse." He winked. "For privacy."

"Ben, I'm excited, but how can we do this?"

"Joe and I got it all worked out. Weather permitting, we'll start tomorrow. He purchased cement, rocks, and lumber for me a couple days ago; it was the same day he bought planks to fix the pump. It's all stored in the shed. You and Lena were too busy baking and doing what not for Christmas to notice." He smiled, but noticed that she didn't.

"Money. I mean how do we have the money."

"I kept that part a secret from you until now. My great uncle gave a small house to my cousin and me because he didn't have a family of his own. Well, my cousin, Jim, lived in it. It's in Galveston. He just sold it because he's getting married and wired me my share of the money. Not much, but enough to do this and have some left over to stash." Ben pulled Katherine to his chest and hugged her tightly, then placed his palms on her cheeks.

"Merry Christmas. I hope you like our present."

"I love it! Thank you." Her kiss was warm and sweet.

"Ben, will we have wooden floors and painted walls?"

"Wooden floors? Yes. I might can afford wall paper if you'd like that instead of paint."

Katherine clapped her hands. "Yes! Flowered. Maybe Joe will build us some rockers to have in there too—if he's feeling generous!"

"I like how you're thinking, Katherine Williams! I'll talk to Carl Justice next week about ordering the paper. Do you know how to put it on the wall?'

"No." They laughed out loud. "Mrs. Justice might show us," Katherine surmised.

Ben guided Gitter back to the road and they made their way to the store. No other carts, wagons, or autos were parked outside the store. He helped Katherine down, then pushed open both the wooden door and the screen door, making the bell above them ring. The smell of coffee drifted in the air. The store felt warm and welcoming.

"Well, look who's here." Mr. Justice came from behind the counter, and Ben shook his hand.

"Merry Christmas, Carl. Katherine brought y'all something."

"Lena and I made these for you two." As Carl Justice unwrapped the bread, Ben interjected. "Goes good with coffee."

"Where's Mrs. Justice?" Katherine asked.

"She's at home undoing Christmas and playing with our granddaughter. We figured business would be slow, and the diner's closed." Their friend pulled a pocket knife from his pants, then unwrapped the cloth from the bread. He cut a big slice. "She may not get much of this bread, but she'll love the cloth. Thank you."

He laughed and Ben liked the way he patted Katherine on the back. They all three shared a cup of coffee, comfortable in one another's company He was glad Katherine loved Mrs. Justice like a mother. Age wouldn't permit Ben to think of Mr. Justice as a father; friendship had broader boundaries, though, and Carl Justice was Ben's friend.

While Katherine went to explore the progress of the guest rooms, Ben purchased her a new bar of lavender soap; hers had gotten thin and small. Glancing toward the doorway that led to the rooms, he smiled at the memory of their wedding night and the lavender scent that wafted from his bride as he held her. With the addition of their own home, Katherine would have plenty of opportunity to bathe herself in lavender scent.

Chapter 15

Early Sunday morning, long before the ladies left for church, Ben and Joe had started building the stone foundation for the new rooms. The air was cold, but Ben noticed that Joe was sweating; his hands were shaking. He was also snappy and unfocused.

Ben had heard him come in from High Cotton only a couple of hours before daybreak. Ben was relieved that one of Joe's friends had picked him up at the house the night before; at least Gitter wouldn't be worn out from a cold, long night tied to the cart, so the ladies could use him to get to church.

"Joe, how's this look? Am I working this cement the right way?" He'd coerced him into drinking coffee to wake him up.

"Sure you are." Joe hadn't even looked at his work when he answered Ben.

"Joe. We're laying a foundation. You best look and make sure I'm doing it right. You still too drunk?"

"Quit judging me. Just 'cause you got you a woman, don't mean you're better than me."

Ben dropped his tools and walked over to Joe and shoved him hard on the shoulder. "That's enough nonsense. You sober or not?"

"I'm sober." Joe looked over to the work Ben had done. "And yeah, you're doing it right."

Katherine emerged from the back porch with coffee in her hands. "I figure you two could use a second cup, so I brewed some more." Ben wiped his hand on his overhauls and took a cup from her. Her eyes were wide as she looked at the work they'd started. "You're really building us some rooms. I can't believe it!" His brother-in-law huffed. "Believe it, Katherine. Ain't nothing else gonna get me out this early on a Sunday morning." Joe took the other cup from Katherine.

"I best go in and check on Sammy and help Lena with the soup for lunch before getting ready for church service." Ben felt a twinge of something—maybe guilt—at her comment. He should join her sometime and take his family to church. Maybe the next time the preacher came to Layton.

He doubted his own intentions.

He shook off the feeling and grinned at his wife. "Thanks for the coffee. Holler when you're close to leaving; I'll get Gitter ready for you and bring Sammy out to watch us men. You just bundle him up good for me."

The men passed the morning in silence other than a question or piece of instruction about the work, and when the ladies returned from church, most of the foundation had been built and could be left to dry.

Warmed by the heat and full from lunch, Ben played Sammy in a game of checkers by the fireplace in the front room. Katherine sat in her rocker watching and mending a hole Ben had gotten in his britches when working at the gin. Joe snored in his nearby room. Lena read a copy of *Little Women* that she had on loan from the school library.

"Everyone was so kind today at the church, wishing us well. I hadn't seen a lot of the folks since before we got married."

"I'd been proud to show you off as my wife. Guess I could have gone with you. But, I was building us a good foundation." Once again, a twinge of guilt ran through him at the irony of his statement.

"Lots of folks asked about you and wanted to meet you. Maybe someday. Soon." Ben looked up from his game just in time to catch her raise her eyebrows at him.

"Gabriel was there. Remember us telling you about Gabriel," Lena asked him.

"Sure do. He's the animal guy. Did he bother you, Katherine?"

"No. He just wanted to tell us that his dog had a litter of pups right before Thanksgiving."

"And he wanted to know if Katherine was still available." Ben and Katherine gasped at the same time at Lena's comment. "Came right up to me and said, 'Did Katherine really get married?' I said 'Course she did. Her name's Katherine Williams now, and she's very happy. Got her a son too.' He looked at his feet and mumbled. 'I figured as much.'"

Again, Ben felt compelled to go to church the next time around—but it wasn't guilt persuading him. This time, it was curiosity. Did he need to worry about Gabriel? He'd voiced the thought without realizing it.

He felt his face heat up as both girls giggled and gave a resounding "No."

Snow came and went and soon mid-March was upon the family. The gin was closed for the season and work at the lumber yard had picked up. Ben came home most days worn to a frazzle. It also seemed that Katherine's mornings started out just as frazzled. He lay in bed next to her, and just like she had for several weeks, she moaned, then sat up in the bed, leaned over the side, and retched into a pot.

They would move into their new rooms tomorrow and he reckoned the household would all be glad. His wife's retching would be behind the new closed door and not echoing throughout the house. His adrenaline spiked. There was one good reason he knew of that a woman would start the day sick. He wondered when Katherine would come to the same conclusion or at least share her secret with him.

He rolled from the bed and went around to take the pot. "Think you're done?" His wife looked up at him. Her smile seemed hesitant, but it came. "For today." He kissed her head. "Let me get you a cloth before I dump this outside. Can you handle some toast or a peppermint?" Katherine covered her mouth, and Ben rushed the pot under her chin just in time. "No." He teased her. "I see that."

Ben walked quietly across the room to the bowl of water and wet a cloth. "Lay back down and let me dab your face." His wife had just lost her contents twice in front of him, yet the sight of her still moved him. "Should I go for a doctor?" His question was an attempt to pry more from her. He wouldn't flat out ask Katherine if she was expecting because he didn't want to rob his wife of sharing the news on her own. Her answer was simple. "No."

He left the room with the pot then came back to care for Sammy's needs. "I can help myself to some coffee and cornbread. You lie here until the sickness passes."

As he had done the past several weeks with Katherine starting out sick, he thought through their situation. When Lena was at school, and Joe was on the rails, Sammy's personal needs would be a lot on Katherine in her condition. Ben wondered if he had overburdened his new wife. He left for work with that thought bouncing around in his mind and dwelt on it all day. Before the sun set that evening, he thought of solution for Sammy's needs when nature called and freed his mind from the concern

When the work wagon Ben was riding in stopped in front of his house, Ben jumped off, bidding the other riders a good weekend. Something out of sorts caught his eye. The cart and Gitter were tied to a tree in the front yard. Ben walked up the porch and into his house. The curtain was drawn over the doorway of their bedroom. Ben's muscles tightened. Why the cart? Why the privacy? Was his wife sick? Was the baby in danger? He called out to her, hoping the answer would come from the kitchen where he imagined her working alongside Lena.

"Katherine?"

"In here." His stomach knotted.

Ben pushed the curtain aside and the sight made him pause. Relief swooped in. "My, don't you look beautiful, Mrs. Williams." He walked over to her. "I'm filthy. So, I have to look and not touch." His wife stood before him wearing the dress he favored—blue check with yellow stitching. The neckline was cut in a small V-shape. Her hair hung loosely in a bun and rested on her shoulders. He leaned in and sniffed. "Lavender." She was as striking as she'd been on their wedding day.

Katherine leaned into him and kissed his cheek. "Wash yourself down. We're eating at the diner tonight—just you and me." He must have looked puzzled. "I skimped on supplies and set aside some money." She slipped out of the room, and Ben stripped off his clothes. His heart pounded as he thought that his wife would share her news with him. He cleaned and dressed himself, then called for Katherine to meet him again in their room. "I married the most handsome man on Earth," she said as led her to the front door.

Lena toted Sammy and hurried from the kitchen to meet them on the front porch. Ben escorted his wife to the cart waiting in front of the house. "Reckon we could find a treat for these two while we're out, Butterfly?" Joe stepped out to join them all. "I'll be staying home tonight, I take it." He eyed the cart. Ben answered him. "That's right Joe." Katherine's arm slid inside Ben's, and they waved good-bye to the others.

As the cart moved down the dusty road, Ben waited for Katherine to start conversation. The silence stretched on. *Is she nervous?* Ben decided to speak. "I met someone at the mill today that I think you know. His name is Jesse; his wife is Celeste."

"Celeste? I haven't seen her since the women's party at the Forder estate. Is he working at the mill now?"

"Yeah. Seems he has a reputation as a hard worker, so they wanted to hire him year-round."

"What a surprise."

"Speaking of surprises." Ben waved his hand to indicate her dress and the fact that they were riding in the cart. "What's the occasion, Mrs. Williams?"

"We're celebrating."

Ben chuckled. "We are?"

"Yes. Pull over there." Katherine pointed to the weeping willow cove where he'd shared the house plans with her.

Ben guided Gitter there and stopped the cart. He turned to her, and without a word, pulled her to him then kissed her to the point of almost pressing then both flat against the seat. "I've wanted to do that since I walked through the doorway this afternoon and laid eyes on you." He heard her catch her breath then she took his hand. "Let's walk."

Katherine's body rested against a tree. Ben encased her with his arms, pressing his hands against the trunk.

"Ben, I'm expecting a child." She rested her hand on his cheek; he watched a broad smile spread across her glowing face.

He tenderly moved his hand to her middle and touched her. "You and me. Our child." He felt his smile spread across his face just as his knees buckled. He caught himself. "I've been through some dark days, Katherine, when I thought I'd never feel joy again. Now I got you and a baby on the way. I'm a happy man." He kissed her on the lips. She bounced up and down on her toes while he embraced her.

"Did you suspect I was with child?"

"I speculated—about every morning for the last few weeks." Ben heard his own laughter fill the air. 'But there's nothing like hearing it first hand from you."

"I'm thinking we'll meet our baby around November. But Ben, right now, get me to the diner before I bite your head off. I want to eat. Sick in the morning. Starving at night. Sure is a funny thing."

Later that evening when they returned home, Ben escorted Katherine to the front door then went to put Gitter away for the night. He noticed that the mule seemed edgy and slightly bloated. He'd mention that to Joe.

He joined the family sitting at the kitchen table enjoying some warm sugar cookies. He chuckled to see Katherine swallow one almost whole. After the meal she'd eaten at the diner, he couldn't imagine where she had room for one more bite of food.

Ben reached into his pocket and pulled out a small brown sack. He watched Sammy for his reaction; sure enough, the boy's eyes widened and a high squeal came from his throat. He reached his hands out for the bag. Lena's reaction was only slightly more mature as her squeal wasn't quite as loud as Sammy's had been.

"Katherine, should we share our treats?"

"Only after we share our news."

He heard Lena gasp and saw her hand fly to her mouth. Joe set down his cookie. Sammy continued to squeal and reach. Ben eyed his bride and nodded a go head.

"I'm with child."

Lena jumped up from her seat and now gave out a squeal that Ben thought put Sammy's to shame. "I knew it! I knew it! All that retching. I know how these things work."

"What?" Ben couldn't hold back the question. Lena's face reddened. "I mean I heard about my friends' mommas being all sick, and then a few months later, there's a baby." His muscles relaxed, and he smiled.

Joe stood up and shook Ben's hand before he glanced at the addition. "Good thing we got that finished, and y'all are moving in tomorrow.'" His brother-in-law patted Katherine on the back. "Guess I'll be building a cradle." Katherine covered her mouth with her hands and released an excited "Yes!" Ben felt so happy, he thought his heart might leap from his chest.

He brought his focus to Sammy who seemed to be moving his attention from the brown sack, to Lena, and to him. He sat down next to his son and pulled out a package of chewing gum. Sammy's small hand reached and took it. Ben held up one finger and the boy went to town opening the pack and pulling out one piece. Good news surrounded the boy, but he didn't even know it.

Ben handed Lena her pack of gum then pulled Katherine next to him and placed Sammy in his lap. He pointed to Katherine and then pretended to rock a baby in his arms. The boy smiled and looked around the room. How do you explain the wait for a baby that Sammy can't see? Lena jumped up and grabbed the calendar on the wall next to the pantry and looked at Katherine who must have read her mind. "November."

Ben noted again that Lena was one smart girl. She flipped each page of the calendar for Sammy to see then stopped at November. She pretended to rock a baby. Whether his son understood or not, Ben couldn't tell, but the small boy smiled, pretended to rock a baby, then turned his attention back to the pack of gum. Ben hugged him tightly and kissed the top of his head. Katherine joined him by kissing the boy on the cheek.

"I have an idea," Lena exclaimed. "I'll draw a picture of our family with a new baby on the November calendar and help Sammy mark every day off until then. I can make it fun!"

"That's a great idea, Lena." Ben smiled at her.

Joe had remained standing by the back porch. "Well, I reckon I'll head out for a bit."

"You can't. I noticed Gitter was edgy and bloated. Best not make him travel anymore tonight. Maybe you should take a look at him. And besides, we need your help in the morning moving our things."

Katherine smirked. "I know more about Gitter than any of you. Grab a lantern, and let's head out to the shed."

"His belly is awful hard. I think he ate something poisonous or maybe he's got something blocking him inside." Ben was holding the mule's head as his wife felt Gitter's belly. "I think we should get Gabriel out here soon as we can. I think he usually comes to town Saturday or Monday twice a month for his mail." Joe nodded his agreement. Ben spoke up. "Reckon we could write a note for Lena to take to his mail slot in the morning?"

The next day Gabriel appeared at the house around lunch time. Ben and Joe had just moved Sammy's bed into his small room when Lena walked through the new doorway with Gabriel.

Ben hoped he hid his reaction when he looked at the young man. As the father of a crippled and deaf son, he knew how painful the looks from other people could be. Ben wasn't taken aback so much by the appearance of Gabriel's facial features as much as he was at himself. He realized the person he'd secretly thought of as a threat to his wife appeared to be nothing more than an awkward child the size of a man. He thought to himself that Faye Forder's past obsession with him wielded way more relational threat than Gabriel's on-going obsession with his wife.

Katherine walked out from the small room next to Sammy's space. "Gabriel, Thank you for coming."

Lena chimed in. "Lucky for us Gabriel wanted to check his mail today. I bet the note wasn't in there an hour before you showed up here, Gabriel."

The visitor wouldn't look toward Ben. "I thought I'd take a look, Miss Katherine."

Ben walked forward and stuck out his hand. "I'm Ben. Glad to meet you Gabriel. I've heard good things about your way with animals." The man-sized boy placed his hand in Ben's. It was sweaty and limp. Ben fought feeling sorry for him.

Ben pointed to Sammy seated in his wheelchair. "This is Sammy. Our son." Gabriel's face seemed to transform right before Ben's eyes. Embarrassment changed into kinship. The man-boy went over to Sammy and shook his hand. "I'm Gabriel. You can call me Gabe."

Katherine spoke before Ben could. "He can't hear you, Gabriel. He's deaf."

The visitor dropped to his knees and was eye-level with Sammy. He reached into his pocket and pulled out a rabbit foot. "Do you mind, Mr. Williams, if I give him my lucky rabbit foot? I got me another one at the house. People like us, we need all the luck we can get."

"He'd like that, Gabriel. And you can call me Ben."

The father felt it in his bones—a friendship of the most unusual sort had just been born between Gabriel and Sammy.

Ben lay in bed that night thinking back on the day. Gitter had indeed been sick, and Gabriel's home remedy that afternoon had done the trick. The family had all settled into their new space. Lena had her old room back, but all to herself for the first time in her life. Joe's spare bed now belonged to Sammy and fit snugly in his new room.

Among the Crepe Myrtles

When Ben had bent down to kiss him goodnight, the pack of gum lay on his pillow and the rabbit foot was clutched in his hand. He wondered how well the boy would sleep alone in a room for the first time in his life then he'd huffed at the thought, for his son looked mighty content. Sammy might have missed the fact that he had a brother or a sister on the way, but all in all, his son had enjoyed one of the best days of his life.

He'd closed the door to Sammy's room and slipped into bed next to Katherine. His wife's back pressed into his chest. Ben tightened his grip around her and rested his hand where their baby lay nestled inside her. The new doors were closed to the rest of the household. He kissed Katherine's neck and she turned to face him.

Life hadn't been this private since their honeymoon.

Chapter 16

"Blast it." As the sun beat down on her, Katherine lifted her apron and wiped the sweat from her forehead and neck. She dropped the britches she was about to pin to the clothesline and sat down on the ground. Her morning nausea had stopped a few weeks ago, but now fatigue had taken over her body. She glanced over at Sammy, who was sitting on a blanket nearby, and decided to join him.

Sammy's brow was wrinkled as she made her way to him. Katherine lowered herself to the blanket then lay down next to the boy. "Sammy, I'm worn slap out. Let's you and me rest here for a while." Sammy seemed to understand and lay down next to her. She took his hand, and with her other hand she pointed to the sky. "See that cloud? It looks like a lump of mashed potatoes." She turned her head and smiled at him then watched him look up at the sky and stare blankly.

"And look over there. I believe I see a butterfly on that flower. I'll have to tell your Papa; he's rather partial to butterflies." She joined her thumbs together and flitted her fingers for Sammy to see, then pointed to the butterfly. His broad smile delighted her. "You look so much like your Papa." A sense of contentment spread through her, and she moved her hand to rest on her stomach. She thought back to last night and a conversation with Ben.

"Oh! Ben, I just had the strangest feeling in my stomach—like a butterfly is inside me."

"I think it's our baby fluttering around in there."

His words had moved into her heart and settled in.

She turned to face Sammy and was met by his gaze. "You have your Papa's smile and his nose." She caressed his cheek. "I love you to pieces, Sammy. I can't believe I almost let you and your Papa slip away. I thought I couldn't love you—what I mean is that I thought I couldn't be what you needed me to be. I thought you deserved someone who didn't think of themselves as not good enough to care for you."

Katherine imagined that Sammy's heart could hear what his ears could not, for he snuggled up to her and let out a sigh—a very loud sigh. Katherine couldn't help but chuckle. At times, she still wasn't used to his unique vocal exclamations. Sammy's eyes were closed; his breathing was rhythmic and deep. With him lying still beside her, she gave in to sleep, soothed by a light breeze that settled around them.

She felt him before she saw him. Katherine awoke with a scream as she sensed someone standing over her and Sammy. The small boy jerked beside her. She opened her eyes, and the figure registered in her mind.

"Gabriel! You spooked me. What are you doing here?'

"I didn't mean to scare you, ma'am. I brought Sammy a surprise."

Until he'd said the words, Katherine hadn't noticed that Gabe held a puppy in his arms. Sammy, on the other hand, must have noticed, for he was already on his feet jumping up and down and letting out the loudest laugh Katherine had heard from him yet.

Gabriel went to his knees and was handing the puppy to Sammy when he caught Katherine's eye.

"Can Sammy hold him?"

"Sure."

Sammy's hands were all over the puppy who began licking the boy's face. Katherine's laugh almost outdid Sammy's. She reached over and placed her hands around the puppy's face. Short white fur covered the squirming body and light brown spots decorated one eye, the right hip, both ears, and the tip of the tail that curled halfway into itself. A shrill bark erupted from the dog's mouth as though the little thing were a threat.

"She sure is cute."

"It's a he."

"Well, then, he sure is cute. How big do you think he'll get?"

"Oh, I reckon just a might bigger than he is now. He's gonna be a small dog." Gabriel ran his hand along the dog's back.

"Does he have a name?'

"His name's Pirate on account that he only has one good eye. I figured out he's blind in his left one."

Katherine laughed again. "He's got a brown, furry patch over his eye!"

"What's happening out here, Katherine?" Lena was running toward them. "I heard you scream." Her sister was covered in flour.

"I'm okay. Gabriel startled me, but look what he brought."

"I see—a puppy." Her sister smiled at Sammy. Pirate began licking the flour from Lena's sleeve. She and Sammy got so tickled, it made Katherine laugh again.

"His name is Pirate," Gabriel explained.

"On account that he is blind in one eye," Katherine added.

"I reckoned he'd be a good pet for Sammy. Pirate can hear for Sammy and Sammy can see for Pirate. They need each other, ma'am."

Katherine pulled her hands away from the puppy and looked Gabriel in the eyes. She was touched by his reasoning. While she may have assumed the puppy was nothing but trouble, she realized that Gabriel understood something about Sammy that no one else, save someone like himself, could. Kinship is bred in what people hold common. Sammy, Gabe, and Pirate—each one was frail, and that frailty formed their friendship.

"Thank you, Gabriel. He's a wonderful present for Sammy." Gabriel broke their eye contact. "And, Gabe, you don't have to call me ma'am. I'm Katherine, like I've always been."

"You're married now, and I'd feel a lot more respectful calling you ma'am." She saw his cheeks turn red.

"Alright, Gabriel. How about some sweet tea?"

"I'll get us some," Lena said as she stood. 'I need to put the chicken pie in the oven anyway."

'Wash your hands, sister."

"Yes, ma'am," Lena exaggerated.

Katherine walked over to the laundry tub and resumed hanging the clothes on the line.

"You shouldn't fall asleep on the ground."

'Why, Gabriel?"

"It's spring and the rattlers are active. You should be more careful."

Gabriel had a point, but his comment irritated her. She would never deliberately put Sammy in harm's way as she thought he was implying. She justified herself.

"I'd hear its tail rattling."

"You don't know that for sure. Sammy can't hear or run, so he depends on you to protect him."

His statement nagged at her confidence. "I'm a good mother to Sammy."

"But you need to be better."

Katherine huffed. No need to argue with the man, especially when what he said rang true. She was a good mother, but yes, she should have thought

132

about the snakes. They were very active this spring. She shouldn't have fallen asleep on the ground.

"You are right, Gabriel, about the snakes." The man-boy smiled at her.

As she hung the rest of the clothes, she watched Sammy and Gabe play together with the puppy. Although he'd always been awkward around others, Gabriel had seemed equal in age to their peers, but seeing him with Sammy and hearing him call her "ma'am," he seemed to have gone back in time and become more of a boy again. She wondered if he would be able to look her in the face at all if he realized she was with child—not that it mattered.

Gabriel stayed a good hour playing with Sammy and showing him some tricks he'd taught the dog, but he wouldn't leave before he saw Gitter. Katherine motioned for him to make his own way to the shed while she worked the garden. Around her, Pirate sniffed everything in sight, getting familiar no doubt, with his new home. Time ticked by. Gabe had not returned from the shed when the afternoon shadows began to disappear as dusk set in. "It's not a family reunion. Come on out, Gabriel," she muttered under her breath.

"Gabriel? Are you alright in there?"

Gabriel emerged from the shed and walked toward her. "Yes, ma'am. But it's a good thing I checked on Gitter. There was a rattler coiled up in the far side of the shed. Gitter didn't see it and it didn't see Gitter. Good thing. I chopped its head off, then tossed it into the woods beyond the outhouse. I told you they's active right now."

Of course.

How had she missed seeing and hearing all that? She shuttered as her skin crawled. "Thank you, Gabriel, very much." She didn't know what else to say to him.

"I better hit the road and get home before dark."

Good. I'm ready for you to leave.

"Yes, you probably should. Thank you for Pirate."

The man who had slipped back into boyhood tousled Sammy on the head, and the two waved at each other. Katherine stood in the yard until Gabriel was out of sight. His visit left her feeling both flustered and grateful.

After she gathered her garden and laundry baskets and set them on the back porch, she lifted Sammy from the blanket and began walking back toward the house. She wondered how she would manage to do this as her belly grew larger. Ben had shown her a way to help Sammy with his bodily needs without lifting him when they were inside the house. She reckoned that soon Sammy would have to stay inside with Lena. That wouldn't fare well for the boy and his dog.

The sound of the lumber mill wagon bringing her husband home caught her attention. She changed her direction and placed Sammy back on the blanket. His Papa could carry him inside. With Sammy's squeals following her, Katherine trotted toward her husband, still struck by his very presence as she'd been from their first encounter. She felt him pull her close.

His arm was warm and sweaty. His kiss was warm and tender.

Before she could speak her welcome, barking filled the air and the puppy whirled around the two of them. Ben released her and knelt, grabbing the dog.

"Meet Pirate."

"You know this puppy?"

"Met him today."

"Who does he belong to?"

"Sammy."

Katherine laughed out loud when Ben's mouth gaped open and his eyes bugged out. She filled her husband in on the day, including the incident with the snake in the shed, which didn't seem to alarm Ben. He set down next to Sammy on the blanket so they could play with the puppy together.

"Pirate. I like that name," he said in a poor pirate imitation. Her husband began to hum "Blow the Man Down." Katherine's mind flashed back to an evening on the front porch when he'd played that same tune on his harmonica. Looking back at the scene, she realized she was already deeply in love with Ben.

"Is that the only pirate song you know, matey?"

"Alas, I'm afraid i'tis."

"I like it."

She smiled at him and headed indoors—a rascal's song fixed in her head and a roguish smile fixed in her heart.

Chapter 17

During their first evening as dog owners, Katherine convinced Ben that Pirate needed to sleep inside the screened section of the back porch instead of outside since he was half blind. In truth, the image of the poor thing being bitten by a rattler he didn't see in the dark kept running though her mind.

When bedtime arrived, Ben filled the washtub and sat Sammy inside it, then headed toward the back porch. Katherine looked up from where she was positioned to wash Sammy and presented Ben with a coy smile. "You're just as concerned about that dog as I am, Mr. Williams." Her husband winked at her and continued making his way to the porch. Katherine heard the screen door squeak. She smiled at herself and then at Sammy who splashed water on himself and guffawed.

Once Sammy was tucked away and sound asleep for the night, Katherine sat on the bed she and Ben shared and brushed out her hair. She watched her husband slip into the tub and splash the used water over his body then lather up with the soap.

"Mr. Forder was at the mill today."

"Do you know why?"

"He came to see me." She watched as he closed his eyes and tilted his head back; a crooked smile spread across his lips.

"Ben Williams, do I have to keep asking you why?"

He winked. "He wants to keep me at the mill year-round as a shift manager. I wouldn't be working the gin anymore." Katherine let out a small gasp and laid down her brush. She brought her hands together underneath her chin. "That's good news! I know you like the mill better."

"I do, so I agreed to his plan. Gets us a dollar more a week too."

"A whole dollar a week! Ben, that's sounds too good to be true." As she spoke, she watched Ben dunk his face into the water then bring it back out, wiping off the water with his hand. "Believe it, Butterfly."

Katherine jumped up from the bed and ran over to the tub to hug Ben. Her russet curls touched the tip of the water and she felt Ben wrap a tendril around a finger and tug gently. Never mind that she was getting her gown wet. She loved this man and knew she'd never get over it!

Sometime in the middle of the night, Katherine saw Ben get out of bed and open the door to the kitchen. She noticed him because she was also awake. Pirate had been whining all night, and she suspected Ben was headed out to fix the situation. Her earlier notions of keeping the puppy safe had all been forgotten. She needed to sleep; the dog needed to hush. Soon the screen door squeaked open. She heard Ben's muffled voice as he addressed the dog. The whining stopped. "Either Ben has smothered the animal or Pirate prefers to roam the yard."

She turned to face Ben as he crawled back into the bed. "Good thing Joe is gone. He'd have shot Pirate by now."

"I would have loaded his gun."

Katherine chuckled. Ben's fingers intertwined with hers as he raised her hand to his lips. "Sleep tight."

Katherine rose with Ben the next morning and made him oatmeal for breakfast. She sat and sipped her coffee, savoring the flavor she couldn't tolerate during the early weeks of her pregnancy. Her taste for it had returned with a vengeance.

"Is he dead?" Lena walked into the kitchen still twisting her hair into a bun.

"Who?" Katherine looked at her husband and shrugged her shoulders.

"Pirate." Husband and wife both laughed.

"No." Katherine would make her sister dig for answers.

"Is he gone?"

"No."

"Is he tied in the shed?"

"No."

"Lands sake, Katherine! It's too early for me to keep asking questions. I'm just happy the dog is quiet."

"He's roaming the yard free and happy. Ben let him out in the middle of the night."

"Thank you, Ben. You kept me from moving out. It was gonna be the dog or me." Lena pointed toward the outside and then to herself in dramatic fashion.

Katherine and Ben both rose from the table. Ben smiled as he leaned over and kissed Lena's forehead. "That would have been a tossup." The trio laughed. Katherine picked up Ben's lunch pail and handed it to him. The couple walked to the front door and kissed good-bye. A smile spread across Katherine's face and a flutter moved in her chest—she already missed him.

All morning long Katherine scrubbed bed linens and hung them to dry; her back ached. Now she needed to help Lena start lunch and looked forward to sitting on the porch to peel potatoes. Sammy was playing next to her on a quilt with Pirate asleep against his leg. She was enjoying the morning breeze when noise at the road drew her attention. To her chagrin, Gabriel appeared for the second day in a row. Katherine rolled her eyes and sat down the bowl of potatoes.

"Morning, ma'am."

"Hello Gabriel."

"I just came by to check on Pirate, maybe play with him and Sammy, if you don't mind."

Gabriel had already seated himself next to Sammy and begun petting the dog. Katherine wanted to feel agitated, but a sense of gratification came over her, and she knew she was happy for the attention Gabriel was giving her son. Sammy's wide grin and guttural squeals assured her that he was happy too.

"You sure you got the time to spend with Sammy? I'd hate for you to let your chores or some business go undone."

"The Baker cow is ready to deliver any day now. I'm just stopping here on my way there." Gabriel showed up the next day too. Katherine realized that until the Baker cow gave birth, Gabriel would be a daily visitor.

After three days in a row of visits from Gabriel, Katherine expressed her frustration while she and her sister did chores. "If I'm honest, it helps us to have him around," she admitted as they scrubbed the kitchen floor. I just get weary of the way he looks at me, like I'm not good for Sammy."

"He's embarrassed around you, but he wants to be friends with Sammy. He's just awkward." Katherine didn't disagree with her sister.

However, when Ben came home that evening, Katherine thought that he was unusually quiet. Perhaps he was also bothered with the amount of time Sammy and Gabriel were spending together. After supper Lena and Sammy played cards by lamplight on the back porch so that Pirate could sit with them. Alone in the small sitting area of their room, with the door open to the sounds of the back porch, Katherine stared out over the Bible in her lap.

"Ben?"

He closed the money ledger he was studying.

"Does it bother you that Sammy and Gabriel spend time together?"

"No. Does it bother you?"

"No. Well, I wish Gabriel wouldn't look at me like he does—like I'm a bad person or something, but I like that Sammy is happy around him."

"I think he looks at you that way because he's jealous. He's been here a lot this week. Maybe too much for you? If you're uncomfortable, tell me."

"No, I'm not uncomfortable. I guess. Anyway, after the Baker cow is born, he won't be out this way as much. If you don't mind his being here, then I reckon I don't either."

"I don't mind."

Ben looked away from her and back to the ledger. If Ben wasn't bothered by Gabriel, then what was on his mind? Katherine sighed, and apparently, it was louder than she realized because she saw Ben look right back up and close the ledger again.

"Something else on your mind? You've not looked down at your Bible for several minutes, so I know you're not reading it."

"I was thinking that something was on your mind. Was everything okay at the mill today?"

"Yes." His reply was curt.

"Ben?" Momentary silence followed her prompt.

"Faye Forder was at the mill today. She came in the office."

Katherine felt her stomach knot up and her shoulders stiffen. It was one thing for Faye to be at the mill, but it was whole other thing that it bothered Ben.

"Does she come often?" Her question was curt. Ben looked at her as if to say, "Settle down."

"I don't think so. Mr. Forder is in Dallas on business. Faye brought her cousin to work."

"Does he work in the office?"

"He does some days. He transfers the load numbers from various customer ledgers into the general load ledgers."

"Did Faye bother you?" The word "bother" was easier for her to spit out than words like "flirt."

"Katherine, do you really want to hear this?"

No.

"Yes."

"I didn't know she was even there until she walked up behind me at the desk and put her hands on my shoulders. She said, 'I heard you were working at the mill. And here you are, in the flesh. All married now.'"

Katherine's supper rose to her throat, but she forced it down. She didn't dare want to interrupt her husband.

"I yanked her hands away, and then she muttered a word no woman—well, lady at least—should say. She walked to the front of my desk and smirked. 'How's Katherine and that boy of yours?' She looked at me as though I were no better than our blind dog. I didn't answer her and she kept on. 'Well, I suppose she's got her hands full, but do give your wife my regards.' Then she walked over to her cousin and asked to see the paperwork on some wood she'd ordered for a table."

Ben stood from his chair and knelt beside her. "You're the most beautiful and honorable woman I know." Panic slid through her body. Was he saying this because he was attracted to Faye and needed to reassure himself?

"Katherine, I don't like anyone mocking you, our marriage, or our family."

"I don't like another woman's hands on you."

She saw a look of shock on his face.

"Katherine, I don't like it either. Everything she said and did made me angry all day long. Don't think for one moment that I liked her touching my shoulders." He glanced at the Bible in her lap. "Isn't there some story in there about a man who ran from a woman?"

"Joseph?"

"I don't know his name. Did he run from a woman because of her actions?"

"Yes."

"Then I'm like Joseph. If Faye had kept talking to me or stayed in the office much longer than she did, I would have walked out."

"Joseph ran because he wanted to honor God."

"I want to honor you." She felt him squeeze her hand. "And remember, my thoughts are not as far from God as you think. You're still praying for me, aren't you?" Katherine nodded yes.

"What if she comes back?'

"I don't think she will, at least not often. That's the first time I've seen her since I started at the mill."

It was the "not often" that bothered Katherine. She'd prefer "never."

"We all live in Layton, Katherine. We're bound to run into her sometimes, even if we live totally different lives. But, if I need to go back to the gin, then I will. Never in all my days have I seen a woman at a filthy gin." As he smiled at her, she felt him pull her up from the chair.

She resisted him. Her mind was tossing unreasonable thoughts and fears her way. Faye was a beauty. Would Ben always want to flee her? His tug grew stronger, causing their bodies to touch. He placed her arms around his neck. "Please don't resist me. I don't think I could bear coldness from you." She moved her hands to touch his shoulders—ones meant for her and no one else.

"I love you, Katherine." He walked over to the door and shut it slightly, keeping them out of view from the back porch. They stood in the middle of the room as his kisses assured her it was her touch he wanted.

Chapter 18

"Count Your Blessings." The tune and words of the hymn came back to him from his church-going days. Ben fought to ignore the sickening feeling brought on by his surroundings—the hard pew, repeated patterns plunked on the piano, four part harmonies, people dressed in their Sunday best trying to cover the evil that lurked inside them.

He glanced to his side. It was not his father, with his head held high like a pillar of the church, who was seated next to him. It was Katherine, wearing a smile on her beautiful face as she sang. Down the row sat his son and Lena. His family—the ones he loved, provided for, and guided. He felt a smile pull on his lips. He loved those three people deeply and knew without doubt that he would die for all three of them. Was God a Father like himself and not one like the wicked man he'd called Pa? He counted the blessings sitting next to him and concluded that yes, God must feel about him the way he felt about Katherine, Sammy, and Lena.

For the last week, Ben had pondered his conversation with Katherine about Faye Forder. He hadn't missed the concern in her words when she said that Joseph fled temptation because he had honored God nor the doubt that Ben could rely on a similar relationship. He had been disheartened at the resistance she'd shown when he tried to pull her to him.

Ben faulted himself that she couldn't comprehend how much his thoughts had recently turned toward God. He'd never shown evidence. She deserved to know that his interest in God had grown, so with the monthly community church service being held in Layton today, he'd determined last night to accompany his family. He had to be honest with himself; he wasn't leading his family—he was coming along with them, but at least he had a desire to do so.

He'd had to hold his laughter captive at Katherine's response and their conversation when he'd told her that he and Sammy would be going with them today.

"To church?" He watched his wife wrinkle her brow.

"Yes."

"No!"

141

"No?"

"No, you can't make a joke about my churchgoing."

He softened his tone.

"No, I can't and I'm not. I sincerely want to go."

"You do?" She spoke barely above a whisper.

"Yes." He smiled and patted her hand.

"Yes?"

"Yes! Can I?"

"Yes." She bit her bottom lip and nodded her head.

"Are you surprised?"

"Yes!"

"Do you mind?" He raised an eyebrow.

"No." He felt her squeeze his fingers.

"Do you want me to go?"

"Yes." A stronger squeeze.

"Then it's settled. Me and Sammy will go with you to church tomorrow."

His wife tilted her head before she spoke.

"Why?"

"Because it's time. It's past time." He rubbed her back.

"Yes. Yes, it is." She had finally smiled at him, and his fingers had caught the tear that rolled down her cheek.

Lena's response to his intentions had been blunt and practical. "That's answered prayer. Katherine, we need to make more food for the dinner on the grounds. Ben eats his fair share and more."Then she'd walked over to him and hugged him.

Pastor Carlson was reading a passage about God not being able to look at Jesus when he was on the Cross. A tinge of anger surged through Ben. How could a father turn his back on his own son? The emotion was too familiar. Then, as the Pastor went on to explain that Jesus had given his life willingly so that all people could accept forgiveness of sin, the magnitude of the sacrifice overwhelmed him.

Hadn't he just thought that he would die for Sammy? He began to realize that this is what God had done for him through Jesus.

He remembered the words Katherine had written him about people accepting the good from God but not the bad. He was guilty of that. He understood more than he ever had in the past that good and bad were both a part of life. A way to reconcile the bad had happened on the Cross.

He felt a tug in his heart and knew it was from God. His reasoning took over and told him that he could ignore the tug for now. By the time the service ended, Ben had done just that.

Ben nodded his head, acknowledging Pastor Carlson when he walked past his pew to stand at the door and greet his congregation. Ben stood up with his family and looked directly at Katherine. He could see the questions in her eyes. What did he think of the service? Would he come again? Had he listened to what the Pastor had said? Had he felt a tug on his heart? Would he respond to the tug? Choosing to answer two unspoken questions, he hoped to bypass the others. "Nice service. I think I'll join you next month too." An angel's face couldn't have glowed more than Katherine's did at hearing his words.

Ben let Katherine and Lena get past him, and then he leaned down and picked up Sammy. Together with his family, he greeted Pastor Carlson and his new bride, Amy, on their way out the door.

"Glad to have you here, Ben." Pastor patted him on the back since his arms were filled with Sammy.

"Good to be here."

"Staying for dinner on the grounds?" Ben liked that Pastor patted Sammy on the shoulder as he asked that question.

"Wouldn't miss it."

Pastor's new wife put out her hand and Ben acknowledged it. "Good to see you and Sammy again, Mr. Williams." The woman had a warm smile as she looked him in the eye and spoke. She had a bigger smile for Sammy.

"It's good to see you too. My wife speaks of you often. I believe she's used the word 'friend.'" Ben chuckled.

Katherine smiled at him before giving her friend a hug.

His family moved out the door and headed to their cart. Ben pulled down the wheelchair and settled Sammy in it while Lena and Katherine gathered their dishes and their blanket then headed to the wooden tables sitting under an open structure with a roof. He pushed Sammy over the black dirt and joined the others under the sheltered food area.

Carl Justice walked over to Ben and shook his hand, "Afternoon, Ben." The handshake turned into a heavy pat on his back. "Right glad you're here. Let me wait with Sammy while you fill up a plate for you both." His friend must have guessed Ben's confusion over his offer. *Wouldn't Katherine fill all their plates?* "The men folk fill their plate first around here and then the women and children get to fill theirs. I'm reckoning you should go ahead and fill Sammy's plate while you're in line, seeing he can't run around to pass the time like the other children." With that said, a line of men had formed——each one holding a plate and moving down the row of tables while the women dished out food to them.

Ben found his place in line and nodded politely to the women as they heaped food onto his two plates. One woman gave him a look that he knew was meant to scold him for filling more than his share. His glance at Sammy had made her face turn red.

He felt relieved when he came to Katherine and Lena. "Reckon we should try this at home? Men first." He winked. Katherine rolled her eyes, but Lena withdrew the spoonful of green beans she was about to dish on his plate. He'd be doing without them.

Amy Carlson was standing next to Katherine, and to her right stood a woman Ben had never laid eyes on, but whose facial expression indicated she suspected who he was. "Mr. Williams, have you met Mrs. Forder?" Amy indicated the woman next to her. A panic ran through Ben when he heard the name. He gathered his thoughts and met his boss's wife, then felt relief when a quick glance down the line of women showed no Faye Forder in sight.

Of course.

As he returned to Sammy and Carl, Mason Forder, his boss, was standing there.

"Ben, just met your son. A fine-looking boy."

"Thank you, Mr. Forder. He's a good soul." Just as Ben spoke, Sammy pulled his rabbit foot from his pocket and held it up for Mr. Forder to see.

"Gabriel gave it to him. He's right proud of it," Ben explained.

"Gabriel is another good soul," Mr. Forder said as he leaned down and touched the rabbit's foot then smiled at Sammy. "I best get in line or Mrs. Forder will say I was responsible for holding up the women folk who were just as hungry as the men." Ben laughed. "I'll go with you," Carl Justice said, walking away and leaving Ben and Sammy alone.

Ben saw the blanket Katherine had placed on the ground for them; he handed a plate to Sammy and with one hand carefully rolled the chair to the blanket. Soon Katherine and Lena joined them there. As though he had been waiting for those two to sit down, Gabriel appeared out of nowhere and stood next to their blanket—but not for long since very soon both he and his Ma were seated with them for the duration of the meal.

When Ben arrived home with his family, Joe was sitting on the front porch whittling. The ladies went inside the house, and Sammy fell asleep on the porch with Pirate by his side. Ben sat next to Joe and observed his brother-in-law. He was bothered by the dark circles he saw under Joe's eyes and the tremble in his hand. He wanted to yank the pocket knife from his shaky grasp.

"Didn't hear you come in last night, Joe."

"I thought the purpose of your new rooms is to not hear anything and to not be heard."

Ben ignored the sarcasm. "You alright? You look a little under the weather."

"If that's what you want to call it, go 'head. I ain't though. Just had a bit too much last night, I reckon. With good reason."

"Good reason? What reason is good enough to drink too much?"

"Prohibition. I better drink up while I can." Joe did a mock toast in Ben's face.

"No reason is good enough to get drunk."

"With the talk of prohibition, Faye's thinking of closing down High Cotton. Moving on to Dallas, she says. To bigger and better things."

Good.

Ben contemplated the image of his brother-in-law. The empty look in his eyes and the tremble were all too familiar to him. A sense of foreboding crept through Ben. Joe's face seemed to transform into that of Ben's own Pa—the younger a shadow of the older. Disquieted, he felt his Sunday lunch rise in his throat. He'd seen Joe's angry when he was drunk. The friend he'd once known was slipping away, and a threat to his family was emerging in his place. Ben realized that his own love and honor would insist he protect his wife and child and Lena from Joe, even if they did not recognize their need for it.

Joe walked away from their conversation, leaving Ben alone on the front porch. As the sun began to set on this Sunday when Ben had gone to church for the first time since he was a teenager, a slight rustling in the crepe myrtle trees to the right of their house caught his attention. Katherine—out for a walk. He watched her as she moved among the crepe myrtles with her hand resting on her rounded belly; the pregnancy had grown obvious to any seeing eye.

Ben smiled, and a warmth worked its way through his inside. He'd never given much thought to the myrtle trees after spotting them that one night, other than realizing they existed, but with his Butterfly flitting among them, they exemplified all that was good in his life, all that he was thankful for, and all that he would die to protect. He captured the image of her among the myrtles and gave it a home inside his heart.

Katherine looked serene and happy, so he chose not to disturb her. He wondered if she might be praying. The screen door creaked, and by the hint of cornbread that wafted around him, he knew that Lena had left the kitchen and stepped onto the porch. Sammy stirred in his sleep. "Oops! I didn't mean to wake him."

Ben didn't move his gaze from Katherine when he spoke. "Big day for him, I guess. But he needs to wake up anyway, or he'll never sleep tonight."

He felt Lena touch his shoulder. "She's pretty, isn't she?" Ben chuckled. "Yes, she is."

"I've never seen my sister so happy. No weeding the garden or wringing out laundry or scrubbing the floor can take her glow away." He heard her sigh behind him. "It's just like a fairy tale."

This time Ben laughed out loud. "Except there's no ugly step sister. Just a feisty twelve-year-old sister with a heart as big as this house" He reached back and patted her hand that was still resting on his shoulder. "Time to go inside." Lena tapped his shoulder and whispered, "I'm practically thirteen." Ben turned his head and faced her. Lena's eyes sparkled. "You got a birthday coming up soon? Humph. I had no idea." He winked, then pulled himself up, but not before she giggled and gave him a swat on the shoulder

He picked up Sammy, whose body was warm against his chest, and carried him into the front room. His stomach growled. "Sammy, let's get you washed up before suppertime." He tickled the boy and Sammy laughed, causing Joe to peek out from his room and shush them. "We're headed to our own room so we can't be heard." Ben didn't even look at Joe as he threw the comment at him.

Later that night while tucked in their bed, he whispered to Katherine. "I saw you walking among the crepe myrtles today."

"You did? You should have joined me."

"I was enjoying the view, Butterfly. Besides, I reckoned you were praying."

"I was."

He squeezed her hand. "I'm worried about Joe and his drinking. He seems to be drinking more. Do you think so?"

"Seems that way to me too. His eyes stay bloodshot. He has tremors."

"I know. I talked to him today. He admitted he drank too much last night. He said there's talk of High Cotton shutting down. Said he was drinking while he could."

"High Cotton shutting down? Good!"

"I agree." Ben wondered where Joe would go for his drinks once the dance hall doors closed, but he kept the thought to himself. "I worry about his temper when he's drunk. If he were to lay a hand on you or Sammy or Lena…"

"He won't."

"I'm keeping my eye on him. I'm not as sure of him as you are.

Chapter 19

Monday morning Joe left for a short work week, and Ben was happy to see him go even if he would be missing Lena's thirteenth birthday. Ben and Katherine had ordered Lena a sketchbook and some pencils with the help of Carl Justice. Joe had carved a wooden pencil box for her and left it for them to give to her.

Katherine also wanted to give her sister something she would treasure, so Ben had suggested she make her an apron because Lena's apron was very thin and well worn. At first his wife had said his idea was too practical, then suddenly she'd kissed him on the cheek and told him it was a great idea and that she knew exactly how to make it special.

For the last week, Katherine had worked on the apron in their room at night. One evening Ben came in from mucking the shed to find Katherine tracing Sammy's hands onto the apron with a pencil. His boy was mesmerized by what she was doing.

"What are you two up to?"

"The apron is going to be from Sammy. I'm tracing his hands, and then I'll stitch over the lines." His wife looked up from her task and smiled at him.

"That's such a good idea, Katherine."

"I'll stitch 'Aunt Lena' around the waist."

"How about I invite Carl and Mrs. Justice to eat supper and have cake with us? I could hop off the work wagon at the store tomorrow and invite them. I'll walk home carrying a new bottle of aspirin with me in case your nosey sister asks why I got out at the store." Katherine agreed.

Thursday rolled around and the family celebrated. Carl Justice brought everyone a cola, and the evening felt very fun and festive. Ben thought about the dark days in his life when he could not celebrate. He was grateful for the gifts God—yes, he realized it was God—had given him in Katherine and her sister. After supper Lena unwrapped her presents.

"Sammy has a gift for you," Katherine stated while Ben tapped Sammy on the shoulder and handed him the package. It thrilled Ben to see his son's eyes light up as he handed the package to Lena; she jumped up and down and then hugged Sammy when she saw the apron.

Among the Crepe Myrtles

Ben watched as Katherine sliced the chocolate cake she had made for Lena. His mind flashed back to a birthday almost seven years earlier when his first wife had made him a chocolate birthday cake. Unexpectedly, a wave of sorrow shook Ben. Guilt accompanied the sorrow, warring with the gratefulness he'd felt moments earlier. Why, with so much joy around him, did sadness rear its ugly head? Sudden understanding filled his mind, and he acknowledged that grief was unpredictable and had no manners or discretion. It came and went as it pleased. He called a truce between his opposing emotions. "Dear God, help me enjoy this moment." He surprised himself when he uttered the prayer. Contentment eased itself back inside him, and his attention turned to the conversation happening around him.

"Ben, if you and Katherine think you could spare Lena, we'd love to have her help cook in the diner one or two days a week. She would receive a little income."

Neither Ben nor his wife had a chance to answer before the birthday girl spoke up.

"I'll do it!"

"Lena," Mr. Justice chided, "I was addressing Ben and Katherine. It would have to be with their approval." Ben saw him smile at Lena.

"That's a mighty generous offer, Carl. But with Sammy and with our baby on the way, I think we'll be needing Lena around here while I'm working."

"I suspected so. The offer stands if you ever want to take it. She's a mighty fine cook."

"Well, perhaps we could spare her a Saturday or two a month." Ben looked at Katherine as he spoke and hoped she agreed with him. "I think that's a good idea, if Lena wants to do it," Katherine added. Ben laughed when Lena shouted so loudly he wondered if Sammy could hear it.

Joe returned from the railroad on Friday afternoon and predictably planned to spend the evening at High Cotton.

"Has Gitter been in the shed all day?" Joe posed the question as he and

149

Ben headed into the house for supper. The two of them had straightened the tools and garden supplies in the shed.

"Yeah."

"Good. He can't be too tired to take me to High Cotton tonight."

Ben huffed and stopped in his tracks. Joe aggravated him.

"None of your drinking buddies can pick you up?"

"Nope." Joe stopped walking long enough to look Ben in the eyes. "Why?"

"I ain't asking. I want to come and go as I please tonight."

"Come home sober and at a decent hour."

Joe resumed trudging through the dirt. "Stop talking like a preacher."

"I'm talking like a friend and a brother. A worried one!"

"You're choosing to worry. I'm a grown man."

"You're choosing to make poor decisions."

With that, Joe let the screen door on the back porch slam in Ben's face.

While the rest of the house still slept, Ben awoke early on Saturday morning to rain with thunder and lightning. He'd been restless all night, and one look out the backdoor told him why. It was evident by the puddles of water that it had down-poured all night. He suspected the sound of the storm had kept him from hearing Joe come in.

Ben made some coffee and poured himself a cup before he pushed back the curtain of Joe's doorway. He flinched and called out to his brother-in-law. No answer. He entered the room and the absence of scent and sound concerned him. There was no smell of alcohol, body odor, or regurgitation. No one was snoring. Joe's bed was empty and didn't appear to have been slept in.

In panic Ben ran to the shed feeling himself sweat profusely despite getting soaked by the rain. Once his eyes adjusted to the dim light, he realized his fear was justified. Gitter and the cart were nowhere in sight. Ben walked the entire yard and ran down the road in both directions, looking for marks in the mud, but there was no footprints or tracks in the mud indicating that Joe, Gitter, or the cart had even come close to the house.

Soaking wet, he slipped into the bedroom and shook Katherine awake. She squinted her eyes at him.

"Katherine, I don't think Joe came home last night."

"What?"

"Doesn't look he slept in his bed, and Gitter and the cart aren't here. I checked the house, the yard, and the road."

Katherine sat up in bed and he felt her grip his arm. "What do we do?"

"When the store opens, I'll run to see if Carl can drive me around to look for him. Maybe he slept in the cart at the High Cotton. Meantime, I'm gonna gather some blankets and bandages just in case there's been an accident."

"I'll help you." He watched his wife rise from the bed, her fullness making it difficult for her. She headed to the door to go outside and attend to her personal needs. He reached for the bed pan. "Hear. Use this. It's too wet to go outside."

Two hours later Ben ran to the store in the rain. He pushed the screen door open so hard that it slammed against the wall.

"Carl!"

"Ben! What's wrong?"

"Joe's missing and so are Gitter and the cart. He didn't come back from High Cotton."

Ben watched Carl come from behind the counter. "I got my son coming to run the store in an hour. Let me ask my wife to come up front and keep an eye on things until then. She's in the back. I'll drive you around in my auto to look for him."

"Thank you." Ben heard Carl call out "Louise, hurry to the front counter!" Mrs. Justice appeared to rush from the back of the store. She blew out a breath and wiped her forehead before she noticed Ben standing there. He saw her eyes widen "Ben, is something wrong with Katherine or the baby?"

"No, they're fine. It's Joe. He didn't make it home from High Cotton last night."

He watched Mrs. Justice put her hands on her hips and shake her head back and forth as she declared, "Katherine must be worried sick about him."

"Yes. He had Gitter and our cart too."

Mr. Justice spoke up. "I'm taking him in the auto to look for him. Can you mind the store until Chester gets here to take over? He's due in an hour."

Ben couldn't help but grin when Mrs. Justice pushed both he and Carl on the back and shooed them away. Carl and Louise were good friends.

The drive was slow and tedious. Numerous times Ben and Carl had to get out in the drenching rain and push the auto out of a rut in the road or out of the thick mud. Ben regretted that Carl's brand new auto was getting filthy. Three miles out of town, Ben spotted what he hoped he wouldn't have to see. His cart was turned sideways in a ditch. Gitter was lying at an angle with his leg trapped under a wheel of the cart. Joe was on the ground next to the cart.

Ben jumped out of the auto, and mud sloshed under his feet and onto his pants. "Joe!" His brother-in-law didn't acknowledge him. Ben reached down and shook him. "Joe! Can you hear me? Wake up." Joe opened his eyes and instinctively sat up. As he did, he turned away from Ben just in time to keep from retching on him.

"Joe, are you hurt?"

"No. I suuuu-po-ssssse I fell a-ssssleep."

"You're drunk! Get up." Ben pulled Joe from the ground and managed to keep his anger toward him under control. He knew that Joe could be hurt and not even feel it. By this time, Carl was at his side and taking charge. "Joe, stand out of the way! Ben, let me help you turn the cart upright so we can check on Gitter." Ben pushed Joe away as he came to help them lift the cart. Joe cursed at him then slumped back to the ground.

With the cart turned upright, Ben and Carl both knelt to examine Gitter. The animal was alive, but it was obvious his leg was injured. He didn't flinch when Ben pressed on his stomach and sides. Ben hoped that meant no broken ribs or internal injuries. His family needed this mule.

The loud rain was making conversation difficult. Ben wiped moisture from his face. "I brought some cloths and some twigs. Let's wrap up this leg to keep him from moving it." The two men worked quickly to bind the animal's leg. When they finished caring for Gitter, Ben noted that the cart was in one piece. Good.

"Let's lift Gitter and put him in the back of the cart. I'll try to pull it home."

"If you intend to pull that cart and Gitter all the way, you can't. Besides, look at the front wheel; its damaged. Let me head back to the store and get my wagon. We'll load it with your cart and Gitter. You wait here."

In his quick examination, Ben had overlooked the damaged wheel. Carl's idea was good, and Ben saw no other solution. He'd keep Joe with him while he waited. He didn't want Carl dropping him off at the house and leaving him for Katherine to deal with.

"Can you stop and let Katherine know there's been an accident."

"Yes. And I'll have my wife leave a note for Gabriel to come check on Gitter next time he comes to town."

"Thank you. I reckon he'll be in town Monday for his mail." Ben sighed heavily as adrenaline coursed through him. Carl ran a hand over his face and through his hair. "Keep an eye on that no-good brother-in-law of yours and give him a piece of your mind. I'll be back as soon as I can."

Ben had already determined to give Joe a piece of his mind, so he didn't need Carl's suggestion, but he enjoyed hearing him say it anyway. He looked down at Joe who was crumpled on the ground and sound asleep. The man stank. Filthy. Pathetic. Alarming. Ben raised his foot stuffed inside a shoe covered in mud and vomit, and propelled it backward. Just as the foot swung forward to make contact with Joe, Ben stopped it and let out a loud, angry grunt. He was hit with the realization that he was about to inflict physical abuse—the very thing he had despised in his Pa and now feared in Joe. The revelation made him feel sick in his stomach and he gagged.

Ben plopped down on the ground a few feet across from Joe. The mud oozed into the seat of his pants. He grunted at the miserable situation and wanted to lash out at Joe, but he would wait and confront his brother-in-law when they were both in their right mind.

An hour passed; the rain ceased; the sun came out; Ben tamed his emotions; Joe awakened. After one more release of the alcohol in his system, Joe sat up. Ben and he were locked in a momentary stare while Ben studied the sunken eyes, the caked mud, and the crusty remains of retching on the pathetic man sitting next to him. Joe finally spoke.

"How bad is Gitter?"

"Don't know for sure. Injured leg. Not sure about his insides."

"The cart?"

"A damaged wheel."

Ben let silence hang tensely between them.

"I'm not damaged."

"Is that what you have to say to me? You're not damaged?" Ben rose to his feet and paced the muddy ground. Then he bent down over Joe and pointed his finger in his face.

"You risked the welfare of our family. Why? For a drink of alcohol that wants to control you. For a glimpse of a pretty woman who doesn't care about you. To gamble money that people you say you love need to survive. What drives that, Joe? Pain? Pride? Loneliness? Stupidity?"

"Casting stones at me, Ben?"

The angry brother and father pulled his finger away from Joe and pointed to himself. "I am not a sinless man."

"Then don't judge me. I'm wise enough to know that you hold a grudge against God for your pain. I know you to reason your way through life instead of relying on God. Neither of us is a saint, Ben. We just happen to practice different sins. One's public. One's private."

"I…I judge the effects of what you do. Your sin affects my family. "

"Yours don't?"

Yes.

Ben perceived that even in his pitiful state, Joe spoke truth. Ben was not naive; in the recesses of his heart he knew one day there would be redemption or a reckoning for his sin.

Ben sat down and the mud oozed into his pants again. The irony struck him. Like his private sin, the black mud stain was hidden for now, but he felt it, and soon it would be visible for anyone to see. He swatted a fly from his face and then looked at Joe.

"You're right about me, Joe"

"I know I got a problem, Ben. I just ain't ready to face it."

"I don't want Katherine and Sammy and Lena and the baby to face your problem. That's really what I'm pleading you about Joe. My Pa…he never faced his problem, but he forced my Mama and me to face it every time he swung his fist at us."

"My Mama took up my Pa's slack when he gambled our money away."

"Katherine's done that for you more than once."

Joe didn't speak. Ben watched him nod his head in agreement, then stand and walk slowly to the cart to place his hand on Gitter.

Ben stood too as he eyed Carl Justice coming toward them in his wagon led by two horses. They'd be strong enough to tote the cart, Gitter, and the three men back home. A wave of relief swept over Ben: then he thought of Katherine. As Carl approached he walked over to meet him.

"You made good time, Carl. Thank you. Did you see Katherine?"

"Yes. I stopped by. She's anxious. It was all I could do to keep her from riding back here with me." He watched Carl snarl at Joe as he came to stand to his right. "I'm afraid she's got nothing good to say to you, Joe. You best get prepared for her wrath. It's deserved if you ask me."

"That's family business." Ben cringed at Joe's cold remark to Carl.

"You made it Carl's business," Ben chided and walked toward Gitter. "Let's get this animal home."

Together the three of them lifted Gitter onto the wagon and laid him against the back. Then with a lot of grunting, they hoisted the damaged cart to the front of the wagon and secured it with rope. Ben looked at Joe. "You sit back there and tend to Gitter."

Just as his house came into sight, Ben looked over at Carl. They were both filthy and smelled of sweat. Their damp clothes stuck to their skin. The wagon was covered in mud. "I don't know how to repay you for your help, Carl. I'm mighty indebted."

"There's no need. Folks help each other around here. The day will come when someone needs you, and that'll be your payment."

Before Ben could speak again, Katherine came running hysterically through the yard. Ben jumped from the wagon and took her in his arms. "Settle down. Gitter's still alive. I'll bet Gabe will have him like new in no time." He moved his hand to the top of her swollen middle. "You and the baby best settle down."

Ben glanced over her shoulder and saw Lena holding Sammy and standing at the window of the sitting room. "How's Gitter?" Lena shouted. "Alive," he replied. The thought crossed his mind that Joe had not even been acknowledged by either of his sisters.

The men unloaded the wagon and Carl Justice went his way.

That night Joe slept in the shed to keep an eye on Gitter. Ben had smirked at his offer. A form of repentance? Punishment? Guilt? Whatever drove Joe to do so didn't matter to Ben. He was relieved he didn't have to sleep out there himself.

The next morning Ben stood in the kitchen and wiggled his shoulders around, trying to get the tightness out of them. His upper body ached from lifting the heavy cart the day before. He sipped his coffee, then set out to check on Gitter and Joe in the shed before the mill wagon arrived.

Both Joe and Gitter were still alive. Ben chuckled to himself; he wasn't sure who was in the worst shape. The women had mucked Gitter's stall and freshened his bed of hay; but Joe slept on a dirty quilt that had been meant for the mule.

Katherine was slow to forgive.

Joe had assured Ben that he could repair the cart before he set out for the rails at noon. With Gabriel sure to stop by and care for Gitter, Ben left for work optimistic that his family would be fine.

Around one in the afternoon, Ben was in the mill office looking over a lumber order receipt when commotion outside got his attention. He stood up and walked to the window to see what was happening. Mr. Forder's son joined him.

Black dust swirled in the air from the speedy approach of an automobile. Ben recognized it as Carl's auto. He curiously watched as his friend brought the auto to an abrupt stop, jumped out of the car, and ran up the steps of the office. Ben opened the door.

Fear jolted him when he saw pain on every inch of Carl's face. Huffing, Carl spoke between breaths.

"Ben you've got to come home! There's been an accident!"

Chapter 20

"Please dear God, no!" Katherine bent across the lifeless body, her belly painfully tight and resting on the chest that no longer moved up and down. She grabbed at her middle with one hand, and with the other she pounded the kitchen floor. A wave of dizziness threatened her consciousness. "No!"

She knew the room was filled with chaos, but the pulsing in her ears and the despair pressing into her body hid it from her. She was separated in her own agony and the agony she had brought to others. Lena's voice crept through her emotions.

She awoke that morning with a sense of urgency. Gitter! She patted the bed with her hand and found it empty beside her. She eased herself out of it and moved across the bedroom floor to the door; at the same time, Ben slipped in from the kitchen. His kiss warmed her cheek. "Back to bed, Butterfly. Gitter is alive." His gentle touch on her back guided her back to the bed.

"Alive?"

"Yes. Now, rest. I'll tend to Sammy and then put him in the bed next to you. I want you to sleep later today after the stress of yesterday." Despite the urgency of her chores, Katherine didn't argue with her husband. Her body was so tired that it ached. She crawled back under the warm covers.

When Ben left to catch the mill wagon, Sammy and Katherine lay in the bed playing finger shadows on the wall. Ben had assured her Joe would fix the cart, and that surely Gabriel would come by and tend to Gitter. Katherine supposed she should be concerned about Joe, but she was more worried over the cart and Gitter.

Her stomach growled, so she signaled "food" to Sammy. He promptly smiled his approval. Ben had positioned the wheelchair so that Katherine could easily guide Sammy into it; she did, and the two of them headed to the kitchen. Her body no longer had room or energy to carry both a baby and a crippled four-year-old.

Lena walked in from the back porch. "Morning. I was checking on Gitter. He's alive, but his leg is swollen. Joe thinks it's broken."

"Ben told me he was alive. I'm so glad. Hopefully Gabriel will be here early this morning." Katherine yawned as she handed Sammy a bowl of oatmeal. "How's Joe?"

"I saw a couple of bruises on him. He says he's fine, but I think he's sore. He's out there working on the cart."

Katherine took a bite of her own oatmeal, and with a mouthful she exclaimed, "Ouch!" The baby was wide awake and kicking her insides. She thought its head must be resting right under her rib cage. "Lena, give me your hand." She took it and rested it on her abdomen. The sisters giggled at the same time.

"She must like oatmeal," Lena joked.

"Or *he* is excited to work in the garden with me all morning." Katherine patted her belly as she spoke, then reached over and took Sammy's small hand. With slight hesitation, she rested it on her stomach. Katherine had no idea how the little boy would respond.

She felt the baby kick again and knew Sammy had felt it too. His eyes widened. His brow wrinkled. Katherine panicked! Had she frightened him? She watched with concern as Sammy moved his hand and rested it on his own stomach, tilting his head to the side. He slid his bowl of oatmeal to her and handed her his spoon.

Katherine sighed with relief. He must have reasoned the only thing that made sense to him—that she was hungry—and offered her his oatmeal. She took a bite from his bowl and reached over and hugged him. She saw Lena smiling at them.

"I think he's going to be a kind big brother. I also think he deserves a treat—two sweet biscuits. Lena, will you fix one with sugar, cinnamon, and butter and one with apple butter?"

With her baby moving inside her and Sammy next to her smiling, laughing, and devouring his biscuits, Katherine felt a sense of satisfaction and gratefulness. "Thank you, God, for giving me this family." She realized she'd spoken the words aloud when Lena offered up a hearty amen.

After Katherine had set up a quilt in the morning shade near the garden for Sammy to play on, Lena carried him outside. Although the sun was bright and there was no breeze, she decided Sammy still needed to get some fresh air during the coolest part of the day. Katherine tied her bonnet around her head then set out to pull weeds, a job she hated almost as much as she hated picking cotton. Lena would be scrubbing the kitchen floor this morning, and they'd be ironing clothes in the afternoon. Katherine patted her stomach and rubbed her lower back. She had a full day ahead of her and was already feeling strained by the pregnancy. Pirate settled himself next to Sammy.

Katherine tugged, and the roots of a weed broke through the Texas soil.

About an hour into her labors, Katherine stopped to take a sip of water from her mason jar and rest on the blanket next to Sammy. Joe emerged from the barn. A knot formed in her throat; Katherine knew she needed to speak to her brother. "How you feeling?"

She observed as Joe squatted down in front of Sammy and rubbed the boy's hair. Sammy pulled out his rabbit foot. He and Joe had developed their own game. Sammy would show the rabbit foot, and Joe would pretend to try and snatch it from his hand before Sammy hid it behind his back. At last, Sammy would let Joe snatch the foot, and the game would begin all over again as Sammy tried to snatch it from Joe.

"I'm a bit sore." He patted Sammy on the head and stood. "I gotta eat and get to the depot. I was hoping Gabriel would come while I was still here." Her brother hesitated. "Katherine, I'm real sorry. It's got a hold on me, ya know, the drinking and gambling. Seems I come by it naturally, but I reckon that's no excuse."

Katherine felt tears well up in her eyes.

"You're a praying woman. How 'bout sending a prayer up for your brother."

Katherine nodded a yes. Her words of both anger and compassion collided in her thoughts and became so tangled none of them could escape through her mouth. She sat in silence on her knees. Joe stood before her; she saw him look toward the shed. "I think Gitter can make it. Gabe just needs to get here." She watched him wave to Sammy then walk toward the house. A half hour later, he emerged, offering a simple good-bye. She stared at him as he headed toward the road. He was the spitting image of their father in more ways than one.

Lena joined her outside for a few moments and carried Sammy to the outhouse. Pirate followed. Katherine had one more row of weeds to pull, then she would gather the vegetables that were ready for picking. Just as she gave her first tug on the last row, Pirate ran past her barking. She looked up and saw Gabriel coming down the road in his small cart. Relief set in.

She met him. "Gabriel, I'm so relieved you're here. Please hurry."

Sammy's squeal caught her attention. Coming from the outhouse, he'd spotted his friend. They embraced in a hearty hug before Gabriel took Sammy from Lena. The four of them headed into the shed. Katherine pulled Sammy from Gabe, but Lena took him from her immediately.

On his knees in the shed, Gabriel looked at Gitter's leg. "I reckon his leg is sprained. I don't feel a break."

Katherine sighed loudly. "That's a good thing, right?"

"Could have been worse, for sure. So yeah, that's a good thing, but a sprain takes a while to heal. Miss Katherine, I need to check him all over, clean him up, and give him some remedy I have for his discomfort. You all best get back to what you were doing and let me work alone."

Katherine didn't argue, and the three of them left the shed. Lena had placed Sammy back on the blanket, and he sat playing with his trains while Pirate resumed his sleeping position next to him.

After pulling the last weed she saw, Katherine gathered cabbage and carrots until her basket was full. She would have to unload it inside the house before she could pick any more vegetables. She glanced at Sammy who was preoccupied with his toys. Lifting her apron and wiping the sweat from her face, she walked toward the back porch but not before turning toward the shed and shouting.

"Gabriel, I need to go in the house for a minute. Can you listen out for Sammy? "

"Yes ma'am. I'll be right out.'

"That's not necessary. Just listen for him."

"Like I said, I'll be right out."

Katherine blew out a breath. Gabriel could suit himself. She opened the door to the back porch then stepped into the kitchen.

"I need to empty my basket, Lena. It's full of cabbage and carrots."

"Set them in the sink."

Katherine emptied her basket, dusting off the chunks of dirt on the vegetables before placing them in the sink. Her face felt flush. Lena must have noticed.

"Katherine, you're red as a beet. Here, drink some water before you go back out."

Pirate barked. Katherine glanced through the window and noticed that Gabriel was heading toward the blanket. Apparently, he hadn't headed right out. "I need to get back out there to Sammy, but let me sit for a minute." She moved from the window over the sink and sat down at the table.

Pirate's barking grew loud and frantic. Katherine had never heard him bark so ferociously. Curiosity made her stand and look out the back porch screen.

She dropped the glass on the floor and screamed. Gabriel was running toward the house with Sammy in his arms. His small, crippled body looked limp. Dread surged through her. She slammed open the screen door and ran to meet them, her heavy middle tightening in pain.

"He's been bit!"

"By Pirate?"

"By a rattler."

"No! Are you sure?"

"I saw it strike his leg!" Gabriel screamed in his agony.

Katherine fell to the ground as darkness came over her. Feminine arms lifted her up; Lena had followed her out and was shouting at her. "Get inside! I'm running to the store for help! Mr. Justice will go for the doctor."

Katherine shook the darkness from her head and walked toward the backdoor in a daze as Lena took off by foot.

Sammy's limp body lay in the middle of the kitchen floor. Gabriel was ripping the pants off him.

"Sammy! Oh, my sweet Sammy." She dropped to the floor opposite Gabriel and bent over Sammy's torso as she rubbed his sweaty hair from his forehead. "Gabriel! He's lifeless!"

"He's breathing! See his chest rise?" She heard Gabriel begin to cry.

She placed her hand on Sammy's chest. "Keep breathing. Oh, my little boy, I let you get harmed."

Katherine saw blood seep from Sammy's lower right thigh. The small crippled leg was swelling around the bite.

Then Katherine and Gabriel gasped at the same time when they both saw blood ooze from Sammy's ankle. He'd been bitten twice.

Katherine rocked back and forth on her knees, wailing. Gabriel was sobbing. "I didn't leave the shed in time. I didn't leave in time. Sammy, I'm so sorry."

Katherine reached over the small boy and touched Gabriel's arm. He spoke through sobs. "Katherine, when I came from the shed Pirate barked, but I didn't see the snake then. I thought he was barking at my movement. I'm so sorry. Then when Pirate barked again and viciously, I saw the snake strike Sammy. I'm so sorry. So sorry."

A sensation of anger filled her, and she pulled her hand from Gabriel's arm. "Sammy! Don't leave us. My little boy. My little boy." Katherine rubbed his chest then began to pull him toward her.

"Don't move him! It spreads the poison. Keep him flat." Gabriel's hand was tight on hers as he stopped her motion.

"Do you have a snake kit in the house or shed?"

"I don't know."

"Think Katherine! Do you?"

She shook her head no rapidly. "No! But, Lena will get the doctor here."

"He's so small and frail. I don't know if..."

"Don't say that Gabe. Sammy can't die! Don't you know a cure? Surely you do, Gabriel. Think!"

"I'll suck out the venom. Get me water or milk or coffee!"

"But..." She felt her eyes open wide and chill bumps run over her skin, but she rose from the floor. She would risk Gabriel's safety to spare Sammy's life.

With her hands shaking, she poured cold coffee into a dirty cup that was beside the sink then fell back down on her knees, rocking back and forth and running a hand through Sammy's hair.

She watched in horror and hope as Gabriel put his mangled lips to Sammy's thigh and began to suck. He lifted his head, turned it to the side, and spat. His spittle hit her arm. She watched him take a sip of coffee then spew it out on the floor. Her stomach lurched, and she lost her contents even as Gabe bent down to repeat what he had done.

"Gabe! It's not working!" She pulled him away. Once again, his spit hit her. "He's not breathing!"

The room began to spin! Her stomach contracted. She watched as Gabriel tore open Sammy's shirt and lay his head on the boy's chest, then let out a loud groan. Katherine shoved him aside and threw her upper body across Sammy's torso and began to wail. "Please dear God, no!"

"Katherine!" Lena's voice broke through the chaos and the darkness. "Katherine, move. Let the doctor see him." She felt Lena drag her away from Sammy and prop her against the wall then felt her rub her abdomen; it finally relaxed. Gabriel was sitting at the table sobbing.

Panic set in as she saw the doctor look at Mr. Justice and holler "Go!" Carl's heavy footsteps echoed in her ears as he ran through the house. The front door slammed, shutting her in with the truth.

Sammy was dead.

Katherine rose from where she was and moved to where Sammy lay. She sat down and pulled the crippled, still body into her lap. No words. No wails. In silence she sat there, feeling tears roll down her cheeks, and rocked him back and forth.

She glanced at Lena who had come and cradled her head on Katherine's shoulder. Her sister, usually so full of life, was weeping and pale.

Time stood still.

At some point, her baby moved against the pressure of Sammy's body. "Life and Death," she whispered finally.

A commotion at the table drew her attention. The doctor was holding a bowl under Gabriel's mouth as he retched.

"Is he poisoned?" Her voice was weak and lifeless. Her heart was vicious and revengeful. She wanted to blame Gabriel, but she knew the blame didn't lie with him.

It would be her that Ben would blame.

"Time will tell. I admire his courage, but fear it could cost him." She heard the doctor's answer, but had already forgotten she'd asked the question. Guilt had moved in and taken over her thoughts and emotions.

———————

"Sammy!" Ben's voice filled the house and pulled her from her trance. "Sammy!" Katherine looked up and locked eyes with her husband while his lifeless son lay in her arms. Her body convulsed with emotion, and she began to sob. "Ben. I'm so sorry. I let him die."

Her husband's body dropped to the floor in front of her, and his arms pulled the crippled body to his chest. The groans and wails that came from this man were like nothing she'd ever heard. She jumped as he fell backward to the floor and held the body against his own, crying out "No!" between his sobs.

Katherine crawled to him and began her rocking back and forth. "I'm so sorry. I left him. I left him." To her astonishment, her husband, the father who had just lost his son, reached out an arm, pulled her down beside him, and wrapped her against his side.

He let their sorrow mingle.

Chapter 21

Katherine supposed that Mr. Justice spread the word to Pastor Carlson, for not long after she and Ben had placed the lifeless body on the table that Lena had covered with a blanket, Pastor and Amy Carlson appeared in the kitchen. Mrs. Justice was at their side. Needing the comfort of a mama, Katherine flew to Mrs. Justice and slumped in her arms weeping freely. She saw Amy gather Lena into her arms.

The voice of the pastor caught her attention. "Gabriel, let me take care of that for you." Though every fiber of her was grieving, her heart made room to be moved by the compassion she saw Pastor Carlson give to Gabriel. He bent down, pulled the young man to him and held him. Katherine heard gentle weeping coming from the man turned boy again—he'd lost his friend and seemed to carry the guilt for it. *I placed that on him.*

The pastor released Gabe, took the rags from his hands and began wiping up the spewed coffee, blood, vomit, and mud on the kitchen floor. The smell of Lysol filled the air. Katherine knew she would forever equate the scent with death.

Mrs. Justice's hold on Katherine loosened, then her hands covered Katherine's wet cheeks. "Let me get some water. Amy, can you find some clean rags? Amy and me will help you wash down the body."

Katherine nodded her agreement, then sat down at the table and began rubbing Sammy's arm. Lena sat next to her and held her other hand. The muffled talk of the men permeated the room.

Katherine, only slightly coming to her senses, muttered, "I suppose, Lena, we should find some clothes for him." She looked to her husband and spoke in a whisper, "Ben? His Sunday best?"

Ben didn't answer, and Katherine's heart ached when she followed his eyes to see what had gotten his attention. In the far corner of the kitchen lay Sammy's rabbit foot, tucked against the wall, clean of blood and other spills, innocent and misguided, as though death had not visited its owner.

Katherine covered her mouth to contain her emotion when Ben walked to the corner, reached down, and picked up the rabbit foot. She watched him run his thumb over the soft fur then squeeze the token with his fist.

Katherine thought he would either pocket it or throw it across the room, but he did neither.

Ben reached out and handed it to Gabriel. The young man took it and fingered it before placing it back in Ben's hand. "Useless," she heard the friend murmur. She watched Ben place the rabbit foot in his pocket, then turn to face her. "Yes, his Sunday best." It was the first time she'd noticed the blood on Ben's clothing and the coldness in his voice.

Katherine and Ben forced themselves to do the things the grieving are called upon to do, and by late afternoon, a wake was scheduled for the evening and a funeral for the next afternoon. The suddenness of the events puzzled her. Ben and Katherine walked into their room to change out of the stained clothes.

"What about Joe?"

"What about Joe? Carl sent a wire to his next stop."

"But he should build the casket."

"Pastor, Carl, and Gabe will help me build it before the funeral. Carl went to the mill to get the wood and have it cut."

"But..."

"Katherine! Sammy's dead! We can't wait on Joe. Sammy's body will start to decay, and I'm not gonna watch that happen on the kitchen table or put him in some potato sack tomorrow and throw him in a hole like he's worthless! I'm building my son a coffin today and burying him in it tomorrow."

Katherine's body shook at his anger and at the sound of Sammy's bedroom door slamming in her face after Ben walked away from her. "Your son?" She shouted through the door.

Katherine fell to a heap on their bed. She had told herself Ben would blame her, but when he seemed to actually do so, Katherine was devastated. She could never make this up to him.

The sound of Ben's sobs carried through the door. Katherine mustered her courage and let herself into Sammy's room. Toy trains and a deck of cards assaulted her eyes; the scent of Sammy's clothing and bedding filled her nostrils. Katherine didn't want to be in there, but she sat next to Ben on the bed and wrapped her arms around him. He didn't flinch or push her away,

166

much to her relief. She sat there silently until Ben turned to her. "I shouldn't have yelled. Katherine, we lost our son. I'm not sure how we live without him."

"I don't know either right now."

"Is there hope of ever knowing?"

"Maybe—yes—we'll live, but life will never be what it was when we awoke this morning."

"Joe can carve him a headstone of some sort."

She touched his cheek. "That would be nice."

Another question was nagging at her. "Ben, do you want to bury him with his mother in Commerce? I'm sure there's a way to get him there—you know—before too long."

She watched him shake his head gently. "No, he belongs here with me. With us. Our yard."

"We can make a spot by the trees—among the crepe myrtles."

Her husband smiled at her. "Good idea," he whispered as he brought his hand to her abdomen and rested it there. "Is our baby okay?"

"Yes."

As if the atmosphere were not grim enough, Katherine sensed a darkness shroud her when Ben touched her abdomen. Something inside her had waned. It was her emaciated worthiness. No longer could it sustain her to be his wife; to mother his child; to take pleasure in life. It was a marked moment.

Friends meandered in and out of the front bedroom where Sammy's body lay on his bed that the men had moved from his small room. Katherine and Ben sat beside him the entire evening. Well intended—but misguided—words plagued her. "He looks as though he's sleeping." "He's walking now on streets of gold." "God needed him in heaven." Could no one speak the truth? That it hurt so bad that he was gone? That for the rest of their lives a part of them would be broken? That the tug between Hope and Grief would never end?

She had a vague remembrance of swallowing the food that Pastor and Amy had placed before her, Ben, and Lena. Sometime when the sky was black and the crickets chirped, Lena kissed her cheek, hugged Ben, then slipped away to Joe's bed. Carl Justice took her seat. "I'll watch now," he told Katherine. She felt a hand clasp hers and lead her to bed. It was Ben's.

With the silence of death surrounding them, Katherine felt Ben pull her to him as they lay beneath the covers. He kissed her neck and rubbed her arm. "I need your closeness, Katherine, to escape my pain." Her body stiffened at his touch and she moved away from him. Feeling unworthy of any pleasure, she breathed in the pain of abandoning him and of losing his son and let it poison her.

Beside her Ben wept.

The next morning Gabriel appeared with a shovel in his hand. "I'm here to dig the grave," he said when Lena let him into the front room where Katherine and Ben sat. The house had emptied only moments ago as Carl, the last to leave, slipped out to rest and return later in the afternoon.

"I didn't see you here last night, Gabriel."

"I didn't come, Miss Katherine." She saw his eyes glance toward the bedroom where the curtain was closed and blocked the view of the body. "Would you like to see him, Gabe?" He shook his head no. "I'll see him when we put him in the coffin."

Ben rose. "Thank you for your help, Gabriel. Let's clear the spot and start digging."

"If you don't mind, I'd prefer you just show me the spot and let me do the work alone. It'd be an honor."

By midafternoon, Sammy's body lay in the ground. With the house filled with friends once again, Katherine slipped out and made her way to the myrtle tree with the fresh mound of black dirt beneath it. Awkwardly she got down and lay her head on the mound.

"Please forgive me, Sammy. I'll never forgive myself." She pulled a wooden train from her pocket, kissed it, and laid it atop the grave. She allowed her body to give in to the emotional exhaustion that pled for relief.

It was Lena who eventually woke her and led her back inside.

Chapter 22

Time was disrespectful of death and the change it forced on Ben and his family, pausing only momentarily to acknowledge the loss. Sunrise and sunset had rapidly produced three weeks since that tragic day—as though Sammy were still at home petting Pirate or playing with his trains. Ben shook the thought from his mind as the cold smoke of morning air surrounded his face. He relished the stillness and quietness around him as he fished, but most of all he relished the companionship of the man sitting next to him—Pastor Wendell Carlson.

Ben chuckled quietly. A year ago the thought of his spending time with a pastor would have been absurd enough to make him either laugh out loud or huff sarcastically. But today, like many others before it in the last month, spending time with Pastor Carlson made him smile and breathe contentedly. He was glad the pastor and his new wife had settled in Layton.

Theirs was a friendship of contrasts, respect, and some form of desperation that Ben had just begun to realize. Wendell was grounded in something—his faith—Ben wasn't, and he found himself desperate for that foundation. Ben was sinking in quicksand internally, and he assumed Pastor realized that and was desperate to rescue him.

"Something funny?" The quiet voice of his friend drew his attention.

"Funny?"

"You chuckled."

"Oh! No, not funny, but good. And good feels, well… good."

"That's good!" Pastor smiled at him. "Care to share some of that good?"

"Katherine's abandoned me—emotionally." Ben felt his eyes well with tears. He stared at Wendell as though the man could absorb the pain for him, but knowing full well that he could not. *If one human could absorb another's pain, I'd have already done that for Katherine.* His friend ran a hand across his own chin. "I'm confused. That's good? And are you sure?"

"No, it's not good." Ben wiped an escaped tear from his cheek. "What's good is your spending time with a heathen, although a good heathen," he smiled, "and yes, I'm sure. She takes care of my day to day needs, but she's closed me out emotionally and…can I speak of these things with a pastor— intimately."

169

"Unforgiveness can harden a person."

"But I don't blame her for Sammy's death."

"She blames herself."

"She has to forgive herself. I can't do that for her."

"No, you can't. Just keep on loving her."

"I do love her. Deeply." Ben's voice shook. "And I think I need her more than I ever have needed someone in my life."

Wendell looked at his friend, and Ben saw both sympathy and sadness in his eyes.

"I know you need her, but not more than anyone else. Ben, there's someone you need more."

"You're talking about God?"

"Yes. And the relationship He has to offer."

"To be truthful, I've done a lot of thinking about God since meeting Katherine. But if He's got love for me, why does He keep hiding it behind death. Three people I've loved have died way too early in life.—my mother, my wife, and my son."

"Ben, seems you don't blame Katherine for Sammy's death, but you do blame God."

"Yes!"

"That's understandable."

"What? I can't believe you agree with me."

"I don't agree, but I do understand. I'll try to explain. You truly know someone when you know their heart." Wendell's hand moved back and forth between the two of them. "Look at us—we're like night and day, but we've come to know and understand each other. It's the same with God. You just haven't allowed yourself to know His heart."

"The pain God brings outweighs the joy—just like I felt growing up with my Pa." Ben exhaled then looked sternly at Wendell. His next words were deliberate and pointed, and his clenched hand displayed his resentment. "What does God have to offer that makes the pain worth knowing Him?"

Wendell didn't flinch at Ben's tone. "Isn't it odd that you don't hold your Pa's death against God?"

170

"I hold his life against God. And I hold God responsible for the pain of losing my first wife and now Sammy."

"He wants you to come to Him in that pain. You said He hides his love behind death. The opposite is true. He displayed His love through the death of Jesus. What He has to offer is forgiveness."

"Not an enticing offer." Ben's chest tightened.

"You're behaving no different than Katherine."

Ben felt his eyes widen. "I am?"

"Lack of forgiveness is suffocating the joy of her relationship with you. Your resistance to God's forgiveness suffocates a relationship He wants with you."

Is that why my chest tightened? Ben shook away the thought; after all, he was the victim of pain—not the cause.

"What do I need to have forgiven?"

"That, Ben, is your real issue. Jesus tells a story in the book of Luke. If two people owe a debt, but it gets forgiven by the money lender, who will love the money lender more?"

"The one who owed the most debt."

"Right. Ben, you don't think you're in debt."

Ben swallowed. Pastor's words struck his soul. He couldn't deny the truth of what Wendell had just said to him. He'd already realized his resentment toward God. But, he also couldn't bring himself to embrace the truth of what Pastor had spoken.

"You're a good friend, Wendell. You and Carl Justice both. You deserve truth from me, and the truth is, your words have hit me hard, but all I can promise you now, sitting at this pond, is that I will think about them."

"You do that, Ben. I'm here for ya...anytime." The moment was broken when Wendell got a hard tug on his line. Ben wasn't sure if the distraction relieved or disappointed him.

The morning turned late. The men packed up their catch and poles and began the walk back to Ben's house.

"I've been thinking about what you said—loving Katherine."

"Yeah?"

"I ordered us wedding bands. I've been holding on to them for our first anniversary next month. I think now would be a better time to give it to her."

"I think you're right."

<hr />

Ben had always loved autumn, but standing at the grave of his son early the next morning, waiting for the sound of the Forder wagon, Ben shuttered. The air was cold and empty. Like Katherine. The memory of his darling, pregnant Butterfly walking among the crepe myrtle trees came to mind. What was once a picture of all he'd come to love and enjoy in life was now tainted by the grave that sat among those same trees and the distance his wife kept from him. He bent down and traced his fingers around the letters on the gravestone. *Samuel Benson Williams.* Joe had done a good job carving the name and dates on the stone.

Joe—he was another worry in Ben's life. His drunkenness and the temper that came with it had grown worse in the weeks since Sammy's death. Ben wondered if that was how Joe grieved. Ben's confrontations had made little difference with his brother-in-law. Ben knew that Katherine worried too. He'd also noticed that Lena seemed to put up a wall around herself when Joe was home. Ben suspected that was a sign of her fear.

He pulled his harmonica from his pocket and began to play "Blow the Man Down." He pictured Sammy, smiling at him as he played, although not one note of the song had ever reached his ears. It was a comforting memory.

His thoughts turned to his wife.

Tonight he'd present Katherine with the ring and tell her he'd marry her all over again if she wanted him to. He was hopeful that what had gotten lost between them might return home. He needed her—body and soul.

At the sound of the wagon, Ben put away his harmonica, patted the gravestone of his son, and headed to the road to catch his ride. He'd come to look forward to talking with Jesse while they commuted to the mill. Jesse exuded a kindness toward him, a sympathy of sorts, it seemed to Ben. It seemed to be the same quality his wife Celeste had shown to Katherine over the times their paths crossed.

Mr. Forder greeted him as he walked through the mill office door. He was looking through documents. "Good morning, Ben."

"Good morning. Glad to see you. What brings you here today?"

"I came to get the plans from when the mill was built. I'm thinking of expanding into Commerce, and I have a meeting with the banker there this afternoon."

"Commerce. I know it well."

"Came from there, didn't you?"

"Sure did."

"Well, if this plan takes off, maybe I'll see if you have interest in running the mill there."

"I'm honored at the thought, but this is home now. I don't think I could ever uproot Katherine. Course, you're my employer…"

"As long as this mill is doing good business, your job here is secure."

"I appreciate that."

"Here it is. Got what I needed."

He watched Mason Forder put on his coat and gather the documents into a satchel. Ben was surprised when, rather than leaving, his boss sat down in a chair beside Ben's desk.

"How you doing these days, Ben? I can't pretend to understand what losing a child is like."

"I'm breathing, Mr. Forder. And that's a good thing. Thank you."

"Sammy was a fine young man. Spitting image of you. Always had a smile for me when I saw him at church."

"Yes sir. I miss that smile." His chest ached.

"You give our love to your Katherine. Mrs. Forder has something for her, but we best keep that between you and me. She wouldn't like me spoiling her surprise."

"Your secret is safe with me." Ben felt himself smile and realized it felt unfamiliar. "Mighty nice of her."

"She's got a big heart." He rose from the chair, "I best get started on my drive to Commerce."

"Good luck." He felt Mr. Forder pat him on the shoulder.

"Thank you, Ben."

After supper Ben put his arm around Lena's shoulders and sniffed the air as she stood at the kitchen sink; the smell of fried pork chops filled his nostrils. "Always love your cooking. Mind if I snatch Katherine for a bit?" Ben glanced over to his wife, who was scraping food from the plates. He saw her wrinkled forehead.

"I don't mind. I can handle the kitchen." Lena smiled at him.

"Ben, Lena's had a long day. I'd feel better staying and doing my part."

"You go on with Ben, Katherine. Rest that baby. I'm going to hurry up and get back to my book. I'm at the best part."

"Still reading *Little Women*?" Ben kissed Lena on the cheek as she nodded a yes. He took his wife by the hand.

"Let's get our coats and sit outside." He leaned inside their bedroom doorway and grabbed their coats off the hooks on the wall, then led Katherine into the front room. He pulled out a record and placed it on the phonograph.

"I thought you said we were going outside."

"We are. And we can hear the music from the porch."

Ben pulled two rockers together and motioned for Katherine to sit down. He heard her breathing heavily. He wondered what caused it. The baby? His nearness?

A pain moved through his chest as the thought of Sammy playing on the porch came to mind. He captured it, embraced it for second, and then sent it on its way before tears escaped his eyes. He was out here to love on Katherine and to bring her back from wherever she was.

"I've got something for you, Butterfly."

"You do?"

He took her left hand and squeezed it. "I miss you Katherine."

"I'm right here. You see me every day." The words were flat.

"I see you, yes. But I don't feel you. You're a butterfly behind glass."

His wife turned to him; he saw a tear roll down her cheek. He watched it fall and land on her baby bulge before he reached into his pocket. "I didn't have this when we got married." He held the small gold band between his finger and thumb. He saw Katherine's eyes widen. "But I have it now. I love you Katherine." He began to slide the ring on her finger. "I'd marry you again if I could, just to show you how deep my love is for you."

Katherine's fingers slid from his hand, and he watched her hold her hand in front of her. Tears rolled down her cheeks. Ben leaned in and kissed her. She didn't turn away from him and offer her cheek like she'd been doing for several weeks, but she didn't return his kiss either. Her lips felt stiff and cold. Ben's hope turned and left. In a quick motion, he slid his own band onto his finger and then stood.

"Forgive yourself, Katherine." He must have stunned her because she grabbed his hand and kept him from leaving.

"Have you forgiven me?"

"I never had to."

She began to weep, but when he reached to hold her, she turned away. Anger tried to surface in him. He'd felt frustrated by her, devastated by her, but never angry with her—not when she turned down his proposal, not even when Sammy died. Anger was an emotion he'd felt exclusively for his Pa. And he knew it led to bitterness. He didn't want to be bitter toward Katherine. He forced the emotion away, but then he let the loneliness and abandonment seep in long enough to acknowledge them.

"I love you, Katherine." He walked to the screen door and pulled it open. "It's colder out here than I realized, and it's getting late. We better go in." He let the door close behind him, then walked over to the phonograph and removed the record.

He tapped on Lena's door. "Need wood for your fireplace?" She answered that she was fine. He wished her a good night.

As he'd done every night since the burial, he stepped into Sammy's room and took in the scent. Each night less of Sammy's aroma was in the air. He walked out. Next he gave a gentle push to the cradle where his new child would sleep. Joe had done another beautiful job making it. Ben changed his clothes, lit a fire in the bedroom fireplace, and crawled into bed. He lay there twirling the wedding band on his finger, listening for Katherine to come in.

"God, please heal our Katherine. And God, I hurt, and I'm not sure how You feel about that."

The thought occurred to him that he'd just prayed. He sat up in the bed, overtaken by the memory of a verse Pastor had quoted at church. It was something about casting your cares on God because He cares about you. "Dear God, maybe I'll do that."

The bedroom door creaked open, and Katherine walked in. She changed clothes. With silence between them, he watched her. How large her abdomen had grown! It wouldn't be too long before the baby would come. Maybe an infant was what Katherine needed—a fresh start.

He pulled back the covers for her as she crawled into bed. She lay down and turned to her side with her back to him.

"Thank you for the wedding ring." His wife whispered. "I don't want to hurt you anymore than I already have because I love you, Ben, and I want to protect you from being hurt."

"You're misguided. You're protecting yourself, Katherine, and that protection is hurting me and pushing me away."

He pulled her to him, but she resisted and scooted closer to the edge of the bed. Ben rolled over and let the tears fall.

Abandonment and Loneliness made themselves right at home in their bedroom.

Through the night, he knew his sleep was fitful because emotions attacked his rest.

Ben felt startled and cold. A figure came to him in the dim room. He recognized her. His heart skipped a beat. He'd loved her once! She'd given life to his son. Feeling desperate to cling to her, he offered his hand, but she refused it. Instead, she looked through him and spoke, "I'm where I should be." Then she lifted her hand and a delicate finger pointed to a window. Ben's eyes were drawn there. A butterfly flitted outside while in the distance a storm brewed. Ben looked back at the figure. She nodded a slow yes before fading away. He raised the window and extended his hand. The butterfly came to rest upon it peacefully until the storm rolled in, then it frantically flew from him and disappeared into the dark sky.

Ben woke and put his hand to his mouth, imprisoning the groan that wanted to escape. He was sweating from the dream. He looked over to his wife and watched her breathe. "Come back, Butterfly."

Chapter 23

Ben sighed. A fretful night had led to a frustrating day at the mill peppered with mistakes and misunderstandings.

When the afternoon wagon passed by the store, Ben jumped off and headed inside. He wanted a cola and needed to walk off his frustration from the day and his dread at arriving at home to a distant Katherine. He looked forward to seeing Carl. The bell dinged as he pushed open the screen door. The store was warm inside from the stove lit in the corner.

"Evening Ben!" Carl stepped down from the short ladder he was using to stock the upper shelves and gave Ben a hearty handshake. "Just getting the shelves stocked for tomorrow morning. How was the mill?"

"Work is good. Mr. Forder is trying to expand, so he's got us pulling records and charts trying to gather information he needs for meetings."

"I heard about that."

"I know you're closing up shop, but I thought I'd get a cola."

"Sure you don't want coffee? It's cold outside." Ben laughed with his friend. "No, a cola's good."

"Help yourself." Ben headed to the cooler and picked out his drink. The bottle was cold and dripping. He popped off the top and began to sip.

"Ben. What a surprise." Mrs. Justice walked over to him. "And good timing. I have something for you to take home to Katherine."

Mrs. Justice went behind the counter of the small post office and pulled a package from the Williams and McGinn mail slot.

"Mrs. Forder dropped it by today when she came in to bring a new spread for one of the rental rooms. Lena had already come for the mail. Mrs. Forder said leaving it here instead of stopping by your house would save her some time since she was in a hurry."

Ben took the package from Mrs. Justice. "I'll take it to her." He reached over and kissed the dear lady on the cheek. Before he left, he paid for his cola and told Carl goodbye.

Katherine was sitting at the kitchen table when Ben walked in. Was that worry he saw on her face?

"Are you alright, Ben? You're late."

"I'm fine. Had a hankering for a cola, so I stopped by the store." He bent to kiss her, and to his dismay, her old, new habit was back. She turned her face so his lips met her cheek. *Why?*

"Mrs. Forder dropped this by the store for you today."

He watched as Katherine took the gift and eyed it curiously.

"Open it." Lena had stopped pouring tea and was standing next to Ben.

He watched Katherine tear the brown wrapping from a small box. Her wedding band caught his eye. Despite her aloofness and lack of affection since Sammy died, seeing the ring on her finger gave him hope. He was glad that she wore it. One day she would appreciate what the ring meant and return to him.

"I saw Mr. Forder at the office earlier this week, and he told me his wife had something for you. I promised not to tell." Katherine looked up and smiled at him then lifted the lid of the box.

He heard Lena sigh beside him just as he watched Katherine bring her hand to her lips. It was trembling. Ben reached and took the gift from Katherine. Inside the box was a small framed needlepoint of a red heart. Stitched inside the heart was the name Sammy. Words circled the heart. Ben read them aloud. "Always in our hearts." He picked up a small note lying in the box and read it aloud. "Praying for your family. Love from the Forders." He felt cared for.

Ben handed the gift back to Katherine. Without displaying any emotions or speaking any words, she took it, rose from her seat, and walked into the front room. Neither Ben nor Lena followed her—the moment was surreal. When she returned empty handed and sat back down at the table, Ben sat next to her.

"Where's the gift?"

"I put it on the fireplace mantle." Ben felt relieved. He'd wondered if she'd tossed it in the fire.

"I'll write her a thank you note tomorrow." With that said, the matter was ended, he presumed, because Katherine bowed her head and began to pray a blessing then eat. Ben looked over at Lena who seemed as stunned as he was. How long would his wife punish herself? He put himself in motion and began to eat. Lena followed suit.

Among the Crepe Myrtles

The following day was Saturday. Joe arrived mid-morning and went straight to bed. Later that afternoon while Ben was working in the shed, Joe walked in and startled him. He held a tin can in his hand. Before Ben could express his curiosity, Joe began to explain what he was holding. "Picked this up at a store on one of our stops. It's a bit late, but I reckon it'll bring some peace of mind."

Ben took the can and read the words on its label. "Snake Bite Kit." Joe's gesture was odd to Ben and very bothersome. A memory of Sammy's swollen leg and limp body flashed before his eyes. Ben shuttered. The sounds in the kitchen the day Sammy passed seemed to resurrect themselves—wails, screams, and the silent sound of utter despair twirled around him in mocking chorus. Ben had to force his hands from reaching up to cover his ears.

He collected himself and spoke as kindly as he could. "I don't know whether to feel grateful, sad, or defensive." He raised the side of his mouth in an awkward smile. "No need to feel anything. I just saw it and thought we should have one here." *No need to feel anything?* "Well, I reckon the shed is the best place for it. Thank you."

He heard Joe clear his throat and begin to speak when Pirate's barking evidently interrupted Joe's thoughts. The dog came running out through the woods and sprinted toward the road.

"Gabriel must be here," Ben stated as he headed out the shed door.

"Gabriel?"

"Yeah. The ladies don't want Pirate around anymore. Said it's too sad for them. So, I arranged for Gabriel to take him back to his place."

"I'll miss the little thing."

"Me too, but I guess I understand where the girls are coming from. They said their good-byes to him this morning before they left to make jelly with Amy Carlson."

Ben uttered his words as though departing with Pirate was a reasonable, unemotional thing to do—much like discarding scraps from the table. In truth, the dog had come to feel like a tangible connection to Sammy. Ben took comfort in the short, soft fur, wiggly body, and warm breath that he felt when he held the dog. Effervescent life! Despite his feelings, Ben would do anything he could to help his wife heal. If departing with the dog would

179

draw her closer to him, then returning Pirate to his former owner was the most reasonable thing to do; but, contrary to his tone of voice, there was nothing unemotional in departing with Pirate.

"Well, Gabriel will be a while, so I was just gonna tell ya that…"

"No, Joe. Since Sammy died, Gabe doesn't come by anymore. I don't think he'll stay long now. Wait, so we can talk about what you got on your mind."

Ben had a suspicion that Joe was going to talk about going to High Cotton and wanting the cart and Gitter. He'd heard the talk that this was High Cotton's last night open and for a cover charge, the drinks were endless. The thought that Joe could drink without the worry of paying drink by drink concerned him.

The transaction with Gabriel was indeed short. Ben handed the dog over to the young man who had refused to get out of his wagon. The three men bid each other hello and good-bye, and Gabriel set off toward his house with Pirate seated next to him. A wave of sadness spread through Ben. Sammy's life seemed to draw people to one another; his death seemed to pull them apart.

He turned his attention to Joe, who seemed fidgety and irritated by the delay in their conversation.

"What's on your mind?"

"High Cotton is closing down after tonight. Faye is serving endless drinks for a cover charge."

"I heard about that."

"Seeing as how ya try to be my preacher and the guardian of my vices, I thought I'd tell ya up front that I plan to make a night of it."

"Joe, High Cotton can cease to exist, but your problem won't unless you do something about it. Partaking in endless drinks isn't a solution."

"Maybe I'll work on my ways. With the place shut down, it'll be easy for me to cut back on my drinking."

"The drinking has a hold on you, Joe, and will force you to find another source if you don't fight the urge. Your problem exists wherever you are."

"I'm not asking, Ben. I'm telling."

"You're not taking Gitter and the cart."

"Don't need to. I got friends coming by to get me."

180

Ben went nose to nose with Joe and pointed his finger at his face. "You're ruining your life, Joe! Nobody cares about you enough to tell you that other than the people living in this house." Ben grabbed Joe's arm. "And, I am not gonna stand by and let you hurt Katherine and Lena."

"I ain't gonna hurt them."

"Not if you're sober."

Joe shook away Ben's grip and blew out a breath that Ben felt on his face. With that, Joe walked away and when Ben came in the house, the dance hall patron was sitting in a tub of water in his room.

"We're done talking," Ben heard Joe say before he dipped his head under the water. Within the half hour, the wagon with his buddies had picked him up.

Chapter 24

The house was quiet with the ladies at the Carlson's house and Joe headed to High Cotton. Sweat dripped off Ben's forehead as he leaned over the large pot and stirred the vegetable soup. When he'd found out the night before that the ladies would be picked up to go to the Carlson's to make jelly, he'd suggested that Pastor and Amy join them for supper.

"I'll make my vegetable soup, and if Lena will write down her cornbread recipe, I'll give it a try. Course, you may find the kitchen filled with smoke when you get home." He pecked Katherine on the cheek. Her acknowledgement was a smile, but no returned affection or humorous retort to his reference of their first encounter.

Standing at the stove and smelling cornbread cooking, Ben fought giving up hope. He'd grieved before and was grieving now, so he didn't want to judge Katherine's form of mourning, but her aloofness brought him anguish and her self-condemnation brought him despair. She seemed to wrap herself in pain and shy away from any sort of pleasure. Needing the touch and comradeship of his wife and wanting to comfort her in return, Ben found himself feeling vulnerable.

It would be good to have friends in the house to dispel the mood that had settled in since Sammy's passing.

Suppertime was pleasant, and although Katherine was quieter than Ben would have liked, he felt pleased that she smiled and talked with the rest of them. The day away from the house with Amy must have been good for her. Ben's hope began to seep back in.

"Well, Ben, tomorrow's Sunday, and I got a sermon to review. We'll see you in the morning at church. We better hit the road."

"Wendell, heard any more talk of your getting to settle in one town and be the pastor?" Ben hoped he had.

"It's still being considered, but I'm thinking I'll be the pastor of Layton within a year. No more traveling to the other towns in the community."

"That would be so nice," Lena chimed in, "church services every week instead of once a month."

"Ben," Amy smiled as she spoke, "that was good stew. Where'd you learn to cook like that?"

Ben swallowed. The pain of Death's latest visit was tender, and Katherine was so distant that thinking of his first wife stung. "I had a good teacher in Commerce."

He saw her turn to Katherine. "Wendell can fry good fish, so it's our turn to cook next. We ladies will sit and sip tea while dinner is being prepared. Course we might have to wait until after the baby comes." The young pastor's wife giggled. Ben watched Katherine lean over and give her a hug. The couple departed.

With a little bit of hope breathing in him, Ben crawled into bed and lay close to his wife.

"I saw you hold your back while we were saying goodbye to the Carlsons. Is it sore? You had a full day in the kitchen."

"No. I'm fine now that I'm off my feet." He felt her start to move toward the edge of the bed. "Katherine, I need to be close tonight. Please." She kept next to him, but turned on her back. He patted her abdomen, clasped her hand, then closed his eyes.

Ben jerked and sat up in bed. In the shadows of the bedroom he saw Katherine pacing the floor. Panic set in. "Katherine! Is the baby coming?" He shook his head to clear it and jumped out of the bed. "No. The baby and me are fine." His hands rested on her shoulders as he held her still.

"Why are you up?"

"Joe."

"He's home?"

"No. And that worries me." Ben moved his hands to hold both of hers, and she let him. "Katherine, he told me he'd be out all night."

"And you agreed with it?"

"No. I argued with him, but he's a grown man and did what he wanted to do."

"His drinking is getting worse. He might be dead on the side of the road. I want you to go find him, Ben." He felt her pull free of his grasp, but she did so without losing eye contact.

"Katherine."

"Ben, I am begging you to go find my brother."

Her arms had grabbed his, and she shook him as she spoke. Ben realized that his wife was scared. He also realized he'd do anything to draw her back to him.

He checked the clock. Three in the morning. He'd be traveling in the dark the entire way. Katherine must have noticed his glance at the time.

"Take the lantern and that new flashlight you got."

"I might not be back for church."

"Ben, just go get Joe."

Within a half hour Ben was headed down the dark road, trusting a small stream of light to guide Gitter's recently healed leg, the cart, and himself. He'd always considered himself a reasonable man, but nothing was reasonable about his heading to High Cotton in the middle of the night. He was going because he loved his wife.

The air was cold and made him sniffle, so he reached up and wiped his runny nose on the sleeve of his jacket. An image of Sammy doing the same thing dashed across his mind, causing a lump to rise in his throat.

Gitter's clopping and the grind of the wheel against the dirt were the only other sounds around him. Alone in the dark and quiet outdoors, a sadness and a loneliness crept through him. He let his shoulders slump and felt tears roll down his face. He knew Sammy was gone from this life. But Katherine? She was hiding just out of reach. His longing for things to be right between them was so intense it made his body ache.

By the time High Cotton came into view, Ben felt emotionally drained. His bottom ached against the seat, and his feet felt cold and heavy. He was shocked at how alive the place was. Light shone through the windows. As he approached, the music pounded in his ears, and boisterous, rowdy sounding voices came from all around. Autos and wagons and horses and carts filled the dirt lot around the building.

Ben pulled Gitter to a stop, jumped from the seat, tied up the mule, and then stretched his stiff body. He dreaded walking into the dance hall and being surrounded by drunken men and women as he searched for Joe.

Before he made it to the front entrance steps, a muffled scream came from somewhere beside the building. Ben crept to the edge of the dance hall and looked around the corner. The air was so cold, smoke came from his nostrils. He heard the sound again, this time more distinctly. A female voice was crying out.

He noticed an expensive looking auto. The next scream was no doubt a cry for help. Ben knew the sound and commotion were coming from the fogged up auto.

He sprinted over to it and began to pull on the door. What he saw before him would be with him far beyond this moment.

"Faye!" He recognized her immediately.

"Help me!"

"Get your hands off her!" Ben reached over the disheveled Faye Forder and shoved the man who wasn't dressed all the way and who had his hands on her in places they shouldn't be.

Pulling back from the man, Ben grabbed Faye under her arms and pulled her free from the auto. She dropped to the ground, sobbing.

Ben saw from the corner of his eye that the man in the car crawled out the back and began to run.

"Faye. You're safe now. Can you stand up?" He lifted her gently under her arms and turned her to face him.

"Ben." Faye fell against his body and wrapped her arms around his back. He felt her body tremble and shake as she sobbed. Before he could speak, she looked up at him—her lips were quivering and pain shown in her eyes. She was no longer a seductress, but a scared, vulnerable human being.

In his frailty, weakness, pain, and humanity, Ben gave in to his desire to connect with another human being, to comfort, and to be comforted. When Faye brought her face to his, he bent down and kissed her trembling lips.

"Ben!" The sound of Joe's voice seemed to rip Ben's soul from his body. He released Faye, bent over and retched, then fell to the ground. "What have I done?" The words reverberated in his head. He rocked back and forth, sitting in his own filth. His words to Katherine came to mind and mocked him, "I'm a Joseph." The memory caused him to retch again.

The commotion around him seemed surreal. Faye's anxious voice crying that she'd been raped. Men's voices demanding to know what going on. His own name echoing around him. "Is that Ben Williams?"

He felt someone yank him up from the ground, and the impact of a fist on his jaw caused him to fall right back down in his own filth. Joe. His brother-in-law dropped on top of him and began beating his face. Ben felt spit and blood leave his mouth. A smack against his nose caused Ben to fell dizzy. Warm blood gushed from his nostrils.

Someone must have pulled Joe from him, because the next thing Ben knew, two men were pulling him by the shoulders and holding him up while across from him two more men were holding Joe. His brother-in-law was drunk and his words slurred. Spit projected from him and hit Ben in the face.

"I'll kill you, Ben! Raping Faye."

"I'm not a good man, but I didn't rape Faye. I didn't do it!"

From somewhere behind him, Ben heard Faye's voice. "He rescued me! He didn't rape me! Richard Byers raped me, and he took off toward the woods!"

Ben began to weep inconsolably.

Joe must have broken loose because his disgusting breath was in Ben's face. He felt Joe's hand pound his chest. "You're nothing but filth! My sister ain't right for you now? Now that she let your boy be killed? Now that she's heavy with your baby? You coming here after other women?"

Ben screamed at his brother-in-law, the sound of his voice echoing off the side of the building. "I came here to get you! Katherine didn't want you drinking yourself to death."

Ben yanked free of the two men holding him.

"You two get out of here. Go home." Some man Ben didn't know shouted at him and Joe, then pushed them to make them move.

With his head slumped to his chest, Ben walked toward the cart. His body was aching with the realization of what he'd just done. He felt his legs begin to collapse and caught himself on the edge of someone's wagon.

A hand touched his shoulder, and he turned to see Faye standing next to him. He loathed himself. "I shouldn't…I was wrong…it meant nothing."

"I know Ben."

"I love my wife."

"I know."

"I'm sorry, Faye, for being no better than that man was. I'm sorry for what I did to you."

186

"You rescued me, Ben. Don't be sorry for that. The other—well, I know you didn't mean it. I don't hold it against you. I don't even blame you. You're a respectable man. You don't belong here. Go home."

He saw her begin to walk away, then pause and turn toward him again. "Thank you, Ben, for pulling me from the auto."

Ben loosened Gitter and crawled into the cart. He'd leave without Joe who could find his own way back. Arriving home to Katherine empty handed would be meaningless once he broke her heart.

He had no idea how he got back to Layton, but when he pulled into the yard, he stepped down from the cart and slumped to the ground. He got on all fours then pulled himself up by grabbing the cart wheel. Sin had sucked every bit of strength from his body; he wasn't even sure if his soul was alive.

He dragged his feet through the dirt, leaving long streaks, rather than footprints in the black dirt. When the screen door creaked, he looked up to see Katherine, and he began to weep as Katherine waddled carefully down the steps, panic in her eyes.

"Is Joe dead?" Ben shook his head no. His appearance must have registered in her mind at that moment. He felt her run her hands over his arms and rest her palms on his chest.

"Ben! What's happened?"

"Katherine, forgive me." He pulled her around the side of the house.

"Ben! You're scaring me! What's wrong?"

He led her through the outer door of their bedroom then sat her on the bed. He fell to his knees beside her and placed his head in her lap. His baby kicked against him. "I'm not a good man."

He heard the words spill from his mouth as he looked her in the eyes and told her everything that had happened at High Cotton.

In horror, he watched her face grow pale and felt her torso collapsing against the mattress.

"Katherine! No, don't leave me! Don't leave me! I'm sorry! I'm so very sorry!"

His wife went unconscious and Ben shrieked Lena's name. The young woman flew into the room and screamed.

"Get a cold rag! She's passed out."

He heard Lena scurry out, crying. Ben stood then sat on the bed, pulling Katherine into his lap. He saw her chest rise and fall. "Keep breathing, darling Butterfly." He rubbed her belly, and the baby moved. Lena appeared before him; he grabbed the wet cloth from her. "Get some smelling salts! Do you have any?"

"I'm not sure!"

"Get anything strong—vinegar!" He hated the fear he saw on Lena's face as she darted from the room. He knew he'd caused it.

"Keep breathing, Katherine." He wiped her face with the cloth. Katherine stirred, and Ben began to weep again. He sat her up slowly, and just at that moment, Lena appeared with vinegar.

"Katherine, are you alright?" His sister-in-law cried and bent over her bulging belly.

"My body is fine. The baby is fine." His wife touched her sister's cheek. "But me and Ben need to be alone."

"Is Joe dead, Ben?"

"No," he whispered to her, He felt both relief and sorrow as she turned and walked out of the room, closing the door behind her.

———————◆•◆•◆———————

He wasn't expecting Katherine to slap him, but when she did, it made him dizzy. "This is your revenge? For me getting Sammy killed."

"No! Why don't you believe me? I don't blame you for Sammy! I never have! I do blame me for being weak tonight. I was wrong. Wrong!"

"I want you out right now. I want you gone—for good."

"Katherine! Let me suffer my shame and penance here and try to make things right."

"How dare you offer to suffer your shame here in this town! To do so would only turn the shame on me. A pregnant wife whose husband cheated on her! You deserve far more penance than embarrassment around those who know you."

"My penance is a lifetime of regret—in front of those I know and love. My penance is a dead son. My penance is a wife who may never trust me again. I'll take it!" He shook his fists in the air then beat them against his chest. "But don't make me try to live without you."

"Then don't!" Her words echoed off the bedroom wall.

Ben knew she was speaking hysterically and emotionally, but he would not tell her that. He could no longer judge what she did with emotions. He'd done shameful things with his. His stomach lurched, but there was nothing left for it to give up. Ben heaved

Katherine clutched her bulging belly.

"The baby! Katherine, please calm down for the sake of the baby."

She didn't.

"I'd rather be a widow and have a fatherless child. But, I'm forced to be a divorced woman or a deserted woman!" He saw her grab at her stomach again. "You deserve a lifetime of regret separated from those you know and say that you love."

Ben grasped her shoulders. "Katherine, I love you. Don't send me away! Don't take me from my baby! I've lost so much."

"Get out, now." Coldness. Hate. Despair.

Katherine lay on the bed and turned her back to him.

Ben stood. The burden of his wrongdoing stood with him and pressed down on his shoulders. He felt his resolve leave him.

Slumped and silent, he pulled open his dresser drawer and took out his harmonica, the small leather satchel that contained his documents, and the one picture of Sammy with his birth mother. Sammy—his boy rested on this property. Now he felt as though he were losing him a second time.

Katherine's butterfly clip sat atop the dresser. He clutched it then dropped it in his satchel. *I'll hold you close, my wounded Butterfly.* Somehow his feet made their way to Sammy's room where Ben collected his son's favorite shirt, the rabbit foot, and one train piece. He put them in his satchel. As he walked out of his son's small room, the baby cradle caught his eye. He had no token of his unborn child to carry with him. He bent and ran his fingers over the blanket folded neatly inside the little bed.

Piece by broken piece, he dragged himself to the outer door, then turned for one last glimpse at his wife. "Katherine?" She didn't acknowledge him. "I love you. I love our baby that you're carrying." His chest had tightened and his throat had closed, trying to imprison his words. "I always will."

He opened the door; the late morning breeze tickled his skin, ignorant of the storm that howled in his soul. Ben moved to where Sammy rested among the crepe myrtles. He lay across his son's grave and wept. Being nothing but bone and flesh, he walked to the only place he knew to go— Pastor Carlson's house. A measure of relief set in when he realized that if Joe were coming home, it would be from the opposite direction. When he arrived at the parsonage, he slumped onto the front steps.

"Ben!" Wendell's voice woke Ben from his dazed state. "Is it the baby? We missed you all at church. Amy and I are worried."

"No, it's not the baby." Ben began to shake. "Wendell, I did a terrible thing." From the corner of his eye, he saw Amy slip into the house while Wendell sat down on the step next to Ben. For the second time in his horrific morning, Ben spewed the story of what had happened at High Cotton and then with Katherine.

Wendell wept with him.

In time Ben spoke again.

"She couldn't love the jagged pieces of my humanity. I'm certain God couldn't love me either."

"Ben, God is gracious and compassionate. He's slow to anger and abounds with love. He does love the jagged pieces of your humanity, as you say. He can repair them through the forgiveness he offers."

"I understand my debt now."

"Are you ready to let Him pay it?"

"No. I deserve the burden of it."

"You do, but He's doesn't want you to bear it."

Ben desperately wanted to accept forgiveness and have the burden removed, but the thought of his having any relief didn't seem fair after the pain he'd caused Katherine. And even as he thought those very words, the irony of his reasoning hit him. It was no different than Katherine's reasoning had been since Sammy died.

"What will you do now, Ben?"

"I'm not sure. Return to Commerce? Can I stay here until Monday lunch when I can catch the train back to Commerce? That is, if she still won't have me."

"Let's go to her, now."

"No, not me. But, she needs Amy or Mrs. Justice."

"I'll handle that." Pastor pulled Ben to his feet. "You go in and eat." *A worthless task for dying man.*

Ben hid himself inside the parsonage, lifeless, other than the relentless breath that kept him alive.

Chapter 25

Katherine stirred from her fetal position where she'd lain on the bed and listened to Ben shuffle around the room. He had called to her, but she didn't answer. The outer bedroom door had slammed shut from the breeze.

"Ben?"

The eerie silence chided her—he was gone. A surge of panic ran through her heart urging her to go after him and tell him that she couldn't live without him either. But Betrayal had hold of her mind and reason, so she chose to let him go.

"Katherine?" Lena's shaky voice sounded through the other door to her bedroom, but Katherine refused to answer her too. Instead, she rose from the bed and shuffled around the room seeing the signs of Ben's pilferage. His dresser drawer was open—every piece of clothing still there. Only his satchel and harmonica were missing. She surveyed the lonely rooms. Tokens of Sammy—gone. Her clip—missing.

The lavender lotion tin caught her eye. She angrily slid it from the dresser top and let it fall into his open drawer; then in anguished contrast, she bent and pulled out his brown corduroy shirt. Her arms clutched it to her chest; her lips kissed its soft fabric; her breath inhaled its scent. She lay again upon the bed and clung to the token of Ben.

"Katherine?" This time she heard her sister sobbing.

"You can come in."

The bedroom door squeaked, and then Lena's body pressed against her on the bed, but her sister lay silent.

"He's gone."

"He left you?"

"I told him to leave—for good."

"Katherine!" She felt her sister tremble next to her. "Why?"

"Faye." A quiet gasp.

"Faye?"

"Yes. He betrayed me."

"He couldn't! He loves you. I saw him turn her away before."

"He confessed it."

Her sister's weeping filled the room.

"What about the baby, Katherine?"

"The baby will be born and never know its father." As Lena rose and stood by the bed, Katherine turned and sat on the edge of it, rocking back and forth.

"How long was he with her?"

"The length of a kiss."

"But…" Katherine sensed the turmoil her sister felt in judging the disparity between a moment and a lifetime. She'd felt that same turmoil too, wondering if she was making a mistake as she listened to Ben shuffle around the room before he left.

"The length of a married man's one kiss to another woman is enough time to ruin a marriage."

Her sister didn't reply. Katherine was grateful that Lena seemed speechless again.

"I'm going to sleep now." Katherine laid herself down, pulled Ben's shirt to her face, and closed her eyes to time and reality.

Light and dark moved in and out of the room. Fuzzy images leaned over her, blurred bodies scurried around the room, and delicate arms set her up to sip something warm or sometimes cold. The images were familiar, but in her fog, Katherine couldn't place them other than Lena, whom she'd sense beside her whenever the dark moved in.

There were constants—fabric clutched in one hand; movement in her belly; feelings of fear and despair.

There were voids—no phonograph; no harmonica; no little boy; no kiss; no butterflies; no joy; no hope. Somewhere in her daze these had slipped away, and she did not know where they hid.

And in the distance, a train whistle blew.

While light was in the room for a visit, alertness slipped in. Katherine fought against the heaviness of her eyelids, blinked, and then squinted at the light hitting her eyes. Her body ached. She felt a moan rise from her chest and heard it fill the air. Someone spoke her name.

"Katherine?"

The fog lifted from her mind and her eyes focused.

"Lena?"

"I'm here." She felt Lena's hand touch her cheek. Gentle sobs told her Lena was weeping.

"Where am I?"

"In your bed."

"Did I die?" She watched her sister's smile spread and her teardrop catch the bottom of it.

"No. You just left us for a while to sleep. I'm relieved to have you back. Feel like sitting up?"

"How long have I have been sleeping?"

"Three days."

Devastation engulfed her as the memories came flooding in.

"Ben."

"Do you remember when you last saw him?'

"Yes." She sat up and rocked back and forth on the bed. With her arms wrapped around her abdomen, she was suddenly cognizant of the softness she'd been aware of in her delirium. She still clutched Ben's shirt; it hung to the side of her thigh.

"Katherine, the baby? Have you felt it?"

"Yes." Her sister began to sob.

"Has he been back?"

"No." Relief and sorrow settled in. He'd surrendered; she was vindicated, but at the cost of being without him.

"Lena, have you been taking care of me by yourself, or is Joe home?"

"He's not home, but Mrs. Carlson and Mrs. Justice have taken turns being here. Feeding you soup. Rubbing your abdomen. Caring for your needs. They'll be happy to know you've returned to us."

"Lena, tell me what happened…after he left."

"You locked yourself in your emotions after you told me about High Cotton. I couldn't wake you. I was so scared you were dying and taking the baby with you." The sound of Lena weeping made Katherine's lips quiver.

"I'm sorry." She pulled Lena to her and hugged her.

"At some point, I heard knocking on the front door, so I ran to see who it was, relieved that someone could help me. It was Pastor and Mrs. Carlson."

Her sister's story paused long enough for Lena to cock her head and whisper her next words.

"They had just left Ben. He was waiting for them at the parsonage when they got home from church."

"So, he's still in Layton?"

"No. He left two days ago—Monday."

"I see. Did you see him?"

"Katherine, do you really want to know all this?" Lena had stopped crying.

"Yes." Her sister sighed heavily.

"Yes, I saw him at the depot on Monday. Mrs. Justice was here with you, so I walked there to see Ben because I knew Pastor was taking him to the train to leave."

"Was Faye there to see him off?"

"Katherine. No. He was no better off than you were at the time. He was breathing and talking, but I wouldn't say he was living. He was a body with sound and motion, but no spirit."

"I'm hungry."

Katherine suspected her deliberate and abrupt change of subject shook her sister's reasoning, for it took her a moment to reply. There was a longing for Ben that Katherine didn't want to acknowledge, and food was her distraction.

"Hungry? That's good. You should try to walk to the kitchen. There's stewed chicken and biscuits. But, maybe you need to make a trip outside first?"

Katherine stood up from the bed, and the answer to Lena's question hit her body full force. "Yes, nature calls." Her sister reached to escort her, but Katherine nodded no. "I'll be fine to go by myself."

The warm chicken began to fill her with energy, but the unusual quietness and awkwardness between she and Lena made her uncomfortable. Did Lena not know what to say or what to ask? Is it possible her sister judged her for sending Ben away? Lena had been aware of his absence for three days while Katherine had been shut out from reality. Maybe she too would begin to feel an awkwardness created by his void. If so, she would learn to live with it.

"When is Joe due back home?'

"Not until Friday afternoon."

"Joe! Lena when did he come home from High Cotton?"

"Some men dropped him off and left him in the yard Sunday afternoon. He was drunk, but Pastor got him into his bed. After that, Pastor drove to the Justice's house and asked for their help in watching over us all. Joe left again on Monday. His concern for you was anything but touching."

"Before Joe left, did he say anything?"

"Just that he'd come around the corner of the building, headed to the outhouse, when he saw them together near a car."

Her sister reached over and grabbed her hand.

"Katherine, you know Joe has his eyes locked on Faye. He's angry. He says he doesn't believe the story about another man taking off to the woods and is blaming Ben for the whole incident."

"Maybe he's right."

"Maybe he's wrong."

Lena made her feel angry and yes, judged. She wanted the conversation to end, so Katherine stood and began to clear her dishes just as Amy Carlson walked through the kitchen doorway.

"Katherine," her friend pulled her into an embrace, "you're awake."

That day and the next moved slowly for Katherine. She found herself roaming aimlessly from task to task or room to room. She supposed that was the way a woman whose heart was severed functioned. She was no longer whole. "Perhaps a bath will settle me down so I can think. Besides, I smell myself." She patted her belly and smiled at her baby who couldn't reply to her comment.

She and Lena set up the tub in her bedroom. The water Lena had boiled was warm and soothing, and she relaxed when the warmth moved up her body. Grabbing the soap that Lena had left on the towel beside the tub, she recognized the scent. Lavender—the soap Ben somehow always had on hand for her. She tossed the purple bar across the room. "Lena!"

"What is it?" Her sister appeared in the doorway with her hands on her hips and her face red from the heat of ironing.

"I'll never use lavender again. Do we have more soap?" Her sister walked out without a word and returned a moment later.

"Here."

Katherine took the homemade soap from her sister. It was rough on her skin. It did not smell good. It suited her just fine.

After she bathed and dressed, Katherine took the iron from Lena. "I can do this for a while. You've been so good to me, Lena." The young woman walked out without a word to Katherine.

Her stomach felt relaxed from the warm bath, and Katherine smiled as the baby moved inside her. She suspected she had about four weeks until the baby should come, but she wasn't exactly sure. The fact that Sammy had been gone about twice that amount of time settled in her mind.

Her throat tightened. She'd gained and lost so much over this year. Ben had said those same words to her just before he slipped out the back door—just as she had slipped into a form of personal death. The baby could be born before their first anniversary date. "We have no anniversary to celebrate."

Katherine knew that Ben had never blamed her for Sammy's death, but she felt in her heart she was responsible. The burden of that was more than she could bear, so she'd become distant from him to punish herself. She had consciously withdrawn even when Ben had begged her to return. She was unworthy to be happy with him since she had caused him to lose such a precious life.

A thought crossed her mind that perhaps she had driven Ben toward Faye. No! The man made his choice to do what he did.

What she did to Sammy was an accident. What Ben did to Faye was a choice. An unforgivable choice.

A tug pulled on her heart. Would God think Ben's choice was unforgivable? She shrugged away the tug. She hadn't talked to God in several weeks, and she didn't plan on doing so now. She didn't want to hear what He had to say because she didn't want to forgive Ben. Or herself.

Smoke! "Blast it!" Katherine pulled the iron away from her cotton skirt she was ironing. A large black mark in the shape of an iron was imprinted on the front of the blue cloth.

"I smell smoke!" Lena came back into the room.

"I got lost in my thoughts, that's all." Katherine pulled the skirt off the board and held it up. "I can't afford to lose this, but I also can't imagine fitting in it again. We'll turn it into rags."

"Katherine?"

Lena was putting the next item to iron on the board. It was a blue chemise shirt. Katherine dropped her ruined skirt and reached over to pull the shirt from the board. She saw Lena startle. Katherine walked into the bedroom, pulled open Ben's drawer, and stuffed the shirt inside without looking.

One day she'd have to do something with his things. One day.

She headed back into the kitchen.

"Katherine?"

"What is it, Lena?"

"You asked me the other day if Ben came back. I told you no, because he didn't. But, he did send this through Pastor." Lena held out her hand to offer a piece of paper. Katherine took the folded piece of paper, returned to her bedroom, and placed it on the dresser. She'd chosen to set it down over crushing it into a ball inside her fist.

Chapter 26

Midmorning Friday, Katherine was in her bedroom sweeping the addition to the house and all the time trying to ignore the desire to read the letter from Ben that still rested on her dresser. She thought she heard an auto come down the road and slow down. Although Layton had hopes of growing into a major stop on the way to Dallas, that hadn't happened and the sound of wagons and carts was more common than the sound of an auto. She stopped sweeping and glanced around the doorway when she heard Lena greeting someone to come in.

"I'll let her know you're here. Would you like some sweet tea?"

"That would be nice. Thank you."

Katherine slid out of the doorway just as Lena walked through it. "You have a visitor, Katherine."

"Who is it?"

"Mrs. Forder."

Katherine gasped and felt her body go clammy. She violently shook her head no, but Lena grabbed her by the shoulders and stared at her, speaking between gritted teeth. "Go to her." Katherine swallowed so hard that she heard it.

"I'll get her tea while you dust the dirt off yourself."

A moment and a lifetime later, Katherine walked into the front room.

"Mrs. Forder. What a nice surprise to have you stop by."

"I'm sorry to barge in unexpected. I'm sure you're right when you said this is a surprise."

"Here's your tea. Please, make yourself at home." Katherine gestured toward Lena's rocker, and as she did she thought how humble her home must appear to her visitor.

"A surprise, yes, but I'm honored you're here." And curious. And afraid.

"Well, thank you, but no need to be honored. I'm here as a woman and as a friend—at least I'd like to become a friend. "

Mrs. Forder's face turned pink and the "First Lady" of the county seemed shy.

"How are you feeling, with the baby and all?"

"Tired and large, but good—all things considered." Katherine fought to hold back the tears.

She heard Mrs. Forder clear her throat.

"Katherine, she's gone—Faye—she left. I thought you should know. And she won't be back, I suspect."

"Is she with him?"

"No. Not at all. She's with a man in Dallas. Uhm, a wealthy businessman. She's been with him for a bit, I understand. She called it moving on, becoming a socialite. Her last tie to life here was High Cotton."

"I thought Ben loved me."

"He does. Katherine, I feel sure of it. Faye came home that morning just to tell us the truth. To defend his reputation. She doesn't do much that is honorable, but she did speak up for him. He rescued her out of that auto where she was being forced upon. She shouldn't have been there, but she was."

"Do you believe her?"

"Yes."

"I sent him to go get Joe. My brother doesn't believe what Faye and Ben say happened."

"I know. He made that clear to Faye after Ben left that night. But they are telling the truth. Katherine, the authorities caught the man who was hurting her."

Her visitor leaned forward in the rocker. "Ben came to the mill Monday morning and spoke to Mason, my husband. He apologized for taking advantage of his niece and said that he'd be leaving Layton."

"He did? Was Mr. Forder angry?'

"Faye had earned her reputation as a loose woman and was always a grief to Mason and me. So, no, my husband wasn't angry at your husband. He was sad for the whole ordeal, for losing a good employee, for seeing a strong man broken by shame and regret, for knowing your family was being torn apart."

"Your husband is a good man."

"He is. Katherine, I hope I haven't imposed on you by sharing what I know. I just thought that if it were me, I'd want to know."

"I'm thankful you told me." Katherine could no longer hold back her tears.

She watched Mrs. Forder stand and pull her handkerchief from her pocket. Without speaking a word, the dear lady knelt and pressed the cloth to Katherine's cheeks. The broken wife felt her wipe the tears away. The clock hanging above the two rockers chimed the hour, and she felt Mrs. Forder rise from where she knelt.

"I best get on my way."

Katherine stood and pulled the woman to her. "Thank you, Mrs. Forder, for coming."

"Call me Abigail."

Katherine's eye caught the heart needlework on the mantle.

"Abigail, the needlework is beautiful and so are the words." She pointed, and her new friend glanced at it and smiled. New friend? Receiving Abigail's offer of friendship felt like inhaling a tornado.

"You've born a lot lately. Take care of yourself and that baby. Maybe I could come by after it's born.'

"Please do."

"Katherine, I do have one more piece of news I want to share with you." Once again, Katherine saw her visitor blush. "I'm with child." Abigail Forder gently laughed. Katherine hoped her own shock hadn't shown on her face.

"Why, that's wonderful, Mrs. Forder, I mean Abigail. Congratulations."

"Isn't it something? Pregnant at my age—the mother of a teenage son. Mason is happy." Abigail extended a hand toward her. "Maybe our children can be friends."

Katherine took her hand and squeezed it. "I'd like that."

"I'll see you soon." With that, the wealthy, kindhearted, pregnant matron of Layton and new friend of Katherine stepped outside and walked to her auto.

Stunned, relieved, angry, baffled—none of those alone could describe how Katherine felt when she plopped back down into her rocker after the visit. Her tangled emotions displayed themselves through a giddy laughter that soon gave way to a tangled muse.

Why offer friendship to me? Because Abigail Forder is kind and down to earth.

Why wasn't Faye in Dallas that night? Because Faye Forder wants to squeeze every ounce from what she gets her hands on—including High Cotton and its customers.

Why did I send Ben to get my brother? Because Joe McGinn's drinking is getting out of control, and Ben could shield her family. That shield was now gone.

Why did Ben give up his marriage for one kiss with a woman who saw him as someone to conquer, but not keep? Because Ben Williams was grieving and needed emotional connection, and his wife was distant and cold.

Why did I send Ben away for good? Because Katherine McGinn Williams felt unworthy of her husband and turned that emotion inside out. She renamed it self-vindication.

Again. Why did I send Ben away for good? Because Katherine has been humiliated and wronged and chooses not to live with it.

You mean you choose not to live with it and be with him; because Katherine, you will live with it for the rest of your life and so will your child.

She absorbed the pain of that truth and mixed it with the pain of Sammy's death and although these truths made her physically ache, she chose them over forgiving him or forgiving herself. She shuttered and pulled herself up from the rocker, in great need of fresh air.

"Achoo!" The sneeze and her crying made her have the hiccups. My goodness, she couldn't recall having the hiccups since…since the day she and Lena had colas with Ben. Meandering around her yard, Katherine glanced to the trees where Sammy was buried. She made her way there. Far too cumbersome to kneel or sit, she bent and ran her hand along the top of the tombstone. The toy train caught her eye. She reached down to pick it up. "The weather is making the paint fade, Sammy." She brought the train to her lips, kissed it, and then placed it back in front of the headstone. "Will anything make the pain fade?"

The grieving woman straightened herself back up. "Ouch!" A sharp pain spread across her lower back, and her belly felt tight and uncomfortable. "Bye, Sammy. Your Papa won't be around to tell you, but he misses you."

Katherine felt strange as she made her way back to the house through the backdoor.

"You've been outside? Where's Mrs. Forder?"

"She left."

"What did she want? Katherine, you have to tell me." Katherine smirked at her sisters pleading hands clasped under her chin.

"She told me that Faye backed up what Ben said and that the other man has been caught and that Faye has moved to Dallas to be a socialite."

"Do you believe her?"

"Yes."

"So, does that mean that you and Ben..."

"No, Miss Happily Ever After, nothing changes between Ben and me." She watched pain sneak across Lena's face. Katherine wondered who the pain was meant for—Lena? Ben? Katherine? The baby?

"She also said that she is with child and that she wants me to call her by her first name, Abigail."

"Out of pity?"

"Out of kindness." Katherine bent and kissed her sister on the cheek. "I need to lay down. I'm real tired." With that, she headed to her bedroom and shut the door behind her.

She was safe from Lena's questions and safe from Joe's imminent arrival and his most certain angry, gloating harassment over Ben's actions.

Her eye landed on the folded letter atop the dresser. Katherine sighed; she knew she was not safe from the written, unread words that taunted her. Not at all.

Her arm reached forward and her fingertips slid the paper to the edge of the dresser where her right hand clasped it. Her left hand rested on her abdomen that was again heavy. "Whew."

Another pain started in her lower back and swept around her middle. Her belly tightened. Katherine breathed heavily trying to keep her composure while sweat beaded on her forehead.

The moment passed. She scooted her way to the middle of the bed and lay down.

Katherine felt warm tears begin to roll down her cheeks. The ache in her heart was more difficult to bear than the ache she'd felt in her back. She suspected the heart pain would never subside.

She pulled the letter to her nose, then ran her fingers along her printed name. The man who had written her letters about stars and butterflies was not the same man who had penned her name on this letter. She missed that first man. She loved that first man. She wouldn't love the other nor would she allow herself to miss him.

"I hate you so much, Ben, because I love you so much."

In contrast to her intentions, she unfolded the letter.

Dear Katherine,

I seat myself to write you and ask you again to let me stay and live with you. I have shamed you. I have shamed our marriage. I have shamed myself.

I know I have done wrong and I will regret what I did the rest of my life. I long to be forgiven by you, by myself, and by God, but I do not think I deserve forgiveness.

I blamed God for my own Pa hurting his family. Now I understand that my Pa made his own choice and shamefully, I am no better than he—the regret suffocates me.

I cannot bear to face life without you or our baby. I knew the moment I walked out our bedroom door that separation in death can be more gracious than separation in life.

If you will let me, I would spend my days beside you both, taking care of you and never expect anything in return except your presence and the presence of our child.

So, darling Butterfly, if you decide to live with me, to raise our child with me, please write to my old address in Commerce and ask me to come home.

I will always love you, Katherine.

I am, as ever, your husband,
Ben

P.S. Please don't think you can't confide in Pastor and Amy just because they took me in.

Katherine dropped the letter on the bed and wept softly. Her hatred and her love for Ben were the front and back of each other. She couldn't separate them permanently; she could only see the side turned toward her at the time.

Drained of common reasoning, she was uncertain how long she sat on the bed, tugging her ear with the letter next to her, trying to make sense of her emotions. More physical pains had come and gone and increased in intensity and frequency.

"Dear God, help me," she heard the words sneak from her lips, not sure if she meant them for the pain racking her abdomen or the pain racking her heart.

She eased her body to the edge of the bed and sat up. Then placing one hand behind her and the other in front of her, she pushed herself up to stand. A pain swept through her middle. Katherine bit her lip. Sweat beaded on her forehead again. She doubled over and held her tight abdomen, blowing out breaths to subdue the pain.

The moment passed, and the realization of what her body was trying to do overwhelmed her. "The baby."

Wooed by the love for Ben that was staring at her, between the pains she found paper and a pen. Her hand trembled as she wrote. The message was short, but not simple.

Ben, Come home.

Katherine.

She folded the letter, sealed it in an envelope, and wrote the Commerce address by heart. She knew he would return to when he read her words.

There was no more time. "Lena! Send for the mid-wife!"

Chapter 27

"**I can't stay.**" He saw the sorrow in the dear woman's eyes as he spoke the words.

Ben had realized the moment he entered Commerce that he would have to leave—again. If departing Layton was Death, then entering Commerce was its shadow.

He'd been broken then revived in Commerce. He'd been revived then broken in Layton.

Ben thought back to his recent return here. He'd almost passed out when he stepped off the train. His throat had constricted. His palms had gone clammy. The scenery before him had spun.

Despite the hospitality and sympathy shared with him by the Cramers, his anxiety continued.

Days had passed with no word from Katherine. Eight to be exact. A telegram could arrive in a day. A letter in three or four.

Each day since his return he'd listened for the train whistle coming from the direction of Layton and then stood at the train depot in desperate anticipation of someone coming to bring him back home. Call it expectation. Call it ignorance. Call it pain. Call it impatience. He could call it whatever he wanted, but all he knew is that with each passing day, the air hovering between Layton and Commerce was suffocating him as though it were poisoned.

He'd written her another letter and mailed it this morning. He told her he was moving on to the town of Flaydada and would work the railroad from there. He gave her his new forwarding address. He assured her that her mail would reach him. He declared again his repentance, his love, his concern, and his hope.

Standing in the doorway of the boarding house with his satchel and a small suitcase filled with a change of clothes and some necessities his dear friends had purchased for him, Ben shook Mr. Cramer's hand, then leaned in and hugged the man. He heard sniffling coming from Mrs. Cramer.

"I can't stay."

"I wish you could. But most of all, I wish you didn't need to stay anywhere except Layton."

Among the Crepe Myrtles

"Thank you for taking me in." Ben leaned into Mrs. Cramer, who smelled of cinnamon and furniture polish, and hugged her.

"We'd like it if you can keep in touch." Ben felt her chin move as she spoke the words, her head resting on his shoulder.

He released her, gave a nod to her husband, and then trudged to the depot. His train would leave in ten minutes.

His hope could leave at any moment.

Chapter 28

"**Dear God, help me,**" Katherine screamed. She panted. She felt herself drenched in sweat.

"One more, Miss Katherine. I see it coming."

Katherine tightened her grip around Lena's hand that held one of hers and Mrs. Justice who held the other.

She screamed again and pushed until she felt her head would pop off. Then, at last, she felt her body release its precious cargo and relax.

Katherine lessened her grip on her friends' hands and opened her eyes to look at her newborn. What she saw caused her to scream again.

"Miss Katherine, your baby was born in a veil." The voice of the midwife, her friend, Celeste, sounded shaky and urgent.

"A veil?" Katherine could only manage a whisper.

Celeste commanded the room. "Lena, hold the baby. Miss Katherine, you stay with us now. Don't you pass out. This baby gonna need you the moment I pull it from this sack." She watched as Celeste reached for the knife that lay nearby. Panic shot through her.

"Sack?" Katherine knew she screamed her question. She felt two hands grab her face and turn it.

"Katherine, your baby was born with the birth sack around it. The sack didn't break. Celeste here is going to cut the sack and pull out your baby."

Katherine felt tears run uncontrollably from her eyes as she began to sob. She was so tired. So scared.

"Is my baby dead?"

"Katherine," Mrs. Justice still held her face, "I'm sure your baby is fine."

Katherine pulled away from her friend's grip and looked to the foot of the bed. Lena was holding a thin, filmy glob in her hand with her infant curled inside. "Hold very still," she heard Celeste say to Lena, then she watched her slit the sack near her baby's face then carefully pull the filmy cover away. She stopped midway and slapped the baby on the bottom.

The cry of a newborn filled the room.

Katherine's shoulders shook as she gasped long sobs. She saw Celeste peel away the rest of the covering. Mrs. Justice ran to the foot of the bed and knelt as though she were about to pass out. Lena's cry reached Katherine's ears.

"It's a girl!"

Lena's shout evolved into laughter and sobbing that caused her to snort.

Katherine laughed and cried too. "A baby girl. I have a baby girl. Is she okay?" She saw Celeste look up from cleaning the baby and smile at her.

"Why Miss Katherine, she's more than okay. She was special enough to be born in a veil, and, my goodness, she's also been kissed by an angel." The dear woman laughed a hearty laugh that filled Katherine's bedroom.

"Kissed by angel?" No one seemed to hear her question because all three of the women were leaning over her baby admiring her face. Then Lena took the child in her hands, swaddled her, turned to Katherine, and reached to hand her child to her.

"Yes. On her right cheek."

Katherine was captivated. The warm bundle melted into her. Tears flowed down Katherine's cheeks. The new mother felt herself rock side to side instinctively as she gazed upon her child. The child gazed back at her.

Then she saw it—the light brown mark on her right cheek. An angel kiss.

Katherine ran her finger along the child's cheek and rested it on the mark. She was mesmerized as the child brought her tiny fist to her mouth and began to suck. "Hello, my darling little girl, Clara Diane."

Only then was Katherine struck by the resemblance. The newborn Clara had his nose. His chin. Katherine bent down and kissed them both. A longing for Ben swept over her.

The wife and mother thought of the words she'd written the husband and Papa. "Ben, come home." Her heart knew he'd waste no time returning to life with his Butterfly and his baby.

Katherine's heart stirred. "Your Papa loves you."

Hope and Joy peeked around the door and smiled.

Author's Note

Almost eight years before the writing of this story, I learned that my cousin had discovered some letters among family heirlooms. These were love letters from our maternal great grandfather to our great grandmother. I was deeply touched by his words that offered a glimpse into their story which was tightly sealed by their generation.

The Letters to Layton series is based upon the deep emotion and frail humanity found in these letters.

"Truth is stranger than fiction," may be an overused cliché, but it was surely the case in my grandmother's life. With my written words, I offer her some closure that evaded her in life.

Many of the characters, names, and locations are derived from the true story. My grandmother's maiden name was, indeed, Williams, and since I'm rather partial to my married name, I kept it in the tale. The cover is a photo of a postcard and envelope mailed to my great grandmother sometime after she married. I found it in an old family trunk that belonged to her brother.

I am grateful to share glimpses of truth in my family's story, but more so to share the truth of God's story. He is a loving, personal, relational, and forgiving Father.

With heartfelt thanks to my husband and children who whispered in my ear, "You can do this." Your support overwhelms me. I love you all. My life is blessed by each of you.

I honor the memory of Mike Massey, the keeper of the family stories, and send love to Jacque, his precious wife and my cousin.

Thank you to my beta readers Michelle, Jerry, and Lynn, for your time and input. I was humbled by your investment.

Thank you to those who stretched me as a writer: Lindsay, who added just the tight tweaks with her proofs, layout suggestions, and edits; Jake, "the fiction reader," who corrected my grammar, offered suggestions for clarity, smiled at the humor, winced at the hurt, and shared his male perspective; my editor, who was forthright, encouraging, and extremely helpful; Leeann, who was the unexpected and unsuspecting push that I needed and who encouraged me with her input and support.

Special appreciation to Lynn, Lindsay, Paul, Jake, Sarah, Jerry, Taylor, Monica, Alissa, Wendy, Marcie, Jo Cherie, Michelle C., Patty, Phyllis, Coleen, and the Portiers for patiently letting me pick your brain at some point in this process, and to Allan—I finally wrote a book, just not the one we had in mind.

Thank you to my readers. I am humbled that you would choose to read my story.

Heavenly Father, thank you for my salvation and for loving me. My prayer is that my life and my work will bring glory to you.

Visit my website kimwilliamsbook.com. Readers can contact me at *kimwilliamsbook@gmail.com* and can also view my *Among the Crepe Myrtles* board on Pinterest at *www.pinterest.com/kimwilliams0903.* You can follow *Kim Williams Author* on Facebook, and my author page on Goodreads. Other books in the Letters to Layton series *When the Butterflies Dance, While The Rain Whispered, and While Evening Fades.*

Made in USA - North Chelmsford, MA
905778_9781545596937
11.09.2021 1243